**Cover Design by Terra Koster of KMS Design Team
Edited by Sara Johnson**

Staccato Publishing Zimmerman, MN

First Paperback Edition: June 2012

ISBN: 978-0-9839341-2-7

Printed in the USA

THOEBA

BY DONNA MILWARD

I would like to dedicate this novel first to my husband Dan Milward. I love you more than you'll ever understand. You never stopped believing in me, and I'll always be grateful to you for giving me my dreams.

It is also dedicated to Dawn Ius, my critique partner. Thoeba would not be the book it is without you. You taught me more than just better writing skills, and I am proud to call you my friend.

I love you both ferociously.

PROLOGUE

Thoeba watched the end arrive with grim fascination. Colors rarely seen in her realm danced a solemn waltz of death in garish display amongst the clouds. Pinks and yellows mated with oranges that became fuchsia, finally surrendering to purple.

Blood and ashes splashed across the sky as her people battled the minions of darkness. She stood on a warm, sandy cliff. The enemy swarmed in the distance, a black swarm of insects flying toward them. It must be the only promise the soulless entity ever kept, Thoeba thought, as she waited for her chance to fight.

For centuries, darkness encroached upon this paradise, this Eden that some called the home of God. For many long years evil promised to swallow the heavens.

They were vastly outnumbered, so much so that the angels were forced to retreat. Thoeba glanced up to see the first wave of refugees rising to the air.

The evacuation had begun.

One by one they disappeared to other dimensions. Not all of them would make it. She drew a shuddering breath. After the struggle to leave their home, she hoped they could someday reclaim it.

Beside her, her lover sensed her worry, and took her hand. A warm and unfamiliar wind blew his long dark hair across his face, partially obscuring his slight smile.

"Are you afraid, Thoeba?"

"No Thani." She squeezed back. "I would prefer not to die."

She sighed, turned her blurring gaze to his face and lifted the corners of her lips. "I rather like it here."

"Think of it as...a new beginning." He stroked the glowing crystal around his neck. "Nothing truly dies, you know that," he said. "Night becomes day, to turn to night again. Flowers die and shed seeds, to grow flowers yet again." He rubbed his hands together, as though this invasion were an ordinary mundane occurrence, something to be dealt with and dismissed.

"Besides, who says you'll die?"

Thoeba, soldier angel of God, stared at the pendant around Thani's neck.

A deity on a string, The Energy, as her kind called It, remained a shining kernel of fluttering life. Without It, all would be lost.

Another wave of her brethren left Eden, and disappeared into the sky.

Fly swift, my friends, she thought, No time for fears, tears, or regrets.

"I will fall defending you," she said. "I will secure your escape."

Above them, the evil arrived and the fight commenced. Other angels met the demonic beings made of ash, and sounds of dying rang through the darkening skies.

Barely aware of anything but the need to destroy, the minions of darkness experienced no pain. They understood only the joy of inflicting it. They slashed at wings, and skewered hearts while their leathery wings beat hot humid winds.

"Wrong," he said. "We will secure *our* escape."

They released each other, their decision an unconscious one. Thoeba plucked her sword from the soft sands, and prepared for her opportunity to do battle. She examined the glowing weapon, tested its weight and heft, and gave it a few practice swings. Her lover busied himself by communing with the gem.

His discussion complete, Thani gave his attention back to her. "Ready?"

He pulled her close. Centuries of love made the kiss perfection, as his tongue eagerly dove into her mouth. She equaled his passion, pressing her bare nipples against his chest. One of hand framed her face the other he placed on the small of her back.

She relished the gentle way he released her lips with a brush of tenderness, only to demand more. She could smell honeysuckle and musk floating from his skin. Her free hand ran through the silk of his hair.

He didn't let her go. Not yet. He tightened his embrace. The hand holding her face gripped her hair, and he trailed wet, sweating kisses down her neck. His arousal burned like fire against her stomach, and she whimpered in pleasure.

He released her with a sigh and a smirk. "Incentive to live through this."

Thani chuckled and grabbed his sword from the ground, grinning at her as he launched into the air.

"Hellspawn." She was not referring to the ashen ones.

Thoeba followed him into the fray.

A molding gray specimen with a protruding lower jaw full of pointed teeth met her. Fangs jutted from every available space in its mouth, and it leered at her, its red eyes alight. The rusty smell on its breath promised Thoeba she would bleed, and she fought to keep her stomach contents.

The monster's intense desire to feed on her rippled through her mind, causing her to lose her bearings. To emphasize its intentions it clacked its many canines at her, drool dripping away from its mandibles as it dove for her.

Thoeba took immense satisfaction in driving her sword straight through it, and pulling up with all her strength. A rib and a leathery wing were sliced away, and the thing tumbled, spinning in a swirl of sooty dust.

The angelic warrior's next victim loomed uglier than the first. Its only eye rolled over her, and a lengthy tongue caressed her face before her sword met the demon's primitive weapon.

Thoeba noted with disgust that the blade and hilt had been crafted from a previous meal. Determined not to be next, Thoeba pumped backward in haste.

The cyclopean pressed the attack, spurred on by the taste of her skin. Its nose spasmed, and a thick line of slobber demonstrated its intent.

She tucked in both wings and dropped.

Creatures of the darkness were not known for their intelligence, and was thus confused by its prey's sudden disappearance. It glanced down, but Thoeba had flared her feathers out to stabilize the reverse dive. She twisted, her own feverish flapping thudding in her ears as she struggled to rise up behind her grotesque victim. She jabbed it in the back, where a heart should have been, and transformed it to powder.

Panting, beating her wings in tune with her heartbeat, Thoeba wondered where Thani could be.

She registered a bellow of rage from beneath her. No time to investigate.

Oxygen became scarce when another gargoyle-like creature plowed into her. Pain dug deep into her shoulder as the monster bit down and pulled. She screamed louder than ever before in her long life. The raw noise echoed back to her, clamoring off the crumbling crags and bluffs.

Thoeba vaguely detected the alarm that Thani radiated before she began to tumble, with her quarry joining her.

Thoeba had her sword, but to her it resembled a twig when she faced the behemoth. It had no weapon, and didn't need one. Its malevolence alone assaulted Thoeba's thoughts with images of suffering she had never before imagined. Her brain ached with horrors she, in all her centuries of life, had never endured. She flailed, weeping as she struck with all the effectiveness of a fist against a mountain.

We are here Thoeba.

Another body slammed into them, separating her from the beast. Relief swept over her for a breath, as she caught herself in a spin, and fought to regain altitude. She searched the skies for her rescuer. *Thani.*

The answer came seconds later, when she heard a distant boom below and his pain shivered through her head. *Thani.* The urgency escalated.

His weak response came late, but she found him. She dropped through clouds without concern for her own safety.

The pain started in her shoulder, but she ignored it in her hurry.

The mists parted for her, and she saw Thani lying broken on the ground. His wings were mangled beneath him, covered in a broth of blood and black film. The beast that he'd tackled ceased to exist.

Thani greeted her with a bloodstained smile.

"Beloved," he said, extending feeble fingers.

Thoeba's heart broke as her toes touched the ground.

"Don't move, sweetness." She dropped her sword, and fell to her knees beside him. "Be still. I need you to conserve your strength. The Energy-"

"The Energy cannot help me," he said. "There's no time." His pendant blinked in sad agreement.

She peered around in desperation for something to stanch the bleeding, and found nothing but the shimmering grains of sand that slipped between her fingers. Another glance at her lover reminded her of the futility of her search. She couldn't tell from where he bled. He seemed to ooze from everywhere, and blood dripped from his beautiful chin. His eyes were losing color and focus.

"Thoeba," he said. "Come to me, my love." She scrambled closer, pleading with her thoughts and grasping his hand.

"Thoeba, I love you," He regurgitated more blood as her tears dripped down his nose. "But I have to leave you now."

She shook her head in protest, but he smiled up at her.

"Yes. You know I must." With his other hand, he tugged

on the cord holding the bright stone around his throat. “Take it.”

“No.” The word came out a whisper.

He held it out to her. “There is no other way. You have to take it to a different realm, any realm.” He sighed, blinked with agonized slowness. “There isn’t much time, Thoeba. If you don’t, the Energy will be too weak to-“ He coughed harder, blood spattering his nose like freckles. “Too weak to restore the balance.”

She knew it to be true. The Energy would not survive in this new dominion of evil that had once been her home. It would fade until It winked out of existence like a snuffed flame.

The darkness gained strength and there were too few guardians left to protect against It. She slipped the crystal from his hand then pushed the hair from his face. She studied his pale skin, his strong jaw and full lips. Her gaze moved to his perfect sloping nose and at last to his fading blue eyes.

“I love you,” she said. “I always have.”

He smiled. Then his visage lost the light.

Grief strangled Thoeba without mercy. For long moments, she allowed it.

She howled her anguish. Her heart filled with torment and rage, like a water flask full of dust.

The living glow in her possession developed an ominous flicker. She might have gone mad from despair had it not been for that presence. After taking another wheezing breath, she nodded.

"You are right," She let her tears fall, but clenched her god in her fist in resolution. "I waste time, and draw attention to us."

But she lingered. She scanned for the enemy above her. Safety existed for the moment. Enough cloud cover hid her and her dwindling party for now.

She tied the crystal around her neck, brought it to her lips.

"Forgive me," she whispered. "But I won't leave him without saying goodbye." Once again she smoothed her lover's long soft hair away from his face, noticing as she did so how his skin cooled in death. Above her swords clashed, demons hissed, and her comrades screamed and died. She planted a delicate kiss first on his forehead, his nose, and finally his lips. She licked his blood off her mouth and reclaimed her sword.

"Where must I go?" she asked. The golden light inside the crystal pulsed with enthusiasm and she made ready to leave.

Thoeba crouched using the power of her legs to propel herself into the twilight and took flight.

She stared straight up, pointing her toes and stretching herself long. She soared, gaining altitude and speed. She accelerated, but it wasn't enough.

She sensed them before she heard them. Dual shrieks ripped through her ears. She'd been spotted and they were coming for her.

Sweat formed on her brow as she flew with desperation, trying to put more distance between herself and them.

The blind flight straight up into the purple nothing began to hurt.

The bite in her shoulder left a stream of scarlet down her chest.

How much longer? She would not waste the energy to call out for help. No one could come.

The demons would fight over who got to eat her eyes. Her screams would be music. Their reveries were more than she could bear.

Thoeba struggled for air, and the monsters were so close she could hear their batwings flapping faster.

She could smell them. The burning sulfuric decay that clung to them like disease hit her and adrenaline gave her a push. A talon raked down her leg, just as an explosion concussed Thoeba's entire being.

She tried to guard her eyes from a brilliant flash to no avail, her limbs no longer worked. She remembered plunging, but nothing more.

CHAPTER ONE

Dawn had crept to the lake when Lt. Colonel Peter 'Socks' Mason brought his German Shepherd, Crash and his Smokercraft to his favorite fishing spot. This little chunk of heaven in the chaos of late May in Cold Lake never failed to bring him peace. With exercise "Maple Flag" in full swing, the whole town swarmed with fighter pilots from the States, France, Germany and more from all over the world.

The annual event meant that thousands of military personnel flocked to this midsized town in Alberta to practice drills and learn new techniques. The base swelled to three times its size.

Peter took leave from it this year. Lucky him. He welcomed the break that came with seniority. Not many other people were allowed to take vacations during the busy event.

At the stony outcropping called Pelican Rock he jigged for pike and walleye. With only twelve feet or so of water, and it being so clean, he could see the fish move below. Sometimes they jumped for bugs on the surface, interrupting the silence with an occasional splash.

He'd had no luck so far, but he didn't care. He could wait. He sucked in a gulp of fresh air. The boat smelled of old fish, wet dog, and lake water. It was a fine perfume.

Nothing stirred but the lapping water and the dragonflies. Even the pelicans slumbered. Crash sighed alongside him.

Peter anticipated a good summer. The rustic A-frame he

stayed at was perfect shelter for his needs. No heat, no water, no phone. No problem. It withstood the strong winds, and stayed dry in the banshee storms legendary in Alberta.

Peter looked forward to snoozing in the massive wooden beds upstairs. At that thought, his chin dropped to his chest. A minute later he jerked his head up with a grunt.

A yawn cracked his face. He rubbed the salt and pepper facial growth he'd cultivated, stroked his German Shepherd.

Peter thought about his kids coming down and smiled. Zack would be home from computer college, and Kayla would be finished Junior High in a couple of weeks.

His ex-wife "graciously" allowed Kayla to spend her weekends at the cabin. Provided, of course, that she didn't have homework or babysitting jobs.

His buddy Jim would come by as well. His big old Prowler sat parked at the Provincial, but at this time of year that campground filled to the treetops with campers, tents, and motorhomes. Jim preferred to jet over for a fire and a few brews.

Now would be a good time to get in some solitary moments before all hell broke loose and the lake crowded.

Peter almost dozed again when thunder clapped.

It startled him into sitting up and scanning the sky for the offending racket. The dog started barking, also roused from his nap.

"Crash," he said. "Be quiet, boy."

What the hell?

Too early for circuits, or any other aviation exercises for

that matter, even for Maple Flag. It didn't sound like an F-18 or a Mig. If he discovered it to be thunder, then he'd better get his ass off the lake. His over-grown dingy didn't handle choppy water that well.

But as he checked for clouds, he realized there were none.

Just the violet expanse turning to gold without a single wisp or aircraft in sight.

So what's with the noise?

Something caught the corner of his eye, making him spin and nearly topple. He saw a sizable white shape hit the water. It caused a splash and ripple large enough to make him brace his footing.

Damn it, what was that?

He had to know.

Crash became excitable, clumsy, and underfoot, as Peter made his way to the back of the boat.

The little trolling motor had some juice left in it. He'd ease his way over to where the lazy circles rang out from the impact point.

Crash pranced all over the hull, anticipation causing his ears to point. Anxious little sounds escaped his muzzle as Peter steered his boat next to the floating shape.

"Down boy," he said to the dog. He worried that Crash would jump right out in to the water to retrieve whatever lay out there. Most likely a dead pelican.

As he steered up close, curiosity became alarm. Crash whined and chuffed next to him, and Peter grabbed an oar to paddle closer.

A girl floated face up, but appeared to be sinking fast. Peter cringed, noting her nakedness.

How'd she get here?

Tendrils of blood swirled in the water around her. His thoughts slammed to Kayla as he dragged the unconscious girl to the side of the boat by the ankle. This young woman looked to be about the same age as her. Somebody must be pacing a trench in their carpet wondering why their daughter wasn't home yet.

"Oh great," he said. "Move outta the way, Crash. This girl needs some serious help."

He leaned farther over the edge, and hauled her up by her waist, careful not to squeeze her too hard. Her long blonde curls had shone like a halo in the lake; now they plastered across her face in a greenish tangle. Her breathing sounded slow and even, as if she only slept. Seemed like a good sign.

He set her down on the Astroturf on the floor of the boat and examined her wounds. It occurred to him she might have been raped and dumped after a bush party. He checked, relieved and surprised to find no bruising and no blood between her thighs.

So where did the blood come from?

Her leg and her shoulder were different matters. Bite marks like no animal he'd ever seen laced her collarbone, and the sinewy muscle of her calf had been clawed.

Peter tried to be rational. He wanted to say 'bear attack', but couldn't believe it himself. The circumference of the bite didn't fit.

He would've given his beer cooler to know what kind of creature in his neighborhood had a mouth that big, but he sure as hell didn't want to meet it.

Placing her flat on the deck behind the driver's chair, Peter searched for his first aid kit.

As if a little gauze would help to fix *that*, he thought.

The wounds would have to be cleaned and the bleeding staunched. He cursed under his breath that he'd forgotten his cell phone.

He had a roll of bandages in one hand and a bottle of hydrogen peroxide in his other hand when turned to face her.

She sat staring right at him.

"Holy," he said. Her gaze startled him speechless. "You're...you're..."

She studied him with the strangest eyes Peter had ever made contact with. Twin solar eclipses in sunset orange.

Strange as well, she didn't seem afraid of him in the least, and she didn't seem to be in pain.

It ruled out his rape scenario. He would have expected a victim would have been screaming the birds from the trees by now. She regarded him with the same point of view as one examining a rather interesting bug.

With nothing intelligent coming from his mouth, Peter edged toward her with caution. "I have some first-aid stuff," he said. "You're hurt..."

Her hand reached out for the supplies. He gave them to her, charmed by her fluid grace.

Peter scanned her face.

Perfect, he noted, but probably not as young as she

appeared. True, he saw no wrinkles, no flaws of any kind.

Just a cynicism in her expression. Almost jaded. Her eyes seemed ancient and world-weary.

His gaze wandered a little farther down, to her breasts. Small, but perky. Obvious strength undulated beneath her skin.

That, and the curtains matched the-

Peter jerked his face away, hoping she hadn't caught him gawking. Heat burned his ears, and he reminded himself not to think with his dick.

He began rummaging for a blanket, anything to cover her. He found his blue plaid flannel, figured that would do the trick.

When he turned to dress her, he saw shock and anger on her face.

She'd been cleaning the blood off her shoulder, but now she rubbed at her back in panic. The bandages and bottle lay abandoned on the floor next to the live well.

"Where are they, human?"

Human? At least she spoke English. "Where are what?" he asked.

Her voice rose in agitation. "Where are my wings."

CHAPTER TWO

Peter glanced back at her from the driver's seat. She caressed Crash while she stared out at the placid lake. Tears trailed down her face to be flicked away with the wind.

"You alright back there?" He had to yell over the drone of the engine. She merely nodded.

The sun brought full morning, along with wildlife activity. He could hear the ducks over the engine, along with the occasional loon. In spite of the calm, Peter worried.

She hadn't said much since she'd asked about her wings. He told her they were there, painted onto her back like strategic burns. The answer hadn't satisfied her. She clammed up and wept without a sound.

Peter didn't like that one bit. She seemed depressed, wallowing in misery and heartbreak.

Who was she? Where did she come from?

He preferred being in the loop with all of the why's and the how's, the when's and the where's.

Facts eluded him here. He'd heard thunder, and a splash followed. Then he'd found a woman sinking in the lake bleeding from unexplainable injuries.

He took a glimpse at her leg. He'd used a spare pair of socks as a tourniquet and the bleeding had already slowed. He'd check on it later. It's possible she might need stitches.

From as far as he could tell, her eyes were clear, no drugs, booze or even shock for that matter.

Although naked, she didn't seem the least bit shy about it. She draped the flannel across her lap instead of clutching it around herself in fear.

She whispered to the necklace. Strange girl. Just popped up in the water wearing nothing but jewelry that seemed to respond to voice activation. And what was with the seared pattern of wings stamped into her flesh? Probably some new fad the kids were doing that he hadn't heard of yet. God forbid if his kids tried that.

He had to do something despite his misgivings about her. Maybe the loss evident in her copper eyes and the pain behind the glare made him want to. Maybe he was just a sucker for a damsel in distress.

~~~

Thoeba's head ached.

The stupid human thinks too loud, she thought. Most of them did.

Still, he'd saved her life, and she appreciated that. With his kind one couldn't be sure. The Energy only knew what could have happened to her if he hadn't found her.

She could have died in this realm. *That* would have been a disaster. Then what might have happened to her soul?
~~~

She shuddered to think of the Energy lying alone at the bottom of some obscure lake on a planet known for the self-absorption of its inhabitants.

Why did the Energy bring her among the Earthlings? She hated coming here. This whole mess started with them.

She hoped their technological advances, and what little strengths they had left would be enough to restore the Energy back to Its glorious self.

How could she save the deity in a world where she could smell the flowers dying?

She pushed the thought out of her head, and concentrated on her pain which she found preferable, although intense. The talon strike on her leg stung. It throbbed like the relentless march of time, a constant drumming reminder of battle. The bite thrummed, she could still feel the fang marks as though they were fresh.

She remembered her feathered appendages, and almost groaned aloud. No wonder the landing had knocked her out.

So now she had to defend the god without her ability to fly. How in the Energy's many Homes of Life would she do that?

Worst of all she reeled from the loss of Thani. She missed him. Tears sprang forth. Centuries together ripped away by one hideous minion of evil. She remembered the taste of his cold lips, heard the whisper of his dying words. She could almost smell the sweet musk and clover scent of him. The moisture from her eyes joined the lake unnoticed.

The Energy pulsed in Its prison. It sent reassurances to her broken heart, soothed her.

Then It sent her a new reason to worry. The demons had gotten close. So close, they would come right behind her through the portal. They should arrive in a matter of hours.

Fear, genuine and sharp, slithered up Thoeba's wingless spine. She remained a solitary seraphim in a hostile world, carrying the most important object in the entire universe. And the hunt had begun.

"Almost there," Peter said, jarring her thoughts. The twinkling god in her hands couldn't be denied. She had to take shelter with the human. The deity gently reminded her that this mortal had a name.

"Can you see that A-Frame over there?" He pointed straight in front of himself. "That's where we're going." She twisted the corners of her lips up for him. She had no idea what 'A-Frame' meant, but the gem around her throat believed in him, loved him.

It made Thoeba wonder. The Energy had boundless affection for all things, all It's children, regardless of ignorance.

~~~

Peter reduced their speed to a crawl, and cruised in. Even the mystery woman seemed impressed at the clean sandy bottom of the shore and the unspoiled purity of the property.

Wild strawberries and bright dandelions peeked from the shade. The log cabin blended with the trees, inconspicuous with its rich brown stain. Sunlight dazzled through the leaves.

He cut the engine. The gentle whoosh of the waves and the pattering of a dog's excited paws soothed Peter's nerves.
~~~

Until Crash nearly bowled him over on his way out. A splash followed, and Crash dog-paddled the rest of the way to shore.

Peter jumped out, grabbed his tow rope to muscle the boat to the white sand.

Already there, Crash shook himself with the *whuppa-thuppa-jingle* sound of a large dog drying off. Peter slogged back to the edge of the boat, where the woman sat rigid on the gunnel.

Her face amused him. Like she needed to force herself to accept his help. It wasn't any great leap to the water. Unless you were injured. He had the distinct feeling she didn't like to admit weakness. He could see it in her defiant sneer.

He spread his arms and waited. It didn't take long before her features softened, but still she hesitated. Just when Peter's arms grew tired from holding them out she reached out to him, and eased into his embrace.

~~~

Thoeba tried not to smirk. It wasn't so bad, being held close to this man. His muscles flexed as he sloshed through the water to dry land. In this position, she could study his profile.

His cropped spiked hair grayed at the temples, matching his stubble. A tanned face displayed a nose straight and noble while the corners of his eyes were etched from years of squinting in the sun.

Those glacial blues gazed at her now, and she found mirth in them. Her heart lurched, surprising her. Even the smell of him made her-

"Oh my God! Daaa-aad!"
~~~

At the sound of the voice, Peter's eyes widened until the white showed all around the pupils. He spun around so fast his neck cracked, and he almost dropped her, which jarred her sore leg. She suppressed a hiss of pain as she assessed the newcomer.

Standing in the shadow of the triangular cabin waited a petite freckled girl with the same sky-colored gaze as the man who carried her.

Except her eyes held fire.

"Kayla. You're early." He wobbled faster to the shore, and Thoeba held tighter, fearing he'd let go. "Kayla, this isn't what it looks like."

"I can-*not* believe what I am seeing. I mean *eeeewww*." The girl protested at top volume. Were all human miniatures so vocal? "I didn't need to see that. Is this your girlfriend? You didn't tell me you were dating, and oh my God. How old is she?" She took a breath.

"She's not my-"

"Mom is gonna freak! You didn't tell her either, did you? What were you two doing? Like, gross, she's naked and everything. You knew I was coming up this weekend, so how could you-"

"Kayla!"

Thoeba winced at the shout. The teenager pressed her lips shut, but continued to scowl.

"I found her in the lake," Peter said. "She's hurt. She's not my girlfriend, so there's no need to tell your mother."

Kayla crossed her arms, and lifted her chin. "Why not?"

He sighed and placed Thoeba gently on her feet in the shallows. "I didn't do anything wrong, sweetie. I'm just trying to help this woman, okay?" He punctuated the statement by assisting Thoeba into the flannel, arms in sleeves. "And if your mom knows I have a woman out here, she probably won't let you come out anymore."

"Oh." Her expression went briefly dark. However, she wasn't speechless for long.

"So did you really pull her out of the lake? What happened, and where are her clothes? Wow, look at her eyes. They're so pretty. They look like that bracelet you gave me for my birthday last year, hey Dad? What did you call it again?"

"Amber." Peter lifted Thoeba with as much care as possible, and brought her into the cabin. Kayla prattled on behind them.

"Wow, is that ever a cool necklace. Where did you get it? Is it one of those laser things with liquid in it? Like a glowstick? Is that it? Or does it have a battery? Hey, do you speak English? You haven't said a word."

Thoeba ground her teeth as Kayla's running dialog pummeled her brain. Two humans thinking at the speed of light, at decibel levels that would kill a mortal. Too intense. No sooner had Peter set her down on her own two feet, she collapsed.

~~~

When she woke, Thoeba became aware of a distinct passing of time. The light outside the balcony window had changed. The sunshine held a deeper color, like a waning day. She'd been out for hours, and she heard a new voice downstairs.
~~~

"No kidding," The voice said. "*This* lake? And you're sure she's not local?"

Thoeba left a soft comfortable bed taking care with aching body parts and followed the sound down a narrow wooden staircase.

Kayla babbled like river water. "Maybe she goes to the Catholic school, cause I would have remembered a new girl with orange eyes."

"She isn't that young Kayla," Peter said.

"She looks it. She doesn't have any wrinkles, or crow's feet, or anything."

"Whoa!" The voice belonged to the man sitting on the futon across from the stairs. He wore dark shields on his eyes, and drank from a blue can.

Thoeba recognized his type. Small dogs barking in large parks.

"Well wherever she's from, I guess they don't believe in clothes," he said.

Peter and Kayla followed his gaze to where Thoeba stood. Peter ogled and Kayla scolded, "Uncle Jim!" before running over to scoot her back up the stairs.

Thoeba heard Peter's guest mutter. "How did an ugly troll like you hook up with that?"

In the loft where she dragged Thoeba, Kayla opened and shut three or four trunks until she found what she sought, chatting non-stop as she did so.

"Last year was all about Billabong, pink was my favorite, so most of my stuff is the color of bubble-gum," she said. "This year I'm into Roxy."

Thoeba said nothing.

"So I hope you don't mind, but I'm going to lend you the pink stuff," she said. "It's just that you're taller than me, and have bigger breasts and I don't want you stretching out my new clothes, is that okay?"

Kayla chose sweatpants and a tank top with burn holes.

"I wrecked this outfit by standing too close to the campfire last year," she said. "You don't mind do you?"

When the fabric landed on her lap, Thoeba stared at it, not comprehending how to go about swathing herself in these garments.

A sigh from Kayla. "You don't know how to dress, do you? Okay. Stand up. I'll help you."

Thoeba handed the clothes back to Kayla and obeyed.

After removing Peter's flannel from her back, the young girl motioned for Thoeba to bend at the waist with her arms up. "I do a lot of babysitting," Kayla said. "But I don't think I've ever had to dress someone taller than me." Her giggle twittered throughout the air as she pulled the tank top over Thoeba's head.

"It's like trying to dress a life-sized Barbie," she said. "Step into here. Watch your leg."

Thoeba ignored Kayla's chatter. Downstairs Peter and his friend were discussing her. She strained to hear the conversation through Kayla's continued monologue.

"Look Socks," Jim said. "Women don't drop out of skies. Not without parachutes."

"Don't you think I know that?" Peter said. "And all she was wearing was a necklace."

"Tracking device? Spyware?" The comments were met with silence. "And what's with the burns on her back?"

"You noticed them too, huh?"

"Yeah," Jim said. "Kinda looks like some weird tribal fetish thing."

So intent was Thoeba on listening to the conversation, she didn't pay attention as Kayla changed position.

Not until gentle fingers traced a line down her shoulder blade.

In one fluid spin Thoeba gripped Kayla's wrist and squeezed.

"Hey!" Kayla said.

Thoeba heard two sets of footsteps thumping up the protesting steps.

"What the hell's going on here?" Peter said. She saw anger flaring in his eyes. "Get your hands off my kid."

Thoeba released Kayla at her leisure. "I wasn't going to hurt her." She glared at Kayla. "Does your kind frequently run around touching skin that doesn't belong to them?"

"Look," Jim said behind Peter, one hand in pocket, one hand waving a can that read 'Kokanee'. "Your confused victim act? I'm not buyin' it, okay? What do you want here?"

Thoeba locked her gaze on the new human. She didn't owe him any explanations.

Perhaps Peter and Kayla required a few answers. After all they'd been kind and had taken care of her.

But this one smelled of day old alcohol, sweat, and the ever-present lake water. Still, the one called Kayla seemed very fond of him, and she sensed his importance to Peter as well.

"I had to escape," she said. "I don't wish to be here, but I have no choice."

Jim twisted his lips. "Uh huh? And where were you escaping from?"

This is going to be difficult, she thought. She crossed the floor to descend the stairs, confident the humans would follow.

Once on the ground floor she inhaled a deep breath. "Your kind calls it Heaven."

The silence that greeted her framed the sound of wind and waves.

Then Jim burst into ripples of obnoxious laughter.

"Oh, that's a good one," he said. "Heaven, eh? If it was Heaven, why would you want to leave?" His mockery filled the room, and Thoeba took an intense dislike to the man.

"I believe her." Kayla blurted. Thoeba rewarded her with a smile. "She has wings etched into her back. Dad you said there were no boats out there or anything. Where else did she come from?"

“Sweetheart,” Jim said. “You believe in Bigfoot. You’re letting your imagination lead you on.”

Kayla scrunched her face at Jim, before addressing her father. “What about the wounds she supposedly had when you brought her here, Dad? Look at her leg and shoulder.”

Peter narrowed his gaze at Kayla as she peeled the water dampened gauze from Thoeba’s tender skin.

No punctures. Splashes of red were all that remained. Thoeba answered the question in his eyes by pulling the leg bandage and sock off.

He squinted at the unscarred limb. “I guess you won’t need stitches after all,” he said. His stance defensive, he licked his lips before questioning Thoeba further.

“What do you want?” Peter asked. “Why are you here?”

“I’m here to save the Energy. To restore the balance.” She drew their attention to the crystal around her neck by cupping it in both hands.

Kayla came closer, reached a tentative hand toward Thoeba’s throat. “Is it…is it…” She licked her bottom lip. “Is it God?”

“It’s what you call God. Yes.”

“It’s beautiful,” Kayla whispered.

“It thinks the same of you,” Thoeba said. “It loves you. All of you.”

The charm of the moment vanished the moment Jim’s braying chortle echoed in the empty space.

“Can you prove it?” Peter asked. “I mean it’s a lovely necklace and everything, but it’s a piece of rock on a string.

You want me to believe this 'Energy," He used hand signals for quotation marks, "Is God, creator of the universe?"

Thoeba came closer to Peter, searched his piercing eyes. "Can't you feel it?" she asked. "Can't you feel the love of your creator?"

~~~

He could. Or at least he thought he could. His heart beat faster. Warmth crept over him, and love spread over him in a wave of...

Whoa. He shook it off. Spock moment. This whole thing was illogical. And fascinating. He walked away from her to clear his mind.

Jim let out a low whistle. "Whoo-eee. Thought she had ya for a second." He took another swig, and a step toward Thoeba.

"Look honey," he said. "We're not into the hippy-dippy, crystal- gazing, moon-princess shit, okay?" He let out a contemptible snort. "Why don'cha go hug a tree or something. Lots of them around here." He wobbled his way to a futon and plunked down.

Thoeba gazed around the room. Peter's inebriated friend sat smirking. His drunkeness made her dizzy. Peter wouldn't look at her. From the hero worship on Kayla's face, she had deified the wrong element.

"You felt It." She stretched forward, and grabbed Peter's arm, turned him to face her. "You experienced It. I know you did."

"Don't tell me how I feel," he said. "You don't know me."
~~~

"I do," Thoeba said. "I hear your thoughts. I endure all your musings." Her voice had the snap of sarcasm. "You humans can't seem to stop sharing them with me."

"Yeah?" Peter took a stand before her, hands on hips. "Prove it."

CHAPTER THREE

Thoeba began speaking to the pendant, as she had ever since Peter yanked her out of the lake. His exasperation poured off him like sweat. She could hear him asking himself why he hadn't taken her to town when he had the chance.

Tell him. We don't have time for theological ponderings.

Thoeba nodded to the sound of the voice in her head, but addressed Peter. "Because the Energy didn't want you to."

"What?" Her statement jolted Peter from his thoughts, and a tempest coiled inside his head. Her conversation with her deity had to end for now. Peter's emotions threatened to explode like a tensed spring, and would have to be quelled.

"It didn't want you to take me to town," she said. "It wants to stay here. We need to regroup and then-"

"Wait a minute." Peter inched forward, narrowed his eyes. "What are you saying? Did you influence that decision? Are you saying *you* controlled my thoughts?"

"We are desperate…." She didn't like his resonance. It seethed like anger and it fed hers. She would have to answer his questions. She needed him to trust her, but this wasn't a good start.

"No. I didn't. Not intentionally anyways." She couldn't help herself as she added, "It would help if you didn't think at top volume."

Peter gripped his head. "Okay, that's it. I call bullshit."

"That won't stop me from hearing you," she said.

She sympathized with the dog. While not empathic as her the tension caused him to whine.

"I'm already sick of you humans. This whole mess is your fault anyway." The exhaustion, pain and loneliness caved in on her. She hated this planet.

Some of her kind had a deep compassion for these beings, but Thoeba could never get around their constant need to rage.

Here she sat, trying to save the Almighty and them, and these beings just stood there with fingers in ears, eyes shut, shouting tired narrow-minded dogma. "In all of the Homes of Life, your kind is always the most selfish, the most inner-involved."

Kayla ventured closer. "Homes of Life?"

"Homes of Life." Thoeba glanced at her, noted how Jim sauntered behind her back, toward the cooler for yet another shiny can.

There went a classic example of the kind of people she had seen in her travels here, a nasty mix of stupidity and arrogance.

"Did you think you were the only ones It created? That yours was the only world?" She shook her head. "I don't know why It brought me here."

Because you have lessons to learn here, young one.

Peter swallowed the contents of his canister, slammed it down onto the counter. “I can’t believe I’m listening to this. Do you have any idea how crazy you sound?”

“Yeah. What institution did you escape from?” Jim asked as he opened another beer.

“I am not crazy.” She begged her deity for strength. “I came here to hide the Energy, and I need you to help me. Please. We need you. There isn’t much-“

“You’re trying to tell me you have God trapped in…” He gestured toward her neck. “Glass, crystal whatever, and It needs us to help? Let God help Himself.”

Thoeba glared at him from across the room. “Stupid, petulant children. Your thoughtlessness astounds me.” For long seconds, no one responded. “You take no responsibilities for your sins, no ownership of the pain you inflict on others.”

“What does that have-“ Jim said. Thoeba sensed the situation getting out of hand, but she wasn’t finished.

“You could have prevented this.” She held the crystal in her clenched fist. “It gave you rules to live by. All you had to do was follow them. It gave you a golden commandment. Haven’t you noticed that the nature of all sin is the pain and suffering you inflict on each other?” Her own sadness threatened to overwhelm her, because her words had caused them none.

“That’s not true,” Jim said. “What about floods? Tsunamis?”

“That is the nature of your planet,” she said. “If you don’t like the weather on your world, you should’ve chosen a different one."

They stared at her. Only Thoeba heard the Energy's inappropriate laughter, like a sparkling in her head. Peter opened his mouth, but closed it again. His brow furrowed with confusion.

"The wars were your doing, not God's. Men tell you to fight for God. Did God build weapons of mass destruction? I saw what your kind did at Hiroshima. I was there. Did God ask you to do that? No. Your government did. You know that, but you blame God. Never mind the everyday things you do to each other."

Somewhere outside, she heard the wind pick up, rustling the leaves on the trees. Jet engines roared in the distance. Outside, life continued unabated. Time moved forward leaving her with few options.

Inside the cedar-scented cabin, Thoeba observed three people full of irritating doubt and decided now would be a good time to share. They wanted evidence? Proof? She would tell them what she knew.

Thoeba glared at Peter, eyes on fire. "She knew, you know. Your ex-wife?" Her chin pointed to Kayla. "She did too. None of your family were fooled."

Her words struck him, but his thoughts proved denial had always been a part of that story.

"I don't know what you're talking about," he said.

She nodded. "You do." Her smile sharpened. "Was she worth it, Peter? Worth destroying your family for?" Peter peered over at Kayla, but she studied the dirty floor.

"Baby..." he said. "I'm so sorry." Bitter tears shimmered down Kayla's face.

“And what about you, Kayla?” Thoeba asked. “Does Daddy know you skip school?” The girl’s head snapped toward Thoeba. Peter began yelling.

“You *what?* How long has-“

“Does he know you steal makeup? From Walmart?” The last questions startled Peter into silence.

Kayla took that as her cue to run crying from the cabin.

Crash loped after her. Thoeba heard the hurried ticking of his claws on the floor in his scramble. Peter and Jim called after Kayla, who ignored them.

Why did I say that? She wondered.

Abruptly conscious of her cruelty, Thoeba reigned in her tirade, and apologized to her deity. It flickered with the negativity in the room, pulsed as though in pain. She couldn’t agree with her god more.

That was uncalled for.

“Wow, you must be great at parties.” Jim said. He lumbered out of the cabin, tossed his empty can into the fire pit, and made for his boat.

“I’m done with this drama. Thanks for the beers, Pete.” Despite her regret at the mean-spirited ramble, Thoeba couldn’t help being happy to see him leave.

“Was that really necessary?” Peter asked. Thoeba had the grace to accept the chastening.

“I was just….I should have...” She gave it up. What was wrong with her? “I’m sorry. I don’t know what came over me.”

Peter shook his head in exasperation. “Look, I get it.

You're not well." His eyes peered through the open door of the cabin. "But you didn't need to be a bitch."

He stomped out of the room, past the rustic kitchen counters, and out the screen door, bellowing Kayla's name.

Thoeba suffered the worst guilt since she'd arrived on this self-forsaken planet. Her deity undulated in Its tiny prison, a slave to emotion from ungrateful creations, herself included.

What had come over her?

~~~

Peter knew where Kayla would run. She'd been coming to the same spot behind the cabin since age six. He bet she didn't know that he remembered that.

Where the fallen tree lay covered in damp fuzzy moss and the pinkish-purple fireweed grew he could hear her sobs. They gouged trenches in his heart.

She would hear him coming. No need to hide anymore.

As expected she slouched in a patch of greenery with her back against a fallen tree. Awaiting a lecture, no doubt. Crash lounged next to her, panting in the shade.

"I thought he was my dog," Peter said.

Kayla shrugged. "Maybe he likes me better." She bit her lip, a gesture she did when she couldn't cover up her insecurity and shyness.

Crash barked, unconcerned, happy to let her pet him. Kayla scrunched her lips together to hide a grin.

Peter did too. Damn dog. Always a sucker for girls.

He shook his head, and sat down next to her on a log.
~~~

“Hey,” he said. “That was…” He paused to roll words in his head. “Interesting.”

She nodded. “Yeah.” A long pause followed.

“So you knew?” he asked. “You, your mom, Zack?”

“Yep.” The silences got longer.

“Do you want to talk about it?”

“No.” She shifted toward him. “Yes.”

“Yes?”

She turned all the way to face him, and nodded. “Yeah.”

Peter picked soft tufts of moss from the old bark, savoring the damp woodsy scent. “I know I don’t deserve your forgiveness for this.”

“And you’re not getting it.”

Peter’s anger rose through his throat, tasting sour like bile. “Watch your mouth. I’m still your father,” he said.

He kicked himself internally. If he wanted a civilized conversation with her about this, he had to tread lighter than that.

He started again. “I mean, let’s be truthful here.”

“Yeah, you’re so good at that.”

Careful, careful. Watch what you say. “Look who’s talking.”

“Hey, I learned it from you.”

Peter’s patience evaporated. “You have no right to judge me, Kayla. You don’t know a damn thing about marriage.”

"I know I'll never marry someone like you." Peter couldn't stop the tearful tantrum that threatened to engulf her. She resembled a fish trying to swallow her bottom lip.

"I hate you. Neither one of you cared about me, or Zack." A sob wrenched from her mouth. "I did that stuff three months ago, and neither of you *noticed*." She wailed as he placed an arm around her and squeezed. Crash sat up and whined.

"No." She drew away, and shuffled off the log. "I will never forgive you for this. *Never.*"

Peter's heart broke. He listened, seated, while she howled in anguish at the sky. A thought wormed through his head.

He would never get his little girl back.

His mouth curved down of its own accord at the same time grief crawled through his heart.

He might have fallen apart with her but something itched at his instincts.

Crash noticed the change first. Peter saw canine compassion abruptly give way to attack mode. Crash perked up, so did Kayla. The air hummed with something he'd never experienced before, in all his years as a fighter pilot. It squeezed the life from the air, replacing it with the buzz of fear.

"Dad?" The word trembled in Peter's ears. "What is that thing?"

Peter brought his face to the sky in time to see a shadow block the sun. Peter sprinted after Crash, who already ran toward battle.

CHAPTER FOUR

Jim pulled the ski boat up onto the sand bar of the Provincial campground. Through the haze of alcohol he noticed the quiet.

"Too quiet," he said in his sloppiest John Wayne.

The air smelled of smoke, overcooked wieners and the distinctive burnt sugar scent of marshmallows. He could hear the snap of burning poplar wood. He noticed a few tents and motorhomes that hadn't been there earlier.

The more, the merrier. Nothing like campers sandwiched together for making new friends. Maybe some of them brought more booze.

Jim kinda liked it, even if he couldn't scratch his ass without someone taking a picture when it got that full.

He trudged up the embankment toward his Prowler, parked just around the dirt curve. Overhead, Maple Flag exercises continued uninterrupted. Shadows crossed the sun, jets soared and dived. Afterburners roared.

It sounded like the Americans were up. Running some drills? A shadow engulfed him as a B-52 Stratofortress skimmed the tree tops. That oughta rattle the dishes in everyone's cupboards.

Jim let out a whoop of delight.

Funny. Nobody else cheered. No one emerged from their motorhomes to watch.

A 'Big Fat Fucker' buzzes the grounds and no one checks it out? Weird.

Silence returned. It gave Jim the creeps.

Hell with them. As soon as he got himself settled, he would take in the some of the action.

Further in it stank so bad on the grounds Jim could taste it. Someone must have caught something, because the smell of fresh fish guts and rot wafted its way over to him. Good thing his camp sat on the other side of the grounds from the cleaning station. The flies were pissing him off. He had to put his hand over his mouth and nose for fear he'd accidently swallow some, they were so dense. Noisy too. Why were they so damn thick all of a sudden?

Even as he got nearer to his motor home, Jim ignored the prickle on the back of his neck.

So quiet.

So what? Everybody must've gone out on the lake. If he wasn't in such bad shape, he'd be watching the jets out on his boat too.

He'd get another lager first. Enjoy the hush while it lasted.

He scuffed his boat shoes in the gravel of the road and inspected his campsite through bleary eyes. His Prowler sat along the back of bush, next to a fire pit. Two other motor homes kept a sharing distance.

Nobody there. That suited him just fine. He opened the screen door to the trailer, sweet trailer away from home. It reeked of barley pops and unwashed lush. Jim didn't even notice it anymore, and out here, there he had no one to impress.

He grabbed another brewskie from the fridge, and enjoyed the brief hiss as it opened.

This was the life. Chilling out by the lake with a few Kokanees, watching the planes. He took a thirsty pull from it and let loose a boisterous belch of contentment.

That's when it hit him. More than just the smell of fish guts, the scent of long ago decay mingled with an undertone of sulfur.

Something strong coming from right behind him.

Jim wheeled on filthy carpet and faced his assailant. Nothing, in all his years of military training had prepared him for this.

A monster filled his vision with the pitch black of volcanic ash and eyes of lava. The beast's teeth were thick and too long to see the entire length from this close to his face. He screamed and swung his beer bottle. Not quick enough.

Before Jim could fully recognize the horror he faced, it had crushed the brown glass with little effort and shards sprayed into his face, drawing lines of red.

The evil before him gripped his jaw with another lethal appendage. It shivered, excitement danced in its eyes as it tasted Jim's cheek with a slimy tongue.

Jim understood then he would not die. No, this would be worse.

Much, much worse.

CHAPTER FIVE

Thoeba's heart lurched. For ten minutes the Energy hadn't calmed down, hadn't come back to Itself. If anything, It retreated further. That frightened her. She feared it would die right then and there, and it might be her fault. Surely her argument with the humans hadn't caused this?

What had come over her?

She asked it of herself over again. It had been awhile since she had dealt with their species, but she didn't dislike them *that* much. She should have known better than to talk to them that way. They were sensitive. Not to mention Peter had saved her life.

She hadn't noticed the profound silence until a familiar scent caressed her nostrils like the touch of an abusive lover.

Sulphuric death.

She turned toward the entrance.

A demon, in all its dark glory, took up the entire doorframe. Two red coals glowed from the shadows. It hunched forward, as though the weight of its single horn were too much for its scrawny neck muscles.

It grinned at her, an expression as welcoming as a dinner invitation from a vampire, with more teeth.

She scanned for exits. Two windows, neither large enough to jump through. The only way out on this floor was occupied. Any weapons she might use were in the kitchen where the monster emerged.

Options? Only the stairs.

Thoeba raced up, heard the beast lurching across the floor. She got to the top and ran for the veranda.

The French doors were open. She took a step, spread her wings…

And slammed to the floor. Thoeba let out a distinctly unangelic oath. Good thing she hadn't tried that closer to the edge.

She mourned the loss of flight with acuity. Tears of pain and terrified frustration welled in her eye sockets. Hope evaporated.

She heard the groaning of the steps as the weight of the enormous demon warped them. She picked herself up and scrambled for position. She needed an escape route, or a weapon. She had neither.

The exits out of the cabin were the door downstairs and the upstairs patio. She wasn't sure if she'd survive a jump from the balcony. At the very least there would be injuries that would prevent running.

But she had to come up with something. After it finished with her, it would find Peter and Kayla. It would most likely torture them before eating them. Never before had she wished so hard to disappear.

Too late. The leathery monstrosity had reached the top of the stairs.

Thoeba crouched next to the open patio doors, waiting for its next move. A low rumble erupted from its throat. She watched it sniff the air, turning its oversized head side to side.

Looking for her.

A smile creased Thoeba's face. She hadn't been to Earth for a few decades.

She'd forgotten, until now, how to be invisible. It wasn't something she did in her native realm. None of them did. But on missions to Earth and other Homes of Life, it proved an essential skill.

She'd bought herself some time and a measure of safety. Thoeba longed for her sword, anything to hit with. Sure, the lamp in the corner might help, but it wouldn't kill the thing, and it would give away her position for no beneficial reason. She had no holy weapon, and no plan.

And it knew she was there. Enormous breaths huffed through a draconian snout with nostrils the size of dates. The beast took tentative steps further, almost half way across the room, between two beds. Malice rolled off its skin like a heat wave.

The sound of angry barking distracted her. She nearly groaned, but closed her lips tight. The noise came from outside and the distance shrank by the second.

The dog. The humans.

They would chase the dog up the stairs and this thing would kill them all unless she did something.

Claws ticked on the stairway, followed by the footfalls of a biped. The demonic predator lost interest in her, and faced his new foes. The German Shepherd's snarls filled Thoeba's ears until the monster roared its challenge.

Crash didn't back off. He launched at the hideous beast, sinking his teeth into a leg. Thoeba watched in horror as it grabbed Crash by the scruff of his neck, and tossed him across the room and into a wall. The dog yelped, but regained his footing after landing.

She saw Peter standing at the top of the steps, holding an axe. She winced.

His protective nature shone like a beacon, looking ready to die a hero.

He had no idea what stared him down. The axe he held would not kill a being from the darkness, but that wouldn't stop the fool from trying.

Humans, she thought. Always acting like they're the invincible ones.

Peter stared at his dog, rage creeping over his features. His face drained of color while his eyes darkened almost black.

The calm facade in which he came for the demon sent a chill down Thoeba's spine. He stayed expressionless, but she sensed anger fueling his strength.

He swung the axe, and the beast grabbed the handle in mid-swing with one hand. Peter struggled to free it, but the monstrosity held fast. Long talons groped for Peter's face.

Thoeba darted from her corner and swiped the claw from Peter's eyes. It would have to be enough. She needed to concentrate on invisibility for a little while longer.

The demon roared in surprise, and let go of the axe to face the new threat. It couldn't see her-and neither could

Peter.

He swung again, hitting the creature in the back with a meaty thud.

She couldn't see the action from her vantage point, but Thoeba heard the sucking sound of Peter extracting the axe, and slamming it again.

The demon couldn't decide between her, the unseen threat, or Peter, the one with the sharp weapon.

Crash made it back to his feet, barking mightily, although keeping a safe distance.

She watched the monster's head sway as it tried to make a decision. It glared at the dog. From the way it focused on Peter, she guessed it did not consider Crash much of a threat. Especially since the human male had already caused it pain.

And it still couldn't see Thoeba. Once again, it shifted away from her.

Just in time for Peter to slice a clean cut across its throat. He seemed surprised that no ichor spewed forth, no torrent of sticky black blood.

Thoeba saw the deep slice and untied the string from her neck. She had an idea, and she had to hurry before the thing hurt Peter.

Thoeba shared the dawning terror slithering up his spine telepathically. The only damage done to the beast remained superficial. And now it was *really* mad.

It stomped toward Peter and Thoeba pounced on the fiend from behind. She clamped her legs around its back, threw her hands over its head with the string between her fists.

She found the gash Peter had sliced by touch, and worked the string in with her deity dangling from it.

Thoeba pulled. She leaned back, using her entire body weight to dig her necklace into her enemy's throat.

She heard it snarl, heard Crash barking, and the girl screaming downstairs. Peter demanded Kayla stay put.

Thoeba tried to tune them all out as her head pounded with terrible visions that didn't belong to her. She closed her eyes, and pulled tighter.

The *pop* that resounded when she decapitated the beast gave Thoeba the soaring joy of victory.

She landed on her knees when it turned to dust, the Energy hanging safely between her clenched hands as the powdery tang of hot demon burned her tongue.

Peter stared at her with wide eyes full of fear and confusion. Kayla screamed from the main floor, begging to know what happened, while Crash padded over to lick Thoeba's face.

She held God with one hand, stroked the shaking dog with the other. She heard Kayla rushing up the stairs, her mind jammed with questions.

"Will someone *please* tell me what's going on?" Peter didn't reply, but hugged his daughter in relief. Her speechlessness, though uncharacteristic, was welcomed.

Thoeba lifted her head to beseech the child and her father.

"That is what hunts me," she said. "That creature is one of many who conquered my world." She got to her feet, wincing at the pain in her bruised knees. "Do you understand now why I need you? Why I must restore the balance? If I don't, more of those will come for your world as well."

Peter let go of Kayla and trudged wearily toward Thoeba. A gentle hand dusted powdered Hellspawn from her cheeks, his expression warm and concerned.

"We'll do what we can to help," he said. "I don't know what, but I'm sorry I didn't believe you. It just sounded….I don't know. Unreal."

A flood of sorrow came then, and Peter rocked her, without seeming to understand the real reasons why she cried.

"C'mon. Sit down." He guided her to the edge of one of the beds. "Kayla, would you make some tea, and…are you hungry?" Thoeba nodded, gulping. She hadn't eaten anything since arriving in this realm.

"Okay. Kayla would you make us something to eat? Toast or something?"

"Sure, Dad. Yeah." Kayla's relief showed in the dropping of her shoulders as she hurried down the stairs.

Peter settled down next to Thoeba, making her long to bury her head in his chest.

"Now. Tell me what's going on Thoeba," he said. "I want to know everything."

Thoeba flinched.

He'd used her name. She'd never given it to him.

CHAPTER SIX

The monster liked his new body. No wings, but that didn't bother him. The demon held all of Jim's memories, all of his thoughts and knowledge. He had something called a truck, and Jim's skill of how to use it. It wouldn't be hard to get around.

He wanted to savor the delights of this realm. This body may be soft and squishy, but easy to control. The stupid human screamed in his head, but since Jim's mind held very little anyway, they were just echoes.

He considered himself smarter than most of his kind, but he took Jim's name and his gender when he transformed to dust to take this body. That way he wouldn't get confused. Just keep things simple.

When the Hellspawn had licked this victim, he tasted the vices this one liked. So many new sensations to explore. He couldn't resist possessing him.

This mortal would be more than just food. He was a doorway to new experiences, and Jim-thing couldn't wait.

He wanted to learn more about this place before his brethren consumed this world too. He needed a little entertainment for himself.

Fortunate also, this human knew where the enemy hid. Jim had met the hated guardian, and her unpleasant god.

So even if his comrade failed in finding the angel, the task of locating the enemy had been completed, leaving the monster extra play time.

Besides, 'Jim' wasn't in a hurry to go over the lake. Silly creatures crossed water in machines.

Jim-thing shook its head. No hurry. He would need sustenance. Perhaps he should eat someone.

Driving proved to be an interesting experience. Thanks to Jim's memories he got the basics quickly. It took him a little while to find the horn and to figure out the single fingered greeting, but the other humans on the road had shown him by example.

Many of these people should probably have paid more attention to the road than their hand signals as they rolled right off the road after he passed them.

It mattered not at all to him as long as he got to Kaos.

He heard sounds of human activity coming from the building he approached. Soothing booming cacophony came from within.

Once inside, he hissed happily at the sights and smells. The space had black walls, and lights flashed and crackled from the center of the ceiling. Stripes of pink blue and yellow pulsed in time with the noise. So many morsels in one place, undulating like wriggling bait...he would need to feed soon.

Something flailed at him with an appendage.

"Hey Jim." It came from behind the...bar? Yes, that was

the word. A man in blue waved to him, twisted open a bottle. The motion made him salivate. "You got time off?"

"Hey...." Jim-thing sifted through the mind of his victim. "...Rick. Yeah, till Wednesday." He accepted the drink, took a pull.

Ahhhh...

No wonder the mortal had been so fond of this substance. It had a woodsy flavor that warmed the belly and pulsed through his veins.

More intoxicating were the smells. Musk. Blood. Beer. Sweaty delicious prey packed the place. Part of him, Jim's part, remembered this to be a rare occurrence for Kaos to be so full during the afternoon.

The military exercise caused this. There were many more delectable humans, in many sizes, flavors, and colors. He drained the beer, and ordered another from the Rick.

He sniffed at a woman in passing. The young and succulent thing had been marinating in wine for hours now. The cigarettes would give her a smoked flavor. Not enough meat, though. He shrugged, and wiped drool of his chin. He *could* just kill her for fun...

He stepped away from the bar to pursue her, when a voice stopped him.

"Jim? Hey, Uncle Jim." A young man with night-colored hair came toward him with an outstretched hand.

Jim knew of this one from his victim. This was a Zack. Jim stretched his face in what he thought might be a trustable expression. He congratulated himself when the Zack returned the motion. Proof that he caught on faster than most demons.

“What’s new?” he asked.

“I just got home.” Zack ran a hand through the black waves on his head, “Haven’t even called Dad yet.” And he proceeded to talk about ‘computer classes’.

Jim’s face nodded.

He tried to bunch his facial muscles into an attentive gaze, but he didn’t care about machines that could talk to other machines. He needed different information, and learned from the old Jim’s thoughts that this was a hatchling of the human called Peter.

Traces of the earthling Jim screamed inside the cranium, making it hard for him to think. Resilient thing, this manling, but the demon remained in control. Between that and the noisy babbling of the hatchling, the monster couldn’t hold the facade.

“Have you seen her?” Jim asked.

Zack’s enthusiasm dimmed. “Seen who?”

Jim backpedalled. The Zack had not seen his enemy of course. The Zack had not been to the nest. “Nothing.” Jim stretched his face again. “How was school?”

“I…just told you.” Zack regarded Jim with narrowed eyes, and the Hellspawn guessed he should leave. Or maybe he should just kill and eat him right now.

“Jim? How many did you have already?”

“How many what?” He studied the Zack’s face. Wrong Answer. The hatchling looked suspicious. Tasty.

“I need a snack,” Jim-thing said.

Yeah,” Zack agreed. “You should eat something.”

Jim scanned his surroundings for the largest person in the establishment. "Later."

Zack nodded and moved out of his path, much to Jim-thing's relief. Any minute his stomach would growl loud enough to drown out the music.

Jim's memories included a catalog of phrases for influencing the lumpy specimens.

Females. He could eat one or he could screw one. He would do both.

Yes, that sounded like fun.

CHAPTER SEVEN

Thoeba dried her tears on Peter's T-shirt, the release unexpected but vital. A weight lifted from her heart. The Energy also seemed at peace.

Tell them everything, Thoeba. They must know.

Of course she had to now. If one minion had followed, others would as well.

She couldn't navigate this planet, let alone fight the demons all on her own. She didn't even have her sword anymore.

"Here. Come downstairs." Peter's voice soothed her.

Thani.

Her Thani stood by her side once again. He'd called her by name. No one else on this world could possibly know it.

His arms enveloped her tight in chivalry. For the first time since she'd arrived, calm washed over.

Thoeba clutched the Energy in one bony fist, demon dust leaving a sooty trail from between her fingers as she allowed him to lead her.

They walked together. She bathed in the warmth of his body and mind while Kayla's mind hummed a song of compassion.

Peter sat Thoeba down on the futon and joined her. She marveled at how he seemed to go from anger to safeguarding in a ripple.

Just like Thani, ever the defender, she thought.

Crash crouched at her feet, at the ready and recuperated enough to defend once more. She rewarded the dog with the scratching of ears that made him rumble and grin, and his energy lifted. The harmony here stayed tentative at best, but a single purpose held a father and daughter together.

That purpose being her and her mission. They believed.

Kayla placed a plate of sandwiches before them. "I hope peanut butter and strawberry jam is okay? With no electricity, and just the three coolers, and one of them is full of beer..." She prattled on, even as she went outside, where water boiled on the Coleman stove.

Without waiting for invitation, Thoeba shoved half a peanut butter and jam sandwich in her mouth. She hadn't noticed her hunger much until now. Peter watched her with some amusement tainted with concern but she paid him no mind. She cared more about filling her belly.

Did mortals always have to make their thoughts so apparent? Peter buzzed with ideas. Fear, excitement and a sense of protectiveness for both her and Kayla raced circles through his brain.

Kayla couldn't hang on to her thoughts. Questions tripped over themselves in her head, and Thoeba tried to shut them out of hers.

So much so, that she almost didn't hear the girl's question.

"I said how do you like your tea?"

Kayla waited across from the futon. She had three ceramic mugs sitting on the kitchen counter, and put sugar and powdered milk in two of them.

"I'll take it the same as you," Thoeba said.

Kayla nodded, repeated the process for the last mug and poured the brew.

Thoeba's ears burned as she endured the weight of his gaze and she slowed her chewing. He studied her again. His wonder and amazement buzzed around his head like a swarm of flies.

It would make her crazy, if the longing for him didn't. Her Thani sat right next to her. In human form.

With his daughter.

He remained unaware of her love for him, and oblivious to her ache. She couldn't remember ever experiencing such pain.

Would he have her back? Would Kayla let her? It wasn't just his face that changed. This morning, she kissed her lover good-bye. This afternoon, he no longer remembered her, and he'd fathered two children.

She wished she'd had the opportunity to pick the time frame she'd landed in. Perhaps one where he hadn't met his wife yet. The turmoil turned peanut butter to glue on the roof of her mouth and formed a sickly ball in her stomach.

She opened her sticky hand to inspect the Energy, her

reason for being here. It shone bright with the love in the room.

Why didn't you tell me?

What would you have done?

It would have made this whole situation easier.

It would have complicated things.

It would have made things better. At least for me.

What would you have done?

She paused. Would she have run joyfully into his arms? Forgotten the importance of her mission?

Or maybe she'd have been distracted, obsessed with Thani's whereabouts while she trying to fight the darkness.

Isn't that what got him killed in the first place?

Kayla appeared with the tea, startling Thoeba. She'd been so deeply in communion with her deity, she hadn't heard her coming. Not good. She let her emotions take the edge off her skill. She must learn to suppress them or people would die.

She put the crystal down, and took the mug in both hands, allowing the heat to seep into her cold clenching grip. Kayla sat on the other futon across from Thoeba and Thani. *Peter!* She reminded herself, his name is Peter. And he is human now.

She drank her tea, savored the warmth washing through her veins. She could learn to like this stuff. It tasted like fruit and roses.

She hadn't forgotten that the two of them were eyeing her with concern. They sat in wait for answers that only she could provide. She glanced down to her god, sitting in serenity in a prison of crystal, waiting for her to tell her story. It pulsed encouragement to her.

How much should she tell them? How much could they handle? She sighed. May as well start at the beginning.

"Your 'big bang' theory is not so far off," Thoeba said. "But it wasn't the birth of this universe. It was the birth of God." She gulped her cooling tea. "It is, as you say, older than time."

No better way to explain that to a mortal. Their minds could not fathom anything older, and she had yet to understand time. "It gathered strength and used all its power to create new worlds, new life."

"We were the first. Angels, as you call us. It created our lives from the power it pulled from stars."

"This is where *you* come in. From the pull of the positive energy, came the negative energy."

Thoeba smiled. This part they had no problems understanding. All Earth's cultures had myths and beliefs about positive and negative, good and evil, yin and yang.

"Polar opposites…" Peter clasped both hands together, blew out a breath. "So the devil exists? Is that what you're telling me?"

"In a manner of speaking, yes. It is a life force without a true soul."

Kayla's confusion tapped Thoeba's brain. "Why doesn't it have a soul?"

"It came to life from the negative push of energy, not the positive pull that brings life. It lives, but with no conscience, no feeling, no true emotion. It is a parody of life."

"So where did that…that…"

Thoeba turned to Peter. "That demon was a creation of the darkness."

"I don't understand," Peter said, stroking Crash's neck.

Funny how Earthlings found comfort in giving comfort sometimes, she thought. A point in their favor.

"When the darkness came into existence, it too desired to create life, albeit in the same mockery of itself." She drained the last of her tea, and walked softly to the kitchen. "We've been fighting them since."

"Fighting them for what?" Peter followed her to the kitchen. "I mean, really. Fight for territory? Fight for souls? I don't get the whole 'us verses them' shit. What's the point?"

Thoeba shrugged as she poured herself another cup of tea, and Peter refilled his mug. He lingered just close enough that she could smell the musk and clover scent of his skin. Inspecting him from the corner of her eyes she drank in the sight of his t-shirt straining across his chest.

And came back to herself. "There is no point." She concentrated on the sweet smell and flavor of her beverage instead of what she really wanted. "It's what they do. They kill, they destroy, they feed. It is their existence. They don't need a cosmic objective." She reached for the open jar of peanut butter, took a handful, and began licking it off her hand.

Nutty and creamy as it was, it took a minute for her to register the disquiet coming from both Peter and Kayla. She peered up to see their gaping mouths as they stared at her.

Embarrassment wasn't a sensation Thoeba felt often, but she recognized the heat spreading across her cheeks. She found a slice of bread, and wiped the peanut butter onto it. The rest of the tackiness she wiped on her shirt.

She had no idea why the gesture made Kayla wince.

"When the Energy created these worlds-"

"Wait a minute." Kayla held up a hand, and connected with them in the cramped kitchen. "When you say, 'these worlds' do you mean there are other worlds? Other planets?"

"Yes. There are other planets and other dimensions." When Kayla smiled at her, Thoeba said, "Yes, Kayla. That means hobbits really do exist, among other things. Dragons, elves, faeries..."

"Aliens?"

The excitement in Kayla's voice reverberated across the room.

"More species from more planets than you can count."

Kayla paused. "Can you read their minds too?"

Thoeba let a grin creep to her lips. "All the time."

Both humans shivered.

"Yeah, okay." Peter searched for words to describe his ideas while changing a subject that seemed to make him uncomfortable. "You were at the 'when' part of creation, here."

Thoeba swallowed sweet and salty deliciousness-she'd begun to thoroughly enjoy these things called tea and peanut butter-before continuing.

“Of course. Your Earth is a marvel, an absolute wonder. I have never seen so many different forms of life in one place before.” She nodded to the Energy lying on the coffee table. “It had really out done Itself. There is life within life on every surface, in every single cell.”

“So did we evolve? Or were we created human as the Bible said?” Peter’s agitation pushed throughout the story, his impatience obvious enough she could have read it even without telepathy.

“You’re getting ahead of me.” Thoeba brought her tea back to the futons and parked on one. Peter sat across from her on the other. “As our Energy created life, evil grew from the darkness.” She tried to come up with a way to present it for their understanding, used the mortal name. “A Satanic by-product, if you will.”

Kayla paled. “That would be the demons then.”

“Satan is the darkness?” Peter asked.

“Yes.” She sipped at her cup, listened to their minds vibrate.

She admired their glass hearts, but worried about their naive knowledge. Not to mention limited senses. Like how neither of them seemed aware of when she could hear their thoughts as though they were spoken.

She rose to pace. She found it burdensome to tell them. “For centuries we have fought them.” How much should she expose? She wasn’t sure she wanted them to know these things about her and her world. If the situation were not so dire, she would leave them without this information.

“Once we were stronger. Most of the time we won. The demons turned to dust as they perished, corrupting even in death.”

Peter and Kayla leaned forward as she gained momentum in her story. Thoeba noticed Kayla had put the kettle back on. Perfect. She would need more liquid to ease the ache in her throat.

"They turn to dust when they die. They pollute the heavens, seep from portals into other realms. They taint the beauty of other planets."

She shuddered. So many battles, too many to count or remember. "Some of them will deliberately transform themselves to powder and they fly into our eyes, adulterating our thoughts."

The tears came again, and Thoeba fought to swallow them. Peter's desire to console her was written in his gaze, but he didn't move. She wished that he could recover those memories, that he could empathize with her pain. He remembered nothing, and perhaps she should be thankful instead.

"Many of my kind died by their own hands, swords at their wrists and throats, driven mad by the essence of the enemy."

"My God..." Peter didn't notice his blasphemy in his horror. She could hear the anguish her story gave him. He shifted across until he sat beside her. She let him rub her back, let the repetitive motion help him cope as well as her.

"It doesn't matter if it is death by battle, or death by suicide, the souls of my brethren scatter. Many come here." She motioned with her arms the vast space around her.

"And no, you didn't evolve from chimpanzees." It made her smile. "I think some of our kind chose that form long ago because of the opposable thumb, and the bi-pedal form. That and the mental challenge, but no. The human form has been designed to hold advanced sentient spirits."

"Anyway, your kind has it all wrong." It might have been amusing had it not been so dire. "You don't go to Heaven and become angels when you die. When our kind dies, we come here."

The onslaught of questions that erupted from both of them became a vocal and mental racket.

"Does that mean-"

"I thought that-"

She pinched the bridge of her nose, and let the babbling tumble from their mouths as both jumped up to stomp around. They talked over each other and asked questions she would answer if they would *just. Be. Quiet.*

Abrupt silence felt like bliss. She hadn't dreamed that would work. Were they picking up her thoughts and feelings? Peter sat back down, and Kayla flopped next to him, both unaware of her influence apparently.

"So...where do *we* go when we die?"

Kayla's voice, scared and small, made Thoeba sad. This would not be easy.

"Your kind can't come back yet."

"Why not?"

"Because," Thoeba breathed a sigh. "None of you can come back to Eden until you learn to deny evil. All of you have some of it in you. Some more than others. Until you are cleansed of it, you'll just keep returning in these forms."

Both humans were picturing historical villains. Thoeba remembered the awful little man with his ugly square moustache, but the man with the crazy eyes and the swastika tattooed on his forehead wasn't one she recognized. Nor did she know the thin one with the black beard and turban. But they got the point at least.

Awful to say, but the next part would be worse. "And now that Eden has been taken, no one ever will get back until I can restore the Energy to Its power."

Kayla drew a shaky breath. "So that's it?" she said. "We just keep reincarnating over and over forever?"

Thoeba sighed. "Precisely."

"Unless we can bring God back to power."

"And tip the balance, correct."

Peter groaned and rubbed his stubble. He massaged the tips of his fingers into his temples.

"So will you help me?" Thoeba asked.

"From where I'm sitting, it doesn't look like I have much choice." He gifted her with a grin nonetheless. "I'll do what I can." He got to his feet, and headed for the door.

"Where are you going, Dad?"

Peter swiveled to Kayla and smiled. "Guess putting those huge shutters on the windows was a pretty good idea, eh? I'm going to board this place up. We'll be safe here tonight, no matter what comes."

He glanced over his shoulder to Thoeba. "Come with me," he said. "I'll show you how to build booby traps, military style."

Thoeba grinned. He sounded just like Thani.

CHAPTER EIGHT

Thoeba helped Peter padlock the massive shutters on each of the windows. One set in the kitchen facing east, and two in the living room, north and west. The creaking wood protested from long years of inactivity, but Peter promised they would 'do the job.' He showed her the locked shed which held the supplies they would need to build defenses. But the winds had picked up too much to set anything up now; they would have to wait for the morning. Until then, the barricades would have to do.

With that done, they retreated to the dark safety inside, where Thoeba told them of her escape to their planet.

Kayla seemed spellbound on the edge of a futon couch while Peter built a fire in the fireplace. Thoeba told them of the chase that brought her here, and her shock of landing on Earth.

She skipped the part about Thani's death. She wasn't ready to talk about it, at least not to them. She swallowed her anguish and pleaded for their help.

“This planet is where the concentration of demon dust is the widest spread. You have just enough technology to turn the tide.”

“But how?” Peter asked. “And with what? You lost your sword.” He tossed kindling into the flame. “Not to mention you’re only one woman. Got any more of your kind coming?”

Thoeba glanced toward the window that had earlier been open to the lake, and viewed gnarled slats instead.

The sunlight visible between the gaps muted to orange. Dusk fell, bringing cobalt storm clouds that flickered and groaned.

More fear came with them.

“I don’t really know. Its possible more angels are already here. More might be on their way. All I know is that I’m supposed to be here. With you.” She cocked her head to the side, listening. “It involves something called ‘satellites.’ ”

Peter moaned. “That is *way* over my head.”

He piled logs in the fireplace. Crash sat panting at his side while Peter coaxed sweet smelling warmth and comfort from the reluctant birch.

“But it isn’t for Zack.” Kayla got up from the couch she reclined on, went to the cooler in the kitchen and returned with a can of cola. “He’s probably here already. I could text him.”

To Thoeba she said, “My brother is a computer genius.”

“I don’t even know what a sat-el-lite is…” Thoeba spoke the word in three phonetic syllables. “Never mind a confuser.”

"Computer," Kayla corrected.

"Doesn't matter. Kayla's right." Peter got up and walked over to the ice chest for a beer. "We need to tell him what's going on. He's my son. You can trust him long enough for him to help us, can't you?"

"Do I have a choice?" She jumped at the peal of thunder, and approached a boarded window with caution. A peek through a crevice showed twilight.

She'd forgotten the setting sun. The smell of ozone lurked through the screens. It reminded her of Armageddon, the last battle of Eden. It remained fresh like a seeping cut that refused to heal.

Thoeba rubbed her goose-fleshed arms as Peter threw another log in the fireplace. He had no idea the true *depth* of her fear. He couldn't...being only mortal. He didn't remember the horrors of his own end.

When night came in our world, it brought destruction with it, she thought.

She heaped herself back down on the daybed, her despair and isolation threatening to consume her.

"Is my son safe in town?" Peter asked. "Is anyone safe?"

"We have no way of knowing for certain." She held her pendant up. "But the Energy is holding up well. If the dark minions were close It would react." Thunder rattled the windows. "Besides, it smells like rain, and demons avoid water whenever possible. It causes them pain."

Kayla sat across from Thoeba and crossed her legs. Peter moved near enough so Thoeba could sip his scent. Musk and clover now mixed with barley, hops and yeast. Crash padded over, his desire for praise radiating from him in a steady pulse like his heartbeat. Thoeba obliged, and pet his flanks.

She liked Crash- he was the quietest Earthling she'd met so far.

Everyone sat alone in their thoughts, unaware Thoeba shared them.

She stroked the good dog, and listened to Peter worry for his children and his whole planet, while he lit lanterns and chunky candles.

Kayla tempered her fear by the fascinating idea of a place where hobbits and elves battled their own evils.

Crash, having satisfied his need for Thoeba's tender caresses, took his post as guardian by the entrance with an air of importance.

The fire and the storm seemed to roar and crackle in conversation.

Thoeba guessed she should be pacified by the gentle flames, but it gave her nothing but trepidation. It reminded her of bloody battles won and lost for centuries.

She recalled the Mongol hordes, the crusades. She'd believed such Holy Wars were the worst things mankind had been capable of.

Then she'd seen Hiroshima.

Her mind drifted to the day when mankind's most diabolic weapon fell like the hand of evil on Japan. Thoeba, along with her comrades were given the warning to retreat. They'd flown at the speed of sound. Some of them didn't make it.

Thoeba's wings caught fire, and it pulled her from the sky. She'd lain burned, broken and bleeding for days in the jungles of Korea before her brethren found her and brought her home.

And she'd never returned.

She wanted Peter to hold her, but his distraction and Kayla's proximity prevented her from seeking his affections. He thought about everything but her it seemed.

He lingered in her heart, but she had no place in his mind. She resented how he couldn't hear her telepathically-At least not anymore.

As she sat in silent contemplation for more than an hour, full night arrived. With it came the clap of thunder that brought rain. Crash paced from the door to comforting hands, back and forth chuffing and whining.

Kayla kept a running dialog about school and homework to Peter while a metal box in the corner droned about the weather and the latest news. Occasionally it barked as lightening flashed, but the blathering never ceased. What was it about humans? Didn't they like quiet?

Kayla eventually drifted to sleep. Peter draped a striped blanket over her, not bothering to pull out the couch for a full bed. Crash snuffed a pathetic sigh from the door.

As the vigorous tapping of the rain intensified, a howl from the wind and the rush of leaves brought a splattering of drops on the ceiling.

Thoeba saw her own worry mirrored in Peter's gaze, like they'd drawn the same conclusion at the exact same time.

The patio doors were ajar.

They ran for the steps, anxious to cut off the last vulnerable spot in the house.

Thoeba assisted Peter as he charged straight out onto the balcony for the storm doors.

He grabbed the left brace. Icy pins of water scratched at Thoeba's skin as the wailing wind tried to blow them off the edge. The tempest pummeled them both. Thoeba's hair clung to her head and shoulders. She pulled on the right hand door as she retreated into the loft, and Peter collected the handle from her to shut them back inside.

Thoeba's heart rattled inside her chest like a caged bird, and her breath came in sputters.

"Does thunder scare you?"

Thoeba met eyes that twinkled in lightning and shadow.

You just don't know me anymore, she thought. The realization brought an emotional pang that Thoeba couldn't identify as hurt or anger.

It took more than a little storm to frighten her.

Thoeba never minded cleansing showers, but positioned next to these closed and vibrating patio doors made her wish these sheets of wet rage would cease.

And that she wasn't so cold and wet.

And that Peter could recall that he loved her.

She shivered there, water dribbling off her nose and chest, and wanted it be Thani here with her in this gloom.

A warm calloused hand took hers, led her away from the noise of the elements.

He'd found a towel, stroked it along her face, drying tears she didn't know had fallen, and ruffling the moisture from her hair.

"You gave me the impression you weren't afraid of anything," he said. "I watched you take the head off a monster." In the flashes of brilliance she could see him grin. "Don't tell me a little Alberta squall freaks you out?"

She shuddered.

No, it wasn't just the cold, or the fear of the storm.

Fighting a single demon was one thing. Saving a deity along with the entire universe would be another. She had the uncomfortable sensation of doubt, that she would fail, and they would all die.

He wrapped the towel around her shoulders and returned her to the relentless pounding on the wooden doors.

He was so close… but not close enough.

"Look," he said. Ribbons of white and pink fluttered across the sky between gaps in the boards. "You can't tell me that's not a thing of beauty?"

Thoeba's eyes stung. Her heart ached from the contact on her back, where her wings should be and his chest brushed against her.

She didn't care about lightning.

Thani touched her here. Now.

Thoeba realized how much she wanted him, needed his presence. Maybe he wasn't the same man. It didn't matter. She had to find out.

She twisted around and cupped his face. She didn't need to be empathetic to sense his surprise. His shoulders tense and his mouth dropped open.

She kissed his lips, using her tongue to gain entry to his soul. She spoke to him then, knowing he couldn't hear her; welcomed him in the silent ways she used to, when they were one, and they called Eden their home.

She tasted his sweet breath before kissing him down the length of his jaw, tracing his saltiness with her tongue. She continued all the way down to his collarbone, raised her face to caress his mouth with hers once more.

He moaned, and held her so tight she could hear his heart beating fast. His mouth took hers, and when she rubbed her breasts to his chest, he hardened below.

Everything. She wanted *everything*.

He pulled away from her. The sudden emptiness in her arms made her gasp.

She barely heard him over the heaven's clamor.

"Why are you doing this?" His voice, thick with longing quickened her need.

"I...I don't understand." Thoeba searched his face in the dark for his hesitation.

"I don't take advantage of women who need my help. You don't need to-"

"What? No." She shook her head in desperation, pushed wet strands of hair away from her face.

How could she make him understand?

"You've been through a lot today. Maybe you should just..." Thoeba stalked forward to claim him. She let her hands wander his growing length. He didn't want her to stop, she could tell by his sigh and the way he cupped her fingers.

"I want to be with you," she said. "I need to..."

I need to be with you, Thani, she thought.

"I want to..." Her whispered words became hoarse with yearning.

"Please. I want to." *Be with you again.*

She ran her hand down his face, shuddering as his stubble tickled her palm. She grasped his left hand, placed it on her breast, and pushed him to a bed.

The back of his knees touched the edge. She nudged him to the mattress, straddled his lap.

He gripped her hips and slid her against his stiff heat as she kissed him with aching tenderness.

He growled as she thrust against him. His eyes gazed into hers with intent, and his hesitation dissolved like morning fog.

She released him long enough to remove her tank top, and dropped it to the ground. She leaned in to take off his T-shirt, even as he bent to take a nipple into his mouth.

Her breath faltered and her fingernails dug into his soaked cloth as she raised it up to his chest.

He stopped only long enough for her to remove the shirt, then returned his attention to the other nipple. Her hands wrapped through his bristled hair. Her back arched in pleasure, and she whimpered.

His arms and fingers traced her body until he flipped her to her back on the bed. Desire gave way to worry, but only for a moment.

She no longer had wings for him to damage. For the first time since she'd arrived on earth, she didn't miss them.

She embraced him in her mind and in her heart, his desires, his intentions.

He removed the rest of her clothing. Her sweats were whisked from her body with surprising efficiency, and he wasted no time tasting her.

His tongue explored without hurry, back and forth, up and down. Making lazy laps at her clitoris.

She surrendered absolutely, opened her thighs for him. She held nothing back, not that she could. Her breathing came fast and hard, on the edge of a scream.

Vaguely aware of him stripping off his sweats and boxers, she welcomed him into her arms. She returned his wet kiss, tasting her lust and moving her body to touch as much of him as possible.

They shared the dizzying anticipation, the animal need.

He entered her, waited as her body adjusted to his size.

She couldn't breathe.

He took her slowly at first, and she ground her chest into his. She wanted all of him everywhere, couldn't control her urgency.

And he went so *deep*. It was so good-it always was with him. Even a human lifetime hadn't taken his skills in satisfying her.

Thunder drowned out whimpers of sweet pleasure.

He got to his knees, and dragged her to his erection by her buttocks. His lovemaking grew frenzied. He thrust harder, faster. Guttural cries came from this throat, his primal self releasing.

She wrapped her ankles around his back, her body clenching of its own accord when she found his rhythm. Her pleasure became louder, and she bit down on her pillow as she rode the wave of sexual euphoria to its crescendo. The sky's rolling growl shook the bed, and Thoeba hoped it masked their passion from Kayla's ears even as she let go.

Peter collapsed next to Thoeba on sweat-stained sheets. She cuddled herself to his chest, and let herself relax in his supple, spent flesh.

Minutes passed without words, their breathing slowed, and she drifted into sleep to the sound of his heartbeat.

CHAPTER NINE

Peter wasn't used to sharing a bed anymore. When he woke up and realized he had Thoeba's arm draped across his crotch it gave him a start.

He opened his eyes to the sight of her unblemished face kissed by rays of sunshine through the slats in the shutters. He studied her pert nose, her creamy satin skin. Golden curls tumbled over the pillow like molten coils. She resembled-well, for lack of a better word, an angel.

Nothing she did last night could be described as angelic, he thought with a grin. His gaze travelled down to her firm breasts, round nipples like pebbles straining against the sheets. It made his cock stir, and he thought about waking her for another round.

Kayla rattled around downstairs. His penis shrank back, the idea of having sex now snuffed out in favor of responsibility.

So much for that. Damn.

He eased out of bed, scratched his stomach, his balls, his ass, and smoothed his facial growth with his hands.

He'd wash up in the lake after some instant coffee and oatmeal.

He sniffed at the hot fried scent in the air. Correction. Instant and Eggs.

God bless Kayla and her love of campfire cooking.

He dressed in a hurry. He preferred his breakfast fresh from the cast iron, and he had a lot to do before he picked Zack up from the marina.

He and Kayla needed to talk about the Wal-mart thing, but in light of last night's bedroom aerobics he'd be willing to drop it for now if she didn't say anything.

He paused to watch Thoeba breathe. She seemed peaceful, sleeping the dreamless slumber of the blameless. He zipped up a pair of cutoffs and decided to let her rest.

~~~

As Thoeba roused, she inhaled the scents of sex and morning dew. Sunlight and birdsong streamed through the windows, and the linens were cool under her fingertips. Peter had left her some time ago.

A sense of loss brought her alert. The bed became unwelcoming without his presence, as though she didn't belong there.

She disengaged herself from the cotton, sought out the damp towel Peter used to dry her off the evening before and wiped last night's sticky lust from her thighs.

Thoeba dressed in her borrowed Billibong tank top and sweats. She could hear sounds of life coming from below, and with the bedroom turning cold for her, she descended the stairs.
~~~

Kayla lounged on the sofa closest to the kitchen, a musical device entrenched in her ears. She raised an eyebrow to Thoeba before removing one of the plugs to address her.

Thoeba could hear adolescent male voices and semi-tortuous squealing emitting from it.

"Good morning." Kayla's smirk suggested secrets. Did she hear them during the night? "Some storm we had last night, eh?"

Thoeba hugged herself. "It frightened me."

"You get used to it." Kayla shrugged, held up the tiny singing box. "Thank God for iPods. I could tune a lot of it out."

"That can't be good for your ears."

"There's Earl Grey and scrambled eggs on the stove if you're hungry," Kayla said.

A rumbling in Thoeba's belly answered. She made her way to the kitchen, poured a cup of hot water and fixed herself some tea the way she'd seen Kayla do it.

As for the eggs...

The stomach that had grumbled before now lurched in protest.

She would *not* eat congealed bird embryos.

She sought out bread, and the stuff she'd had yesterday.

What had Peter and Kayla called it? Peanut butter, that's it.

Breakfast in hand, she sat across from Kayla on the other sofa. She sipped at the hot liquid, shut her eyes and let the caffeine bring her back to life.

She thanked me for iPods. I would never have given them Ipods. That was definitely their doing. The Energy's whispering voice sounded amused.

Thoeba spat brown liquid all the way across the living area until it reached Kayla's crossed legs.

The girl sprang up, wiped tea from her knees. "Ow! What did you do that for?"

This is why I didn't tell you about Thani. You forgot all about me, didn't you?

If a god chuckled in the forest, only Thoeba would hear. It sounded like bees in a fan.

Guilt and panic put a ball of hair in Thoeba's gut.

Where was It? She scanned the room. Her breath came in little gasps as her sights flew to the futons, counters, and coffee table. Her hand clutched at her throat, where the crystal should have been.

"Relax," Kayla said. "He's right here." She groped into the pocket of her hooded jacket and produced the deity. The crystal pendant twinkled, safe and silent in her hand.

Kayla and I are getting to know each other.

Thoeba peered into Kayla's sky blue eyes. She tried not to let her anxiety show, but it didn't stay hidden when she snatched the necklace back.

“I found it under the coffee table,” Kayla said. “Must’ve fallen off your neck when you and dad ran up the stairs.” Her lips turned up, and her eyes narrowed.

Thoeba sucked air in shaky heaves until the Energy sat on her collarbone once more. She changed the subject.

“Can you speak to It?” Thoeba asked.

Kayla shrugged a shy acknowledgement. “Not really. It’s more like feelings.”

Thoeba pondered this, wondering if humans could learn that level of communication.

She’s a frequent visitor to this world, an old soul.

Why hadn’t she seen this possibility before? Thoeba scrutinized the girl, half expecting to see her many lifetimes etched on her spirit like rings on a tree.

You underestimate them. And you were busy.

She endured the mild rebuke from her god but it brought heat to her face and a delicious tremble to her knees.

Speaking of trembling. Peter.

“Where is your father?”

“Setting up the booby traps,” she said in a matter-of-fact tone, as though her father fortified his domain on a regular basis.

So it was true. Earthlings *were* desensitized to violence.

“His phone’s dead so he called Zack on my cell a couple of hours ago.” Kayla checked for messages. “Dad’s gonna meet him at the dock.”

Thoeba shoved the remainder of her snack in her mouth and hastened outside.

Crash nipped at minnows in the shallows while Peter trudged back and forth between his boat and the shore.

He loaded life jackets, spare boat shoes, socks and a cooler.

Thoeba perused the cabin's perimeter, saw that he had checked and reinforced the defenses. Her acute senses deduced the trip wires had been fashioned from fishing lines. They shone like spider silk in the daylight.

She also picked up the scent of ammonia drifting from the floorboards of the cabin porch.

Homemade bombs.

Thoeba had seen enough war contraptions such as these to understand how humans used them for killing each other. With any luck these tactics would work on demons as well.

Peter glanced up at her, and a pang of nervousness fluttered in her throat.

What should she say? Thanks for last night, do you know we were lovers in another lifetime? *That* would go over well, no doubt.

"Good morning, Thoeba." He continued packing supplies.

That's all? Just 'good morning'? After all that happened between them, he greeted her like an acquaintance? She had a difficult time dealing with his casualness. It poisoned her heart.

She shifted on one foot, pushed a lock of hair behind her ear. "Peter. Hi."

He rambled back toward the boat and placed the ice bag on the co-pilot seat, unaware of her discomfort.

She missed Eden.

She longed for her old life and her union with Thani. This existence made him a stranger where love and familiarity used to be. Here on earth he would always be oblivious to the echoing sadness of her heavy heart.

His current thoughts were on his son, his excitement reserved for the mission ahead. Everywhere but here and now with her.

She strayed to the shoreline in her bare feet, let the sand sift between her toes. She could hear her pulse and the playful splashing of the dog. The green scents of a forest lingered after the storm along with the smell of clay.

Peter thought of her as just another woman, and when she'd seduced him, she hadn't considered how much that would hurt.

She tuned into his thoughts, suddenly aware they involved her after all.

"Peter, you can't leave without me," she said.

He lost his footing when he spun to meet her. He cursed and splashed, regained it.

"I hate it when you do that," he said. "Get out of my mind." He shook his head, beads of sweat rained on the lake. "You have to stay here. With Kayla."

She inched forward. "No, you don't understand." She longed to touch him. "I have to go with you, in case there is another attack."

He sighed. "Look, I have to go get my son. There are no roads to these cabins. Kayla is safer here." He surveyed his property, his expression confident. "Those explosives will stop a tank."

"We can take her with us."

"No." Peter kicked sand out of his boat shoes, refused to make eye contact. "I've set this place up like a fortress. She's better off with you." He raised his eyes and pointed to her neck with the crystal resting there. "Bear in mind, you need to protect that."

Thoeba glared at him. It wasn't just that she needed to be with him. "If Zack is as smart as you say he is, we need to protect him as well. Can you program satellites world wide? He's critical to saving your world."

Thoeba heard the war inside his head echo like shouts.

"If you want her to stay here, fine. Zack is the one who needs protection, and I'm the only one here with anything resembling a holy weapon." She tapped the pendant. "Don't think for one minute I'll let you take this with you."

Peter made a slashing gesture with his hand. "You have no idea what it's like to be a parent." He glowered at her, his blue eyes icy. "You just don't seem to understand, she's my little girl." He twisted away from her, continued to wade out into the shallows to finish loading the boat.

She smouldered, clenched her fists. "You think you are the only one afraid of loss?" She decreased the gap between them, and grabbed his arm. "You don't know how I feel. Don't presume I would not *understand*." She tried to squelch her ire, think reasonably. The Energy at her throat always responded adversely to her negative emotions. "I'm just being practical."

"Are you?" He smirked. "Are you sure it's not just because you want to stay with me?"

Volcanic irritation heated her face in sharp contrast to the chilled water that tickled her knees. She became angrier by the moment. "Don't overestimate your importance," she said.

Peter chortled, and it colored her ears.

"Okay, let's think about *your* practicality for a minute." He propped an arm on the gunnel. "Do you think it makes sense to come with me, and leave her alone, out here, with creatures from another dimension flying around?" He gestured to the air. "And yes, *you*." He jabbed a finger at her, "You have the only holy weapon."

"Who will shield you?" she asked. "You are being over-protective of her. You would leave yourself wide open while she sits in a fortified cabin."

"You really don't get it, do you? I'm her father." He leaned in so that Thoeba could smell stale coffee on his breath. "Protecting our children is what parents do. Don't they have kids where you come from?"

"Well no," Thoeba said. "Only mortals bear young."

Thoeba steered the conversation back to the problem. "The demons, if there even any out there…" They both glanced up to the endless blue. "They won't be interested in her."

"They'll be far more interested in me," she said. "We'll be leading the demons away from her." If that didn't convince him, nothing would.

Thoeba heard the hitch in Kayla's breath from behind her. She'd come down the grass to where they argued in the shallow waves, the silence broken only by Crash bounding through water to greet her.

"Dad?" Kayla said. "I think I'd like to stay here." An emotion flashed in her blue gaze. Thoeba picked up on something grinding through Kayla's heart. Perhaps resentment or jealousy. "Crash can stay with me."

Peter regarded his daughter. Thoeba became aware of his thoughts again.

He'd noticed it, that momentary glare Kayla shot at the woman he'd slept with. He didn't want to leave Kayla alone, but he didn't really want Thoeba with him. And he couldn't leave the two of them alone in the confined space of the cabin together.

Thoeba waited for him to think it through.

He checked the morning skies, searching for kites of black on the wind. She'd won this one.

One demon. Only one has come thus far.

They had listened for chaos on what she now knew to be a radio last night, and Thoeba hadn't heard anything out of the ordinary. No sightings, no reports of mass murders or destruction…yet.

"There hasn't been any signs of others so far," she said, repeating her god. "We would have seen them by now. If we move quickly, we can be back to the cabin before more of them arrive."

Peter made a decision. He shouldered past her and took Kayla's arm. "You stay inside the cabin." He ushered her toward the door, double-checked his handiwork of boobie traps. "Go to the bathroom now, and then lock yourself and Crash inside."

He gestured to the outhouse, all the while surveying the outside walls, the surrounding grass, the floorboards. His sense of urgency as he rushed around in earnest infected her as well.

No time to waste.

He stopped long enough to direct her. "Go ahead and get in the boat. I'm going to check everything." He led Crash by his collar.

Thoeba sloshed back to the boat, tolerating the cold bite on her lower legs while the soft sand gave beneath her feet. She found a small ladder on the back end that allowed easy access into the boat. She settled in one of the rear seats, waited for Peter to finish.

Kayla met her father at the door. He embraced her, and she returned it with equal ferocity. The sight made Thoeba's heart do a little flip.

"And you don't let *anyone* in until we get back. Got it?" he said.

Thoeba smiled as Peter kissed Kayla on the top of her head and ushered the dog into the cabin with her. Peter slammed the screen door shut and waited.

The next sounds she heard were familiar to Thoeba. They reminded her of medieval times of wars and plagues in earlier visits to this realm. They were the thuds and scrapes of a wooden door being bolted tight.

"All locked up?" Peter asked. A muffled reply came from within the log walls.

Peter nodded and made his way to Thoeba. Fear now etched creases in his handsome visage. His mouth pulled down in a grimace better suited to an older man.

Peter didn't spare her a glance when he hoisted the anchor into the boat. He said nothing while he pushed the bow out to deeper water, merely grunted as he climbed the ladder to get in. He stumbled his way to the pilots chair and the little watercraft rocked with his efforts.

Finally he met her gaze. "Happy now?" he asked. She bit back her retort, knowing he'd snapped at her out of worry. The journey to the Cold Lake's marina began without conversation.

CHAPTER TEN

Jim-thing liked mornings on this planet. True, the sunlight seared his eye balls forcing him to wear protection and cover his head-but these were minor inconveniences.

He kept taking off these 'sunglasses' and checking the shiny white squares in his mouth with their reflective surface. He liked the eye shields. He could see his face in them.

The air stayed still and ripe. The previous night's storm seemed to have discouraged more campers from coming to the campground.

Strange beings, these humans. They liked to play in water, but didn't seem to enjoy it so much when it fell on them. He didn't like rain either, but at least it didn't cause him pain in this form.

He put the sunglasses back on his face, and surveyed his territory. His ears strained for the slightest movement, anything that might be good to eat. No new snacks had arrived. He would have to eat leftovers.

A chill slipped across his body. Oh. Yes. Perhaps he should cover his nakedness with something as well.

Jim-thing stalked back inside the Prowler.

Flies languished over last night's dinner as he admired his work. He went to shoo them off, and picked them out of the air. They made delightful appetizers-he loved their crunch.

The girl's blood washed the walls in scarlet. Chunky gobs of burgundy that glistened in the light.

His prey had been stupid enough to come with him to this campsite. He loved it when he outsmarted his food.

She'd tasted like a smoked ham and screamed in pleasure, then pain. It was music to his borrowed ears. Made him feel *alive*.

But it also gave him a strange sensation of nausea. The demon gloated. The desire to vomit and the smoked ham reference belonged to the real Jim inside, not to him. The human knocked around his head howling in vain.

He enjoyed experimenting with mental abuse, and this new method of torture excited the former demon. Especially when he could mix it with physical pain.

He wanted to linger. The desecrated body of his young prey lay like breakfast. She tempted him to stay for seconds with her glazed eyes and open mouth crawling with tasty treats.

But he had work to do, things to destroy. He searched around the trailer for something to keep him warm, and found a garment on the floor. It hurt his eyes to gaze upon the material, bright yellow color and purple trees. But he soon figured out they went on his legs and he wouldn't have to see them if he didn't look down.

Something under a pile of beer cans smelled of old alcohol and regurgitation. He tried to use it to cover his chest area, but he couldn't figure out which one of the holes he should put his head through.

No matter. On the wall hung a garment that reminded Jim-thing of his old skin. Even the demon could see he could put his arms in it and be shielded from the elements.

Much better. But he needed to feed. One could not accomplish mayhem of such magnitude on an empty stomach. He eyed the disemboweled woman and licked his lips. He'd eaten all the good bits, like the heart and liver, but plenty of meat hung on the bones. He wrenched one of her limbs free with a wet rip. Inside his head, the real Jim shrank in disgust.

Gnawing on a human arm like a drumstick, Jim-the-thing marched down to the docking area, wondering how these beings chewed their prey with such flat teeth. Good thing he still had demonic strength. He needed it to tear his food into smaller pieces.

The boat waited to take him to the enemy, which he knew from Jim's memories hid across the lake in an A-Frame cabin.

~~~

Once they were on the open water, Peter increased speed. The engine roared in his ears and spray from the bow sloshed against his forehead. He squinted, watching the shoreline for other boaters. Or more demons.

How'd he get himself into this? Oh yeah. He dragged a woman out of the lake and brought her to his cabin instead of bringing her to a hospital like a smart man would have. First she'd caused shit to fly between him and Kayla, then pissed off his buddy and lastly she'd brought her demon
~~~

friend down on his home. Then there was the mind-reading crap-If that's what she did. He hadn't convinced himself she'd really done that.

Then she seduced him and thought that gave her the right to call the shots. Not to mention, she'd started clinging already.

He had the worst taste in women. The sneering curl of his lip exposed his teeth to the wind, causing a ripple of agony.

It would be better once he got back to the fortified cabin with Zack and Thoeba. He'd be reunited with Kayla and Crash, and the four of them could hunker down and come up with a better plan. He had ideas, but he needed to get Zack in on this. He had the brains: Peter would have to be the brawn. Maybe he could talk Jim into helping them for a few beers. He'd tell him chicks dig heroes.

Peter peered over his shoulder at her. She sat at the back of the boat, her eyes also watching the water, her hair blowing like a radiant curtain in the wind. Damn.

She raised a graceful hand to pull away a stray curl, and his heart thumped. Sunshine turned her pale skin to pink.

Sunscreen. I should have given her sunscreen.

Her coloring suggested they didn't have ozone depletion where she came from. He scrounged in the cubby under his seat, watching his direction while his left hand rummaged for the plastic bottle of lotion. He didn't want to look at her anymore. She pissed him off. She made him want her. She confused the hell out of him.

"Thoeba." He twisted around to toss her a full tube of SPF 50. "Rub that all over your body. Your face too." He would have preferred to do the job himself, he remembered how those curves squirmed under hands, but he had to steer.

Yeah, steering. Much more important than massaging creamy wet lotion all over her thighs… Judging by the anger that glazed her eyes, she wouldn't want him touching her anyway.

He couldn't resist glancing back as she opened the tube and splattered a huge blob of white cream into her hand. She appeared to be disgusted, and it made him chuckle.

"Go on," he said. "All over. Everywhere." She glanced askance at him, but rubbed it on her legs. She covered both calves and Peter swallowed. If he watched her any longer, he'd run them up on a deadhead or something. Better to concentrate on the water and getting Zack from the marina. In an hour they would be there and back, and he wouldn't be alone with her anymore.

The smell of coconut on the wind tickled his nose. He couldn't help thinking how it blended well with her sweat, and he shut his eyes, just for a second, and breathed deep. He opened them again, but his mind went elsewhere.

Last night defied description. He remembered her taste, her smell, her passion.

He wanted her again. He thought about taking her now, on the boat. His grip loosened on the throttle, causing the engine to flounder.

No. Not here. Not in the middle of the lake in open spaces while his son waited at the docks. He watched her slide sunscreen down her neck to her chest, lift the strap of her tank top to get beneath. Someone would have to do her back.

What the hell is the matter with me?

He'd heard that danger created some interesting sexual tension, but it didn't strike him as being that simple.

From the minute he'd seen her take the head of that *thing*, he'd been turned on.

True, he hadn't believed her at first. Deity in a crystal and demons chasing her, yeah sure. But that leathery black monster hadn't been a National Geographic phenomenon from the Amazon rainforest. Unless it was *really* lost.

And he admired her warrior spirit. Great. So he had a thing for Amazonian warrior women, got his rocks off on watching them kill monsters. No wonder he got bored with his marriage.

He couldn't stop staring at her.

She stayed put with her knees together and her chin down. Poor lost angel. He shouldn't have bitten her head off at the cabin. He resisted the urge to go to her, wrap his arms around her and tell her it would be alright. He let his breath out. But would it be alright? Or was it too late?

~~~

Jim–thing throttled down when he spotted the cabin he sought. His host had been friendly with the owner, and spent his days and nights at this place whenever possible.

Ah, the memories that weren't his....Warm fires, good conversation and *lots* of beer.

Jim-thing guided the jet boat to the sand bar. The engine barely rumbled, and he remained undetected as far as he could tell. No one greeted him. No sounds but the sigh of nature in the trees.

A stench wafted to him that he didn't recognize. The reek made his eyes water and his nose sting. Jim's memories-the real Jim's- registered this odor as 'Windex', a substance used to clean windows.
~~~

Something rustled in the cabin. He sniffed for clues. He inhaled until his adenoids rattled in pain. Stupid limited senses. This human had a stunted sense of smell.

The eyesight of his host body seemed good enough, not great, but he found the gleaming fishing line right away.

He grew suspicious. The real Jim had ceased his internal bellowing. The abrupt silence told him Jim knew something Jim-thing didn't.

He approached the tight strings with caution, and ran a finger down a sharp edge. It cut him, and a red streak rose to the surface. He put his finger in his mouth, almost ate it. The blood tasted good, like beer on a hot day. Actually, he detected alcohol in it.

He should probably go around all the shiny strings, in case they cut him again. It wouldn't be good to get distracted now, not with the enemy within his grasp.

CHAPTER ELEVEN

Thoeba couldn't wait to get off the boat. What a way to travel. It was the only way to get to the marina from Peter's cabin, so she'd concentrated on keeping her breakfast down and staying dry.

He'd been thinking about her, she'd picked up on it, but she couldn't quite concentrate with the roar of the engine and sprays of water soaking her face and hair.

His thoughts as always, were drumming around through his head in wild abandon. She didn't care enough to focus. She could sense the lust near the surface of his awareness, but didn't share it.

Her anger with him held fast, but not for the argument at his cabin. One minute he had separation anxiety about his daughter, the next he wanted sex. Were all humans so conflicted, or just the males?

They neared the town. He switched the throttle lower and his thoughts shifted back to Zack. He scanned the busy marina.

Leisure craft of all sizes and styles bobbed in rows along

the docks. She saw Smokercrafts like Peter's, as well as jet boats and behemoths that churned wakes big enough to rock their humble boat.

It looked overpopulated. Thoeba snatched Peter's flannel shirt on the co-pilot seat and draped it around her shoulders. With all these people she feared someone would see the burns on her back. It wouldn't do her any good if someone got curious about her little anomaly. From what Peter described, they would make her memorable.

"That's him." Peter pointed to his left, began puttering toward someone waiting on the edge of a pier.

Thoeba straightened for a better look.

Zack had short black hair and a skinny frame. Mischief dimpled the corners of his mouth as he ducked his head. He resembled Peter, but lacked his father's confidence.

Thoeba's heart gave a painful jolt. If she had been able to give Thani children, this is what they might be like.

That's a very human wish, Thoeba.

She wondered at her god's observation. Never before had she desired to be a parent.

They must be rubbing off on you.

Zack caught the rope his father tossed to him. Love and pride radiated from Peter.

She had no concept that humans possessed this intensity for their young. She herself had never experienced that with any being other than her deity and her lover, and even that paled next to Peter's emotions for Zack and Kayla.

Zack got down on his knees to tie the rope to the dock

and pull them in. Peter held a hand out to stop the sideways drift of the boat once they touched the wooden planks of their destination. Zack acknowledged Peter, nodded to Thoeba, and proceeded to get in the boat. He'd done it many times before judging by the quickness of his entrance, but he resembled a gazelle negotiating a cliff while doing it.

He wore the standard garb worn by the few earthlings she'd seen since her arrival: T-shirt, shorts, rubbery shoes and sunglasses seemed to be a kind of uniform for people living on the lake.

Strange how Zack's thought processes were so reasonable. Too bad his father wasn't this normal. She sensed a calm rational mind with great intelligence. His shyness made her comfortable with him.

Except for that last thought. She couldn't see his eyes behind the glasses, but they were locked on her chest, and she abruptly crossed her arms over it.

Peter gestured with his hand toward Zack. "Thoeba, this is my boy Zack."

The young man flashed a brief smile filled with crooked pearls, betraying his concern that she'd caught him staring at her bust.

"Nice to meet you," he said, extending his hand. Thoeba let go of one her shoulders long enough to return the greeting, and decided to adjust the flannel accordingly.

"You as well," she said.

Zack turned his attention to his father. "So what's going on exactly?"

"It's a long story. We're really gonna need your, how do you say it? Expertise?"

"Now, when you say 'we'…" Zack glared at Thoeba. "You're part of this?" he asked. Suspicions sniffing around his mind like a pack of wolves on a trail of blood. He didn't trust her.

"Dad? Are you, uh…"

"Not your business," Peter snapped. "But yeah, she's the one who got me involved with this." He inched to his son, as though to whisper. "You haven't seen what I have seen. The stuff I told you about on the phone? These things are *real*."

"Demons?" Zack's voice rang out, making both Peter and Thoeba cringe and search around for eavesdroppers. "You made it sound like a horde of bat-things were taking over the planet. Well, check it out, Dad." He spread his arms wide, encompassing his surroundings. "Life goes on as always. I don't see anything."

His priorities shifted, his eyes narrowing behind the sunglasses. "If it was really that dire, you wouldn't have left Kayla behind."

"She's okay," Peter said, as if to assure himself as well as his son. "Crash is taking care of her." Thoeba noticed Peter's grin had a wicked curl to it. "She has a lot of protection."

Zack arched an eyebrow. "Dad…" he began, "…Did you booby-trap the cabin?"

Peter threw both hands up in supplication. "Not without reason, right?"

"Uh huh." A chord of panic struck inside Zack's head. She didn't think he liked his father's ideas.

"I suppose you've got a real plan?"

"I promise I'll tell you everything," Peter said. "Just get yourself settled. It'll be better once we get back to Kayla and Crash and we're safe. We can't do anything until after dark anyway." He removed the rope, and shoved them away from the dock.

Zack's alarm rose like a tapped spring. "After dark? Why? What are you going to do?"

"Son," Peter squinted up and around at the sky. "I know this sounds crazy." He fired the engine back to life and brought them out to the open water. He brought a hand up to shade his eyes as he checked the sky for the eighteenth time that morning. "But we are up against beings from another realm, and they're gunning for her." Peter swung his head at Thoeba, who met Zack's eyes with her sternest glare.

"Zack, demons are coming to invade our planet, and we need your help to stop them."

Thoeba wondered if she should catch the boy. She thought he would faint. His thoughts roared through her head.

Gone were the logical thought processes and the quiet intelligence. Terror spread through his mind like a forest fire sparked by an arsonist's glee. It wasn't fear of hellspawn that made him this way.

In fact, she couldn't be sure if he feared Peter's apparent insanity or his expectations. Thoeba rubbed her temples.

Just as suddenly as the inner turmoil began, it silenced.

Certainly got a hold of himself quickly, she thought.

"Is that all?" Zack scratched at his peach fuzz, made himself at home in the co-pilot seat. "No pressure or anything."

He'd calmed too fast for Thoeba. Then it hit her. He'd decided not to believe them.

I never promised you this would be easy. The Energy said.

How would she convince him?

~~~

Jim-thing noticed the walk-traps all over the ground. Good thing his host had seen this kind of thing before, otherwise he might have stepped on one. Jim stirred in fury inside his mind, and Jim-thing sighed in happiness. No matter how hard he tried, the human could not hide secrets from him. He relished how it angering this soul.

He never tired of the new game. Jim tried to take his body back, but Jim-thing retained command. He could go back and forth like this all day.

Examining the perimeter of the cabin, he found the floor board traps, and the trip wires. All the windows and doors were boarded up and locked. He needed a way inside. This shelter housed his enemy. Jim's memories had told him as much.

Ferocious barking cut through the cabin door, paired with scratching and growling.

From his host's memories Jim-thing learned that a four-legged furred being waited within.

He didn't eat furry things. Their skins got stuck in his teeth and gave him indigestion.

Not to mention the fluffy flavor that made him want to hack it up.
~~~

This one had a name: 'Crash.' Jim's mind told him this creature banged into things often as a puppy. Apparently he hadn't got any smarter because now the dog slammed himself into the door trying to get at Jim-thing. Which meant it sensed him.

Not the Jim he wore, but the monster inside. Crash wanted to fight, to defend. Jim-thing let his mouth curve. He would enjoy killing this creature for the sport.

It made the human crazy inside his head. It caused Jim-thing a great deal of pain, like his body was being strained through mesh. It made him sneeze rancid black dust, but delivered intense satisfaction.

"Hey hello," he called. "Anyone home?" The barking became piercing, the snarls more urgent, but behind it he heard a succulent sounding voice.

"Crash, be quiet! That's Uncle Jim out there. What's the matter with you?"

"Hey kid." Jim-thing could see her eyes shimmering through slats in a window. The real Jim loved this one-the Kayla, and she loved him back. He decided to practice his grinning technique. He would make her help him.

"Uncle Jim, why are you wearing your leather jacket backwards?"

The smile on his face faltered. Stupid garments.

"Kayla, where's your dad? Are you alone in there?" The dog's frenzied vocal assault forced Jim to shout. "Can you open the door?"

He didn't dare touch the walls. Humans were smart, but Jim-thing considered himself smarter, and he wouldn't fall victim to 'booby traps', thanks to Jim's old friendship. He even knew what kind of weapons Peter had inside.

"Uh..." She hesitated. Surely she'd let him in? Her loving Uncle Jim? What made her so reluctant?

Then he understood. These traps were meant for *him*.... Not Jim the man, but his demon self and his kind. The enemy was wary of him, ready to fight to the death.

He needed that little bitch to let him in.

"Please, Kayla." A plan quickened in his overcrowded brain. "There's *things* out here. They're going to kill me."

"Oh God." He heard her shuffling toward the door, and his muzzle widened in victory.

"Um....okay," she said. "I'm coming, Uncle Jim." She scolded the dog as she made her way to the cabin's only way in or out. "Move, Crash. Outta the way."

He listened to the hurried sounds of padlocks being disengaged, barely audible over the incessant noise of the German Shepherd.

Soon, soon.

"Hurry Kayla."

Large pieces of wood were scraped away from their brackets inside.

Jim-thing dropped into a fighting stance, and clenched his hands until they resembled the talons he once used. He began to salivate. Battles always gave him an appetite. He could hear the roaring challenge from his adversary.

The door opened with a creak and the dog charged for him.

Ivory fangs protruding from the black maw at eye level, his hands reached to embrace the beast's throat. One hand grasped the dog's collar, the other slid below the jaw and pushed up with all his strength.

A yelp escaped from Crash then the crunch, and the dog went limp. Jim-thing flopped the head of his foe over to meet his gaze, just in time to see life leave the dog's eyes. He sighed, tossed the carcass to the ground.

Awesome.

He met Kayla's round cobalt eyes as she trembled in the doorway. He saw recognition there. No, he wasn't her Uncle Jim.

She spun on her heel, and he gave chase with the layout of the floor plan fresh in his memories. She had nowhere to go.

CHAPTER TWELVE

Thoeba decided skipping across a lake on a sliver of wood wasn't as pleasant as flying. Nowhere close. Their speed, coupled with waves created by sharp changes in weather, launched the boat short leaps through the air. She couldn't remember experiencing nausea often, but she made up for lost time now.

She gazed up to the cloudless blue expanse, envious of the machines speeding and swooping in curving patterns overhead. Peter called them jets. He'd told her the military he worked for would let them use some of them for their quest.

She missed soaring through the wind. If she'd flown across Cold Lake, she'd have been back at the log house long ago.

She remembered, with bitterness that the demon she'd slain at the cabin had possessed wings. Yet she'd arrived without hers. Not fair.

You're assuming they obey the same laws, her deity said,

that they play by any rules at all.

She hadn't considered that. But it didn't explain why she couldn't keep her wings.

And how would you accomplish your mission being the only woman on the planet with feather-covered appendages on her back?

Thoeba could almost hear It smiling.

You would stick out a little, yes?

The Energy, as usual, had reason's for the things It did. It understood this race better than she did, and could only imagine how humans would have reacted to her original form.

She concentrated instead on the complete lack of conversation between the father and son sitting in front of her. Even a non-empathic person would have noticed the dense tension.

An ache existed between them like a song silenced in anger. Why didn't humans simply tell each other what they needed?

She could sense Peter's absolute love and delight in Zack and his accomplishments, but also recognized his fear of being unwanted in the boy's life.

Zack believed he'd never be good enough, strong enough, manly enough for his father.

She sighed. Humans. One would think a race of beings without the ability to read minds would work harder on verbal communication.

As the cabin came in sight and Peter slowed the boat, she

vowed she would right this wrong between them. If she couldn't make them talk to each other, she'd spill their secrets like she had for Peter and Kayla earlier.

Her pendant pulsed in alarm.

She brought her hand up to soothe her god.

Alright. Perhaps she should stop interfering with the affairs of these humans and keep quiet.

That's when she noticed it. The quiet.

"Peter," she said. "Peter, something's wrong."

He shut off the engine, his full attention to her.

"What?" His voice rose an octave, and anxiousness appeared to stretch his mouth downward in a grimace. "What do you know?"

"Nothing," she said.

"What do you mean, nothing?" he asked. "You distinctly said *something* is wrong."

"That's the problem." She picked her way to the front of the boat, her heart straining. "I don't hear or feel *anyone*." From this distance, she should have at least been aware of the dog's presence, but she couldn't focus on either Crash or Kayla.

She heard lapping waves, hushing winds, and distant jet engines, but nothing more. The cabin remained silent.

She vaulted out of the boat before Peter did, right off the bow. She couldn't slog fast enough to the shore. He splashed behind her, trying to push through the unyielding lake, screaming for his daughter and dog.

His voice chafed her sensibilities with its edge of hysteria. Peter's heartbeat droned in her ears. Zack's confusion and fear pummeled her until she nearly dropped from the weight of their anguish.

Peter reached the sand first, his body surged forward like a juggernaut.

"Kayla?" He yelled. "Crash?"

Thoeba dragged herself past the shore, dug her hands in the yielding dirt while Peter's fear sliced through her, weakening her.

Behind her, Zack leapt off the back of the Smokercraft. His mind locked onto the possibilities of walk-traps he needed to avoid. But the gravity of the situation soon crept into his heart like a poison and his father's agitation started to affect him.

Thoeba could hear something else in her mind. It started as a soulless hum of flies feasting, defecating, laying eggs. It sounded of frenzied consumption without thought. She smelled rot, the presence of death. The truth hit her and –

She vomited. Peter screamed.

"Crash." And his pain seared through her brain. *"God, no."* But God lay powerless against Thoeba's throat, sad in It's impotence.

"Dad, what is it?" She could hear Zack stomping his way to shore. Thoeba forced herself to stand. She had to go to Peter.

She made her way to him, careful not to trigger any of the hidden bombs. She scanned for traces of silver or clear lines, strange lumps of dirt.

Finally she succumbed beside him, wrapped her arms around his shoulders. Peter's tears rolled down his rugged red face as he cradled the loose head of his cold friend. He stroked the fur, but only once. His thoughts shifted to more important matters. He gulped a breath and swallowed grief.

"Kayla." Peter got up so abruptly Thoeba slipped to the grass. She got a jolt of foreboding, but she couldn't find his daughter anywhere. Everything became Peter's rage. All else dulled in comparison.

"*Kayla.*"

Peter stormed for the cabin door. It sat opened wide, the summer breeze tapping a query. He disappeared from view, but his stomping and bellowing could be heard outside.

"Peter *wait.*"

"What the hell is going on?" Zack asked. "What's wrong with the dog? Where is Kayla, damn it?" Thoeba ran to follow Peter. She may have been compromised by the barrage of emotions, but she couldn't let him do this alone.

Zack came after them, asking more questions that went unanswered. "Won't someone please tell me what's going on? Oh God. Is Crash *dead*?"

"Don't come in too far." Thoeba stuck her hand out to Zack in warning. "The whole thing is a trap. You might get hurt."

"Hey don't worry, lady." Zack gestured to some disturbed pockets of dirt and sand covered with grass. "I can see them. I'm not an idiot."

Thoeba gave him a warning glance and ran. She waited long enough to let her eyes adjust to the gloom, relying instead on her hearing to tell her what awaited. Peter trudged upstairs, footsteps burdened with a heavier heart.

"*Kayla, where are you?*" His voice held the over-brimming edge of a sob.

Whatever had been here had long gone. Thoeba perceived nothing, not even Kayla's death.

That meant she might be alive somewhere.

The stairs from the second floor squealed under Peter's weight as he came down. His state of mind caused the bridge of her nose to throb.

This would hurt.

He marched past the futons, through the kitchen to grab her by her shoulders. Squeezing hard, he shouted in her face.

"This is your doing." He shook her until her teeth clacked, but she made no move to defend herself. "*Where the fucking hell is my daughter?*"

"Dad, what are you doing?" Zack braved the porch, leapt over any loose floorboards and separated his father from Thoeba. "What's the matter with you? Whatever's going on, it's not her fault."

"That's where you're wrong, kid." Peter backed up, but his eyes never left hers. She absorbed his resentment as though she deserved it. She *did* deserve it. "It *is* her fault. She brought all this shit on us." He rubbed his hand down his bristled jaw and fear trickled down Thoeba's neck.

She'd never believed she'd be afraid of him, not her Thani.

But this man isn't Thani, she reminded herself.

Then she saw the piece of paper he held in his hand. He

thrust it in front of her eyes.

"I found this," he said. "What is this?" His anger simmered beneath his skin. The taint of Zack's alarm crackled through her mind, but Peter's breathing remained the only sound to break the silence. "*What is this?*"

Thoeba extracted the paper from his shaking hand. Words scrawled in blood flowed across the page in ribbons.

Latin. The most common language spoken in their universe.

That could only mean one thing. She read the first line to be sure. The demon, for it could only be one of them, addressed the note to *Inimicissmus*. Greatest enemy.

She read on, certain the letter was meant for her and The Energy. It had Kayla, and it wanted her to come to the portal.

"What does it say?" Peter hovered behind her, his breath hot on her neck. "Translate."

"It wants an exchange." She licked her dry lips. "It wants us to give up The Energy, and it will give us Kayla in return."

"Where?" Peter began to gather supplies-the kind used for war. "Just tell me where to find this thing."

"It says it will wait at the portal." She watched Peter stalk around the room. "Do you remember where you found me?"

He seethed at her and Thoeba reeled from another pang of regret.

His, not hers.

"She might still be alive. Just because she isn't here…." She searched for the words to make him understand. "I didn't feel her death."

If she had hoped to soften his heart, she'd failed. He grabbed more weapons. First the rifle, then the pistol, and the axe.

"Zack gimme that box." Peter nodded to a crate next to the fireplace, which no longer held logs for burning. "Fill it full of those..." He pointed to the small collection of homemade Bangalore Torpedos sitting on the coffee table. "Be careful."

Zack began the task by spreading a blanket from the couch inside the box. He cradled them like deceitful children asleep next to each other and giving no hint of the destructive power that slumbered within, laying them out, side by side, along the bottom. He said nothing, but Thoeba knew at this moment he dreaded his father's actions as much as she did.

"You..." Peter pointed the axe at her and her pendant. "Can you use that to make this a holy weapon?"

"How?"

"Would it work if we tied that thing around the handle?"

She wasn't sure. "It's worth a try."

"It had better work." He shoved ammunition into the pockets of his sweatpants. "It'll be a quick fight if it doesn't." His hatred dimmed the power of the Energy, and Thoeba held it away from him.

"I had better hold onto this," she said. "You're hurting It."

"I'm going to hurt a lot more than that," Peter said. "Now. Where do I find the thing that took my daughter?"

CHAPTER THIRTEEN

Jim-thing hopped up and down on the jet-boat, almost dumping himself overboard in the process. With flailing arms and a grin wide enough to collect bugs Jim-thing congratulated himself.

Such a brilliant plan!

He had weighed anchor here, at the white outcropping of stones called Pelican Rock. Though he couldn't see the portal yet, he was certain it stretched above him in the sky.

Others like him would come to this place seeking the enemy, the hated Energy. The closer his adversary came, the wider the door would open. His siblings would be drawn through the portal just as he'd obeyed the urge to enter.

Then he could eat the Kayla.

The kid quaked in the corner of the rocking craft. Her teeth and forehead still bled, making him salivate. She didn't dare defy him, not after he'd been smacking her face into hard surfaces all morning.

He exposed his incisors at her because he could see it terrorized the hatchling. He'd learned that adrenaline gave humans an elusive tang he enjoyed. Not that she would need much seasoning at her age.

Jim-thing gave the side of his head a resounding smack that made his ears ring.

Well, that hurt.

His host protested--didn't like Jim-thing thinking of the girl as a food source. He resisted Jim-thing's control more and more every hour.

How annoying.

It made him want to bite things. Maybe he should have eaten the dog after all.

After checking to make sure Kayla sat sufficiently docile, he scrounged through the boat for food.

Thanks to his host, he had all manner of knowledge of things in this world. Like what was edible and what was not…well, at least in the humans opinion.

He pawed through the live well, under the bow, and in the cubby holes that ran along the gunnels. Nothing but empty… granola bar wrappers? Yes, that's what they were called. Couldn't eat those.

Edible things swam in the water below him, but he didn't like the idea of getting wet. Moisture didn't cause him pain in this form, but even as a mortal man he disliked its intimate sliding touch of liquid on his skin.

That and he would have to leave the Kayla unattended. He couldn't do that, not with glory obtainable.

He took a quick glimpse around. He could hear a few boats growling across the water. They were too distant to see Jim-thing and his hostage, and too far to hear Kayla scream had she mustered the energy to try.

The one he wanted would be with him soon. The Energy and the angel's presences neared, causing an itch between his shoulder blades.

Hateful god…protecting all the food simply because they had souls. Once he destroyed It, Jim-thing and all his kind would devour everything in a never-ending orgy of fresh bleeding flesh.

Even with the sunglasses he could make out the circle churning in the air above. A darker blue in the sky mixed with wisps of clouds. It undulated with a timeless patience that nibbled at his nerves and made him whimper in agitation.

When the Energy approached, the sky would rage open and rain evil upon this realm.

He couldn't wait.

When his stomach rumbled he focused once again to the water lapping against the boat. Maybe he should grab a fish or two?

Something slender glimmered just below the green surface.

Jim-thing's face hurt with the leer that widened it. He recognized that shape, and he understood what it meant.

The long strip of metal could only be the hated weapon of his adversary. Swords weren't often found in this lake, if Jim's disbelief meant anything, yet there it lay buried halfway to the hilt in sand.

He remembered chasing the angelic being through purple sky, and almost snagging her when she disappeared in a skull-splitting clap of thunder.

She'd been leading with a holy sword, he recalled. Even from the surface he couldn't miss the shimmering white light of the metal.

He'd chased her and that blinding glow, and he found himself here, stunned and tumbling through empty space until he hit the ground.

The sight of the weapon driven into the bottom of the lake told him one thing: His hated nemesis would show up unarmed. It made him chuckle. He liked the sound of his happiness. It reminded him of burbling lava.

The teenager tried to shrink into the corner. Dried blood caked her bottom lip. Her eyes pleaded with his, she didn't understand the true danger of her predicament.

He wanted to do more than just devour her. He would savor the pain he inflicted on her first, his idea of an appetizer or foreplay. Both.

He sneezed twice.

Not again.

Black dust blasted from his nose, smelling like sulfur.

Stop resisting human!

Jim, the real Jim, rattled his cage. No matter. Jim-thing still had full control.

He admired the expanding ripple above him as clouds puffed away in rings. Excitement gripped him, and his brain throbbed in pain as Jim battled for his body.

Another violent sneeze. Soot launched from his face, covered the floor of the jet boat, and striped the left side of the Kayla's face.

"Kayla, jump in the lake."

Jim-thing lashed out in confusion. Who said that?

"Hurry, princess. Grab that sword. It's in the water. Right, right. Jump to your right."

Jim-thing felt his lips moving, but he wasn't the one speaking.

For the very first time ever, Jim-thing panicked. Sweat pooled in strange places like under his arms and in the palms of his hands. His breathing labored, and his mouth dried up. The situation slid from his control. He didn't enjoy the vibe.

Kayla wasted no time obeying the host, diving into the lake. Droplets from the splash slapped him. Jim-thing couldn't bring himself to follow her.

She could lap circles around him if the swim didn't kill him, and she would find the sword as well. His host assured the demon of that.

He glimpsed at his own backside. Why would the human want him to kiss that particular body part anyway? It seemed impossible.

He heard a buzzing approach, louder than anything else on the lake. Jim-thing glanced toward it and saw a boat headed straight for them.

He caught sight of his feminine foe, with her yellow hair blowing away from her sneering face. Two men were in the boat with her. One drove and the other stood behind her like a rear-guard.

They were prey--and he would eat them all.

Jim-thing sneaked a peak at the growing portal. The men would be food for his siblings, but he would linger with the guardian. And he would eat her in front of her god...after playing with her of course. He would defile the hated divinity by drenching It with her blood.

He waited on the gunnel, satisfied. Not long now. The closer she got, the wider the portal became. He spared another glance.

Ah, yes.

Thunder shook the world, so noisy the boat beneath Jim-thing vibrated. His ears hurt, and his host tried to make him expel mucus and powder yet again.

The portal, one sky-blue eye in the entire horizon, wept tears of ebony. Nightmares scrambled, free to pillage and consume this new prize.

He became aware of the approaching boat throttling down to join him. They would fight him, but they would lose. He wasn't alone anymore.

Yet before he could take pleasure in his victory, Jim-thing began retching between his knees. His hands clenched his throat as though trying to hold the angry soul down into the depths of his belly.

Jim fought him, harder now than ever. While Jim-thing tried to call out to the other minions of darkness, Jim succeeded in silencing him.

Jim-thing pushed the human back behind his temples, causing weeping tar to leak from his eyes.

Neither one existing in the body would give quarter.

Death would claim the loser.

Jim-thing heard a splash erupt from behind him, and a sharp stab rendered him stupid.

He'd forgotten about the Kayla. He peered over his shoulder to see her-one hand steadying her on the side of the boat, while the other held the pilfered sword...in his flesh.

Jim-thing decided that having a sharp object sticking into his back inflicted a lot of dizziness and nausea. Definitely the worst sensation he'd experienced in this shell.

The blade twisted through intestines and slid from his body as the Kayla dropped back into the lake.

Holy power chased him from his dreams of supremacy, and from his very existence.

~~~

Jim's presence at the portal and his violent conflicting emotions confused Thoeba until she watched the black powder explode from Jim's orifices. She never thought she'd ever express sympathy for him, not after the way he'd treated her, but no one deserved a death such as that. Not even a stubborn drunk like Jim.

She'd heard of possession, but never before had she witnessed it. It made her soul curl into a ball to think of one of those *things* invading and controlling her mind.

Surely a fate that welcomed death.

She'd endured Kayla's turmoil and fear from a distance, and her gut churned when Kayla dealt the killing blow.

The girl paddled her way to the back of the boat, scrambled up the ladder in her haste to reach Jim's sideways
~~~

slumped body. She kept the sword in a whitened grip.

"Hurry," she called to them. "He's still alive!"

Thoeba's heart rolled over. This passing would linger. Peter knew it too. He steered sharp and slammed his boat against Jim's vessel. His frantic desire to help his best friend showed in his shaking hands.

Zack cut the engine. Kayla struggled to stay upright, but she regained her footing and got to Jim first.

At first she hesitated. The girl's conflicting desires were difficult to endure. Part of her wanted to embrace her Uncle Jim, the other part feared him.

Zack stabilized them by tying the boats together while Peter and Thoeba crossed over to reach his fading friend.

Kayla's strike had hit Jim in the kidney as well, and the blood oozing from the wound mingled with black sins.

Thoeba's couldn't help but notice the glorious shine of bright steel, the square of emerald on the pommel blinking at her in the sunlight.

She swallowed. Kayla had her holy weapon.

"*Do* something." Kayla's agonized face made Thoeba wish for her deity's power. "He saved my life."

The damage is too great, and I don't have enough strength to heal a fatal wound.

Thoeba empathized with her god's sadness like the weight of gravity on her missing wings. It sang hollow like phantom pain.

"Kayla?" Jim's voice had no energy behind it. "Is Kayla okay?"

Peter reached an arm around him, holding the other man like a child. "She's fine, buddy. She's just fine." He peeked at his daughter's face to assure himself.

Kayla's hurt dripped in silence down her face, and she knelt to touch the man she'd worshipped much like a father all her life. "You saved me, Uncle Jim. I love you."

Jim's dimming eyes focused on Peter's. "It made me do...*things. Horrible things,*" he said. "It wanted to...It wanted to *hurt* Kayla." Jim coughed, and Peter wore the red flecks from Jim's mouth on his T-shirt.

Jim lived alone in his head now, Thoeba was certain of that. His memories, as well as the strength required to fight the demon spoke of a true champion. It didn't seem fair that they couldn't help him, that her weakened God could only sit and watch while Jim's life drained away.

Jim struggled to focus on his chosen family as he faded. "I've always loved you Kayla." His eyes softened on Zack, who rushed to say goodbye.

"You too, Zack. I hoped I'd have a boy like you someday." Zack's face crumbled in response, trying in vain to stifle a sob.

"And you." His gaze found Thoeba. "I know who you are. I know *what* you are." His grin demonstrated a change in attitude. It charmed her despite the blood slicking his mouth. "Take care of my brother."

His gaze rolled toward Peter. "Socks," he said. "You are..."

He would never finish the goodbye.

Thoeba remembered why she'd stopped coming to worlds like this. She couldn't bear the mortality, couldn't bear the agony of those who lived through loss. This time didn't differ from any of the other tragedies she'd seen in her travels.

Death snuffed the light out in Jim's expression like the extinguished wick of a kerosene lantern. He dimmed away, abandoning those who loved him.

Only the wind disturbed them with its moaning.

Until leathery reverberations approached.

You have company.

The words of her deity snapped Thoeba back to the present. She squinted to the sky only to see shapes of horror racing across it.

"Zack." Thoeba eased upright, her eyes tight on the onslaught coming for them. "Zack, untie the boats. We must go."

"We can't just leave-"

"Yes, Peter, we can." She pointed to the raven dots that grew in size as they watched. "Those are not birds."

He stared in amazement before whispering a crude oath. Zack straddled both craft with his legs, unraveling the ropes holding the water vessels together, aware that their lives depended on his speed. Kayla, who had moments earlier killed an evil spirit with a sword, stood in slack-jawed wonder.

The new arrivals resembled a cloud of insects, only larger, and even from the vast distance, Thoeba could see pin pricks of red eyes.

Many of the monsters dispersed, seeking violence for

entertainment and meat for their appetites. Many more focused on the tiny floating device holding a god and a small selection of snacks.

The demons formed a ball of deadly hate, and bore down on their location.

As always, they hungered.

CHAPTER FOURTEEN

"*Move move move.*"

It impressed Thoeba how both his children sprang to action at Peter's command. Kayla managed to keep her grip on the sword as she abandoned Jim's body and sprang for her father's Smokercraft.

Zack doubled his efforts until they were free to drift from Jim's jet boat. He swung himself into the pilot seat usually occupied by his father and fired up the engine. Peter and Thoeba leapt across the gunnels and into their seats even as Zack picked up speed.

"What are those things?" Zack had to shout over the engine. Thoeba got a strong dose of his fear, his need to escape. It stung like a lightning strike.

"Those things are related to what got your Uncle Jim," Peter said. "Whatdaya say, kid? Any doubts now?" He wasted no time stumbling to the crate holding the pipe bombs.

Thoeba once thought a smarter man wouldn't have brought such dangerous things on the boat, but now she marveled at Peter's foresight.

"Kayla, you hang on to that sword like a baseball bat, and swing for the fences," he said. "Go for the heads." He faced Thoeba. "That's a true holy weapon, right?" She nodded. He turned his face back to his daughter. "Hell, hack and slash, sweetie. Kill 'em all."

Thoeba tested the edge of the old axe Peter had given her. The twinkling crystal lay tied there with a slip of leather string. She wanted her sword back, but reasoned Kayla would need it more.

Peter better know what he's doing, she thought.

Humans are resourceful when desperate.

Thoeba jumped when she heard the voice inside her head once more. Her powerful Lord had been quiet for awhile. At first she believed separating the god from her person created the distance.

But that didn't feel right. Something else made her deity keep Its thoughts deliberately away from her.

She realized it held a secret. That reason alone made Thoeba's knees weak.

Her God, her reason for existence, the most powerful force in the universe...experienced mortal terror. Worse yet It would hide that truth from her.

Time grew sluggish as she stared around the floating escape vehicle.

A terrified young man perched in the driver's seat, steering with a tension that could crack his knuckles.

A teenaged girl welded her rusting and damaged sword with the grace and skill of a Neanderthal.

A middle aged father snarled as he tossed aside his ineffective rifle and opened a crate of crudely constructed destruction.

No wonder her god feared. Shame crippled her. She would fail. They would all perish here and now. She would die with them, and...

What of her soul? Where would it go?

I have faith in you.

The love of The Energy overwhelmed her, she took a deep breath.

But they are supposed to have faith in you, she told It.

They do.

She became conscious of her god's strength returning as the humans made themselves ready for battle.

And that is why we will live through this.

"I hope so," she said.

"What did you say?" Peter asked. Time and reality returned.

"I'm hoping you'll let me throw some of those." She beamed at him and received a rush of pleasure at the manic grin that crept over his face.

"Sure," he said, presenting a tube of chemicals with a short string. "Would you like to go first?" His exhilaration made her shake her head.

This crazy human *enjoyed this* she thought with affection.

She dragged her attention away from the explosives to the unholy horde approaching them from behind the boat. The Hellspawn gained on them.

Peter's instincts matched hers, and he turned to call to Zack.

"Hey," he yelled to be heard over the engine's howl. "Is this as fast as we can go?"

"Yeah." Zack put more pressure on the throttle, no doubt hoping he would squeeze a little extra speed from it. "You could get out and push."

Thoeba almost laughed. All the souls alive on the racing craft smirked but no one let down their guard. The dots off their stern grew bigger.

Kayla tried a few practice swings. Peter held the bombs as though they were hot in his hands. Thoeba realized she held hers across the pendant with a grip that made her glad her god didn't need air.

She let go, and tried to relax long enough to make assessments.

At this distance throwing bombs would be a waste. She didn't even know if they would work. They had one holy weapon and an axe with a deity swinging from it against a flock of demons.

Thoeba wiped sweat from her brow, realizing for the first time in many centuries, she perspired from fright. She caught a whiff of her own body odor in the summer heat, and wished for a waterfall shower.

The hate emoting from the enemy touched her and made

her anxious. Peter and Kayla both bore the same sickly pallor of doubt and fear.

The bat-like creatures were close enough now that Thoeba saw the loathing in their eyes. Slits of hostility focused on her, on the glowing charm around her weapon.

One of them broke from the pack and surged forward. The air from his flight strokes pounded in Thoeba's ears as it inched through the sky.

Its eyes were twin red dwarf stars as it sailed toward her. She braced herself for the attack.

Kayla chopped off its arm and black powder showered them.

The demon's shriek pierced their skulls, but the determined comrades shielded their ears and held their ground. Thoeba heard the scream inside her head, experienced the rage as though it were her own, but refused to buckle.

Not this time.

Zack swore loudly while Peter cheered.

"That's my girl," he said, poising himself for his role in the battle. The other demons, incensed by the injury of one of their own, pressed harder.

Thoeba understood Peter wanted a little bit of vengeance-just a little bit of payback for things lost. His eyes darted to Kayla, but not quick enough for Thoeba to miss. For things he *almost* lost. He would enjoy this, but his face never betrayed that thought.

Until he grinned. The demon horde had come within range.

Thoeba found herself impressed at how a calm Peter lit a fuse and pitched one of his toys into the cloud of enemies. One of them snatched the pipe in its teeth.

Like a dog with a bone, Thoeba thought.

Four demons disappeared in a swirl of ebony mist. More demons bellowed in unexpected pain, as remains of the weapon and fiery toxic chemicals sprayed on them as well.

Thoeba laughed to see human weapons, not even blessed, defeat the most violent and evil beings in their universe with simple alchemy and pure will.

Told you. You can destroy anything with explosives. Even the unholy.

She smirked and reminded her god not to act like It knew everything.

The mirth on the boat became short-lived. Monsters came forth again undaunted, unafraid.

"There's so many of them." Next to her, Kayla began to waver. Thoeba's nostrils withered with the vinegar odor of Kayla's defeatist attitude.

Peter also peered around himself in dismay. The demons had caught up, and Thoeba's keener eyesight saw some of the faster ones were trying to come in from the front.

Zack made the mistake of glancing up from the lake. "Holy freakin' shit, Dad. What the hell is that?" A demon wheeled over his head, too high and too slow to hurt Zack, but it chanced a bite anyway. The young man dodged incisors the size of his index finger. Thoeba choked on his terror.

"Just drive, Zack." Peter waited for the evil to fly far

enough away from his son before he lobbed another bomb. The monster dipped to avoid, and the projectile splashed into the water without causing further turmoil. Thoeba waited for the boom, but disappointment reigned.

"Well, that was a waste," Peter said.

"Are we losing power?" Kayla asked, "They're gaining a lot of ground."

Thoeba double-checked. The enemy surrounded them and kept pace. The boat had not lost power. The demon's determination gave them an edge. Hunger gave them purpose.

She readied her weapon. Hopeless as it had become, she would never admit defeat, never surrender.

The Energy twinkled a reminder through her mind.

Yes.

That would help very much.

"Kayla," she twisted the girl around to face her, almost getting a jab in her stomach from her sword. "Do you trust me?"

As she studied the girl's eyes and heart she rephrased her question. "Do you trust me not to let you, your father and your brother die?"

The girl's expression changed. Thoeba had won her over for the time being.

"I'll trust you that much," Kayla said.

"Good," Thoeba said. "Just do what you need to do. Watch out for yourself and them." Thoeba jerked her head toward Peter and Zack. "I won't go far."

Thoeba willed herself away, and prayed to The Energy that Kayla and Zack understood her actions. She had a strong feeling that Peter would.

CHAPTER FIFTEEN

"Dad?" Kayla's voice sounded panicky, like a revving jet engine. Her eyes grew wider as she realized she waited on alert against the "boogie men" alone. Thoeba had been beside her, behind Zack one minute, winked out of existence the next. "Where did she go?"

"It's okay sweetie," he said. "I think I know what she's doing."

He glanced over to Zack, who huddled over the steering wheel of the boat like a NASCAR racer, eyes intent on the horizon. "You doing alright, kid?"

"What the hell did you get us into?" Zack asked. Peter barely heard the question over the loud engines and the screech of the screaming beasts.

"What did *I* get us into?" He took a breath to deflect some of the blame, and watched Zack take a face full of black ash instead. The engine wavered, throttled down until Zack finished spitting demon residue from his mouth and nose.

Apparently Thoeba had taken position at the port in front of Zack.

No time to squabble. Peter brought his attention back to the battle. He faced the wind and used his Zippo to spark another fuse. This time he waited an extra heartbeat before throwing the bomb. A good sized explosion took out three of the advancing swarm.

Nice.

Monsters powdered the waves behind the boat and Peter whooped his approval. Another cloud of supernatural bat-shit pelted his head and shoulders, and he grinned. He hadn't seen the demon behind him, but it hardly mattered.

"Thanks, Thoeba." He grinned over his shoulder at thin air. "Glad you got my back."

He took a moment to check the horizon. At this speed they'd reach the marina in minutes. There were more and more demons and Peter, along with his crew, were leading them straight to the populace of Cold Lake. They couldn't turn around, but they couldn't fight them all either.

Shit. Now what?

Kayla cleaved the head off a monster that dared to gnash teeth at her, bathing herself in more soot.

"Do you have a plan?" Her voice barely carried over the caterwauling of the enemy and the grind of the engine. "Cause now might be a good time to tell us." She continued to hack away at body parts, grunting with each small victory.

Explosions erupted from the back of the boat. Howls of agony and black meat exploded from the front of the vessel.

Peter couldn't think what to do next.

His military training kicked in. Only one place would keep them safe in a crisis of this magnitude.

"We'll go to the base."

A resounding clang tolled through the air, followed by a near-sonic scream. All fighters hit the floor, dropping weapons and covering ears.

One of the nightmarish beasts fluttered away with half a tooth.

"Nice one, Kayla," Peter said.

Zack steered a steady line despite the black spray Thoeba generated from in front of him "Good idea as any," he said between gagging fits. "You think that'll help?"

Peter peered at his daughter.

She stared at the portal, which vomited enemies in a steady stream. Water crawled off her face in shaky drops.

Were they sweat or tears?

"It has to." The fear in her eyes played with his emotions, but he kept lighting fuses and tossing bombs overhand with all his strength. "We can't keep up with them alone, and our guns did nothing."

A variety of jet boats and yachts bobbed or cruised by the docks. The mayhem hadn't reached them yet, and they were leading the demons to a smorgasbord.

"Your military base..." Thoeba's voice found his ears above the chaos. "Can they protect the Energy?"

Peter ignited another fuse while his daughter sliced the

wing off yet another monster with a well-executed backstroke. He timed his throw carefully, tossing the pipe into a cluster of four enemies. A satisfying bang transformed them to fireworks, and he roared his pleasure.

"Sure." He couldn't see her, but the tar spatter all over Zack told him she worked in his defense. He smiled reassuringly at the windshield. "They have bigger bombs and better weapons than we do."

Zack slowed the boat, causing Kayla and Peter to reestablish their stances. A Bangalore torpedo tumbled overboard, and Kayla jabbed her sword into the astroturf in an accidental effort to regain purchase.

Peter realized they were approaching the docks. He peered skyward and even from this distance he could see more black shadows forcing their way through a scar in the sky. The river hadn't slowed yet.

In that instant he saw the end. They were all doomed.

A soft touch on Peter's back soothed him. The sweet breeze of Thoeba's breath tickled his ear, and the scent of honey soothed his nerves.

"No, we're not doomed," she said. "The demons will follow the Energy like a moth to flame. We can draw them away to your safe place.

He jerked his chin to the people on the docks, who were gradually becoming aware of the approaching menace. They shielded their eyes from the sun, focusing on the coming tide of black. Many of them pointed, but none of the fools had the sense to run.

At least not yet.

"What about them?"

"We can't save them all. Can you send them a message? Tell them to leave?"

He navigated his way to the co-pilot seat, checked on Kayla. She swung back and forth with her weapon in a clumsy but effective arc of death. The demons dodged just out of reach like huge black seagulls.

Peter knelt on the seat, and blew the horn with his right hand. He waved at the growing crowd with the left.

"*Get out*." He screamed, but the group remained to gawk.

Peter noticed the demons were no longer interested in their entourage. Even as his voice began to break, they'd zeroed in on the throng of flesh waiting on the shore like salmon on cedar planks.

A cacophony of shrieks chorused through the sky when the minions of darkness came to feast. Only then did the people flee.

To Peter's horror, demons were plucking people off the pier like fleshy grapes. Body parts were consumed mid-flight. Blood and gore splashed the wood of the docks, splattering the running crowd.

Only dimly aware of his surroundings, he almost didn't notice Thoeba's reappearance.

~~~

Thoeba braced herself against the onslaught of violence and the sound of breaking bones. Waves of confused horror assaulted her.

She would *not* succumb. The longer she remained on this planet, the more she realized how fragile humans were, why her god wanted to protect them. It started to affect her as
~~~

well.

She gripped the axe, reminded herself that she held the power to kill the beings that terrorized this place. She could appear and disappear at will.

She would use that to her advantage. She slowed her breathing, calmed herself. She understood, even if she couldn't see it, that the Energy dimmed in the midst of the evil. Its silence spoke of prudent inconspicuousness.

Inhale. Exhale. Just breathe.

She knew what she had to do. Zack slowed the craft considerably to avoid ramming into the boards of the pier.

Her enemies coasted over them in a steady stream to engage the humans who were now trying to scurry to safety. Hundreds, perhaps thousands poured forth from the portal, showing no signs of stopping.

She willed herself visible once more, startling Kayla who let out a yelp.

"I thought you disappeared," Kayla said.

"I did." Thoeba agreed. "But I didn't leave."

"I like that trick of yours." Peter turned to address them. "Can you do it again?"

Thoeba nodded. "That's the plan."

Zack cut the engine.

"I hope you've got more than that," he said. "These things just keep coming."

Thoeba held her right hand out, palm up. "I do. Kayla, I'll need my sword back. Your father's out of bombs." The girl did so with reluctance. Thoeba gave her a stern look.

"It's *my* sword," she said.

"I know, I know." Kayla handed it back, hilt first. "I was just starting to like it."

With her left hand, Thoeba handed the axe to Peter, deity and all. His eyes met hers, astonishment etching his features.

Over them tar curtains of evil descended on humans running like cattle. She raised her voice to be heard over the screams.

"I fight better with my own weapon, and I need you to make sure your military people protect the Energy." She sighed at the mayhem. "Take care of It until we get to your safe place."

"Do you have another vehicle of escape? One for travel across dry land?" She took a swipe at a demon that ventured next to Kayla's head. It hissed at her, shying away from the biting metal, and flapped away unconcerned. It would seek out something weaker, she knew.

Peter glanced to Zack, "Where's your truck?"

"Over by the store." He gestured with a hand, and Thoeba followed it to see a four-wheeled rusting rectangle with wheels within running distance. "Now I'm *really* glad I found that parking spot."

"Excellent," Thoeba said. "As soon as this water vessel reaches the edge, run." She chanced another look around. Nothing threatened them for the time being, but that would change now that there were more ravenous monsters than humans in their midst. "I will be following behind."

"But you'll be invisible?" Kayla asked.

“Yes, just make sure the Energy is safe.” She pointed to the twinkling crystal dangling from the axe handle. “That is all that matters. Without The Energy, we are all lost.”

She searched Peter’s eyes for hope. “Your military people…they’ll be able to help us?” For a chilling moment no one spoke.

Peter turned away from her, but she read his fear. “I sure as hell hope so.”

The boat bumped into the dock harder than Thoeba expected, and they all stumbled. Kayla made frightened mewling noises while trying to scramble back to her feet. Zack’s shoes squeaked across the gunnels in his effort to tie off the boat to the dock.

“No time for that, Zack.” Peter helped Kayla toward him, while Thoeba skewered another minion. “Help your sister.”

When Thoeba joined them, Zack and Kayla were dashing for Zack’s vehicle. Peter crouched on the dock, hands outstretched for her.

“Let’s go,” he said.

She didn’t need any more encouragement. She grabbed his hand and let him haul her from the watercraft.

Peter’s strength and adrenaline affected Thoeba as well, and when he lifted her to her feet, she kissed him ferociously.

“For luck?” he asked. She had no idea, but she heard an old engine struggle to start in the background.

“We must go,” she said, tugging him by his hand into a sprint for the sound of Zack’s vehicle.

Zack greeted them on the road next to the marina by slamming his brakes and raising a small cloud of dust.

"*Get in.*" Kayla waved at them from the passenger side of the vehicle.

Where? Thoeba wondered, but Peter steered her toward the back.

"Jump on the tailgate," he said, tossing the axe irreverently into the truck box. "Get in the back."

He peppered his words with a boost to her rear end. She crawled across metal, never letting go of Peter's hand. She yanked until he joined her, his feet barely leaving the ground before Zack tore them away from the lake.

CHAPTER SIXTEEN

Thoeba squinted upward and saw a swirl of enemies diving for them in a whirlwind of death. They came so quick, their eyes formed a crimson ribbon of hate that lengthened and snapped like a whip striking toward them.

She licked parched lips. "Are you ready?"

Beside her, Peter swallowed his fear and brought the axe in his hand to his forehead.

He was praying, she realized, and the Energy thrummed love and encouragement.

You will be strong. You will be victorious.

"The Energy heard you," she said. "It believes in you."

Peter sighed. "Then I guess I'm as ready as I'm gonna get."

"Good." Approaching bellows of rage drowned her

words. “Because they’re here.”

The monsters preferred easier pickings, but they couldn’t resist movement. Their speed of travel made Thoeba and her friends tempting prey.

Not all of the monsters were armed. Some carried clubs, some fashioned crude weapons from the corpses of former victims, but many used only their claws and teeth. The later kind rarely attacked anyone armed-they had just enough sense to leave well enough alone.

Thoeba willed herself to vanish, timing her disappearance with the first strike of her sword. A demons head tumbled away from them, and the body followed, exploding into a pitchy residue.

Thoeba tried to crawl forward to better defend her lover and her god.

Not that she didn’t trust Peter to fend off the evil. But more were on the way, and she’d relax a little if they went through her first.

Around them, buildings flashed by her vision, torched and crumbling while human screams echoed in her ears.

Thoeba did her best to ignore the carnage. Their mission meant protecting the Energy, Thoeba had to remember that. If the Energy didn’t find sanctuary, no one on this planet would survive. So she kept her wits and listened for telltale hissing sounds, sniffed the breeze for the sulphuric odor of her enemies.

The truck barreled along, gaining momentum. The pandemonium around her subsided only slightly when signs of civilization gave way to trees, foliage, and ditches.

Death surrounded them. Any life that might have existed

along this stretch of road had been terminated. Cars burned and beasts lapped at pools of blood on the edges of the highway. Thoeba saw three of the brutes fighting over a charred torso.

Inside the cab of the speeding truck, Kayla screamed for Zack to drive like less of a crazy person, but his sense of horror spurred him on.

Thoeba glanced behind her. Peter stretched out with his weapon, gleefully killing monsters. His body covered in sweat and dead demon powder gave him a manic look.

He resembled Thani again. A powerful rush of twitching pain hit from her loins to her fingertips. She couldn't be sure if it hurt to see him like this or if it turned her on, but there wasn't time to dwell on it.

She prepared to help him defeat the next foe, but the sound of crunching metal made Thoeba spin to a crouch. One of the demons had landed on top of the cab of the vehicle, talons digging in to keep its grip.

It cocked its head, considering its options. Red orbs of loathing darted from Peter to the Energy, no doubt wondering which it wanted first. Kill the ultimate enemy? Or eat first?

Thoeba smiled.

Always thinking with their appetites.

She would solve its dilemma.

She rose on the balls of her feet, cleaving its head into two halves before it could react. It shattered like eggshells to dust, blinding her.

Frantic with fear, she wiped the grime from her eyes with

her free hand, and leveled her sword to maintain her precarious balance.

She needed to lower her center of gravity. Now.

Before she could get back to her knees, Zack took a corner-too fast. Peter swore. She heard him hit the side of the truck, bellowing in pain. She extended her hand.

"*Thani.*"

Not Thani, she thought. I must keep my emotions out of this.

"*Peter.*" But she never touched her lover.

Instead of moving forward, she tumbled back.

Reality hit hard, much like the searing hot sidewalk on which she landed. Pain slammed through her body. Her knuckles skipped like stones off the cement. Agony scraped her arms, legs, and face. She could smell and taste the metallic tang of her own blood mixing with the earthiness of dirt baking in the sun.

Her ears, unharmed, picked out the sound of screeching tires and acceleration, followed by murderous howling that faded.

She couldn't find the breath to cry out, couldn't get air. She had no wind left in her lungs, and her deity couldn't tell them she'd fallen.

The sounds of their racing battle faded away, leaving her to smell the blood and burning, to hear the roar of fires, the sobs of the dying, and the satanic screaming in the skies.

~~~

Peter almost dropped the axe trying to right himself in the
~~~

truck bed.

He had to hand it to the boy, that sharp turn had thrown a lot of the black bastards off their tail. Some of the beasts were still trying to keep up with them, but Zack's maneuver created some breathing room.

"Great driving, Zack." He doubted the kid could hear him from the driver's seat, but he yelled it anyway. He felt pretty damn good right now. Like they had a fighting chance. Even the gem on his axe fluttered like Christmas lights. He took it as a good sign.

Which reminded him-he caught a glance of the damage done to the roof of Zack's truck. Finger-shaped punctures demonstrated the need for observant invisible allies. He smirked at the opposite wheel well.

"Nice work," he said to the thin air. She didn't respond, but that didn't surprise him.

In fact, she probably wouldn't. These ugly bastards resembled giant bats. It just occurred to Peter they probably had the ability to hear like them too.

Only a few stragglers attempted to follow them as they accelerated away from the Grand Central part of town. He lay against the back of the truck, took a deep breath, and checked his surroundings.

They were well on their way to the base, but for now, they had nothing but highway. Not a lot of traffic, most of the motorists were crashed or half eaten in the road. No one passed them going north. He figured most people would evacuate the Cold Lake area altogether.

In minutes they'd find help from the Canadian military and all their international guests.

If we don't become roadkill ourselves, he thought.

He raised his gaze to the air, grimacing at the chaos. Jets from several nations scrambled to meet the threat, all guns firing.

He couldn't see the cerulean skies anymore, only the charcoal and tar of thousands of frenzied flapping menaces attacking and swooping at anything that moved.

He witnessed an F-18, one of Canada's own, crippled like the victim of a bird strike. The engines flared and exploded as several demons were sucked through the intakes. Peter noticed the pilot hadn't even had time to eject.

Just as well, he thought, a quick fiery death might be preferable to being eaten alive.

Peter heard the roar of Migs and Hornets taking to the sky. An A-10 Thunderbolt lived up to its name, growling just over his head, missiles blazing.

Peter heard Kayla and Zack cheering through the glass, and he joined them in spirit.

The monsters kept coming in sheets of black, taking up airspace, causing the jets to flounder upon impact.

Demons burst and died, sending ash down to the ground like a dirty blizzard. Visibility became nil, until no one had control of the earthly heavens.

Peter watched the pyrotechnics, envying his comrades in arms for a brief moment. At least those pilots weren't going to live with whatever became of Earth if they lost this war.

The truck lurched beneath Peter and they lost speed.

Why were they slowing down?

He sat back up, shifted to peer over the cab of the truck. They were on Kingsway, but he recognized the streets coming up.

"*Hey*." Peter slapped the glass next to Kayla until he got her attention. "Tell him to take Queensway." Comprehension dawned in Kayla's gaze. He saw her lips move, repeating his words. She gave him a thumbs-up sign, which he returned.

Kayla's eyes grew wide, she pointed and screamed. Peter caught the darting reflection in the glass window, lashed out with his axe.

It bounced off the horn, making a resounding ping as the metal skittered off. The weapon's vibration stung his hand, and the demon barked in anger before snapping at Peter's arm. Peter gave it an elbow in the snout instead.

Peter scuttled sideways to the other side of the truck box, ducking a windy swipe with a club.

Another demon joined the first, clawing at its comrade in an effort to steal prey judging from the strange otherworldly argument that ensued.

The two exchanged a brief but scarring tousle before Peter dared to move. He tried to gain a better position, farther away from them.

The truck made a quick zigzag turn, jostling Peter and his enemies back and forth into metal. His offspring shouted so loud, Peter could make out their words.

"Daddy! Zack DO something. Get them off him."

"What the fuck do you think I'm doing?"

Tires squealed, and momentum carried both beasts back toward Peter. He shuffled dangerously close to the tailgate when a talon snaked out for his ankle.

The demons hissed at Peter, their claws finding no footing on the slick steel. They swung for him with a bashing tool and their arms, only to slide away while Peter clung to Zack's Ford with his left arm.

"Thoeba," Peter said. "What are you doing? I need some help."

Nothing happened. Zack drove like a man possessed, Kayla crying in fear the whole time.

But no help from Thoeba.

"What's the hold-up?"

His energy waning, Peter swung the axe with his free hand. The bizarre circumstances were taking their toll.

The first demon shoved the other behind itself, grasping for Peter with a razor-like hand large enough to squeeze his entire face like a bleeding sponge.

Desperation taunted Peter into swinging, and he lopped the appendage off at a gnarled wrist, promoting a deafening screech. Its breath and spittle smelled like a slaughterhouse bone barrel.

Powder sifted from the wound until the beast blew away like drifting sand.

The small victory bolstered him enough to press the attack on the last one. He inched forward on his aching knees, axe held high.

Now would be a good time for Thoeba's help, he thought. But it appeared that he faced the monstrosity solo.

Good thing these things were stupid.

He faked a downward swing, and the beast moved to block with its club. Peter reversed his swing and gutted the hideous creature with a slice to its abdomen, spraying a fan of ash all over the truck. The club continued its path, swiping Peter across his cheekbone and forehead until Peter heard the jagged rip of his skin.

Peter covered his mouth with a filthy hand, trying not to breath in any monster fragments. Zack took corners as if he drove the General Lee. As hard as he tried Peter couldn't stay upright.

He collapsed on the floor of the truck bed, trying to swallow air in sloppy uneven gulps. He'd never felt so vulnerable in his life, like a man standing against a tsunami. He stared at the head of the axe. The light of the crystal shone sallow, but it twinkled madly at him. Too bad he couldn't understand it.

Peter experienced sharp tweaks of pain as the Ranger squealed to a halt. Truck doors opened and slammed shut. He wanted to sleep, but the sound of his children bickering kept him awake.

That and the realization that the one person acquainted with destroying demons regularly had gone missing. He fought the cold terror leeching into his gut.

"You could've gotten us all killed."

Peter shifted his focus on his daughter's anger. Was she talking to him?

"What did you want me to do?" Zack asked. "It's not like I could help them fight those things from the driver's seat."

Kayla hated Zack's driving at the best of times, but that must have been one hell of a trip.

~~~

He heard his son speaking from just above his head. "Dad?" his voice betrayed an edge of fear. "Dad. Are you alright?"

Peter groaned, tried to push himself up, but his arms trembled. Something sticky seeped into his left eye. "I'll live."

Kayla approached the tailgate. "What's wrong, Daddy? Are you hurt?"

Peter wormed his way to her, his knees protesting with shooting pinpricks of torment. He looked up to see the worried expressions of his children waiting with their arms extended to assist him. Thoeba had not appeared.

"He's bleeding." Yeah, that sounded like Kayla. "Zack, get him out of there."

"Thoeba?" he called, "Are you here?" He checked for signs in the ash for her presence-- a footprint, or a clear spot, but his vision dimmed. He fanned his hands along the steel, fumbling for flesh he couldn't see.

If she were dead, would she stay invisible? How would he know?

Only the wind answered, spitting demon soot in his face and hair.

Somewhere behind him, human voices barked orders and Peter heard a bazooka fire.

Bazookas. Peter grinned at the welcome idea. Why didn't I think of that?

"C'mon, Dad," Zack tugged at Peter, and Kayla helped
~~~

drag him off the tailgate. "We gotta get inside."

"Thoeba." He let his kids lead him toward the military base, but he scanned for signs of her blonde hair, her amber eyes. "Where are you?"

Fatigue robbed Peter of his senses. He could just make out the chainlink fence in front of them, and the single storey brick building behind it. Men and women in battle gear hustled in and out of bay doors.

Zack held him up while Kayla's greeted a soldier whose fading voice he didn't recognize. The man sounded as though he spoke through a pillow.

"Stay with me, Dad." Zack sounded strange too. Distant. "We need to get you some medical attention."

How had it turned dark so fast? And in his last brief thought he wondered again what had happened to Thoeba.

CHAPTER SEVENTEEN

He soared over cliffs of warm orange sand and waterfalls so pure they shone like falling diamonds in the low sun. The breeze cradled him like a precious child. He dipped and swerved through the air in timeless joy.

In the twilight of day the lavender skies seldom realized true nightfall. But stars shimmered bright, adorning the horizon like a bracelet on the wrist of a goddess. In all the Realms of Life, this land had no equal. Its holiness extended to the corners of the universe and he never grew bored with its soothing beauty.

Nor did he tire of the magnificent creature swimming the wind toward him. Her shining curls bounced and twirled around her head in a brilliant spray like a golden peacock unfurling her plumage.

Her radiance shone from her face as she thrust her hands out to him. He lunged to her, snatching her up in his arms, and spun on air.

His perfect Thoeba.

"Do you know how much I love you?" he asked. "How my heart beats for no one but you?"

She answered with a tender kiss. "Do you know?" she said, "That I'll love you until time stops?"

"Time could stop and I would still love you," he told her, but only in his head. Such a thought cheapened when spoken.

She owned a beauty so rare the heavens could not compete. Her flaming eyes outshone the sun and moon. Her lips tasted of cinnamon and roses, her skin softer than the kiss of clouds.

Her gaze brightened at his declarations of adoration, and her breath hitched.

He heard nothing else but the steady thrum of their wings. Even their thoughts quieted.

As ancient soul mates they climbed the sky, holding each other close in safety and love.

He kissed her, taking her mouth as though it belonged to him. He'd heard her heart and knew it to be true. Playfully, Thoeba pushed away and he let himself go.

He tumbled in freefall. He could see her flutter away from him, her presence sharp in his soul. He took a deep breath, and dragged his wings out, catching a vortex of air.

He could hear Thoeba's laughter riding the wind. She coasted back to him, eyes glowing bright.

"I love you, Thani."

~~~

Peter jolted awake.
~~~

For a brief panicked moment he didn't recognize his surroundings. A humming fluorescent lamp kept the darkness at bay, but not by much, and he could make out a drop ceiling two meters over his head.

He lay on an old army cot- he'd recognize that mildewed canvas scent anywhere, not to mention its rigid discomfort.

From the other side of a closed door he heard voices issuing tense commands and confirmations. The well-oiled machine that is a military command post, he thought.

My kids.

He sat straight up, dropping the axe to the floor with a loud clang. He'd dumped himself from the bed onto his stomach.

Where the hell are my kids?

His panting echoed in the little room, sounding like desperation to Peter's own ears.

He rolled to his back again, took a shaky breath.

Get a grip, he told himself. Calm down.

It came back to him then. The wild ride in the back of Zack's Ford, the screaming horde of evil tailgating them as Zack raced for the military base.

He licked his lips in a futile attempt to moisten a mouth gone dry in terror. He forced his brain to think clearly, push the fear away.

Then Peter remembered. It had been his kids that dragged him out of the back of the Ranger. They'd been in better shape than him.

His aching fingers rubbed the dried blood on his shirt.

The shirt felt crusty, smelled coppery.

He'd almost been killed there, when a demon landed on the cab of the truck. Zack had swerved to dislodge it, back and forth across the two lane secondary road.

Thoeba had taken care of it, hadn't she? He hadn't seen her, just the explosion of her victim. But then he'd been attacked again, and she left him to fend for himself.

That didn't make any sense. She had a warrior's heart, and besides being angelic meant it was in her job description to protect humans, wasn't it?

He groaned, the noise tinny and lonely in the oversized closet. He could smell fear on himself, like acrid body odor.

He and the kids would be safe here, for the time being.

But what about Thoeba? Had she survived? Would she be able to stay invisible?

Surely, it had to be pretty damn hard to kill an angel, but she would be friendless out there.

In the background he could hear few remaining F-18s roaring, peppered by occasional explosions. There seemed to be very little aircraft in the sky.

Good or bad? He couldn't be sure. But he could no longer hear screams or smell burning flesh.

Peter became aware of the axe twinkling next to him. He'd almost forgotten about it.

Odd, Peter thought, they let me keep the weapon?

He shook his head as he sat up. Sloppy work, even if they were under attack.

His fingers were cold and stiff. They tingled, a charge seemed to surge through his veins. He groped for The Energy, surprised to find It thrumming with the same pulse he experienced in his hands.

"What was all that?" he asked. "Was that you?"

He turned the weapon over, inspecting it. The crystal flashed.

The grin on his face faltered and realization dawned on Peter. "Did you give me the dream?"

The visions returned with such vividness they were more memory than anything else. It seemed so *real*. He thought about the air blowing past his face, the flavor of her kiss. How he'd burned in her passion. He clenched his teeth.

Thani. He'd heard Thoeba use that word, no-that name before. *His* name. And he remembered his wings. But he didn't have wings. Yet he missed them.

The nerves in his back tingled like phantom loss. A single tear trickled down his cheek.

He wiped it away, and brought himself back to the present. He couldn't let his guard down now. He didn't have time.

Nothing good waited for him outside that door, he bet. But he needed to investigate.

He had to find his kids.

CHAPTER EIGHTEEN

He got to his feet, worry hustling his movements and making him noisy. Caution took over once he got to the door, and he used stealth to turn the handle. Not even the click of the bolt gave him away. He gaped at the scene.

The lights flickered unreliably, no doubt due to the pandemonium outside. Camouflage uniforms rushed past him, calm but busy elsewhere. No one paid him much attention.

Afternoon daylight still shone strong through long windows. Demons abruptly plastered themselves against them, gnashing teeth and beating fists against reinforced glass trying to get in.

The staff were startled into moving away from their desks, but soldiers waited at the ready with high-powered C-7 Colts. Just in case.

The windows held up well.

"I see you're up, Sir." The young guard's voice made him

jump, but Peter refrained from swinging weapons or appendages. "We were getting a little nervous."

Nervous about what? He wondered. Then he remembered the head injury, and touched his sweat-damp forehead.

"What happened? How long was I out?" He read the soldier's rank and name tag. "Private Brewer? And where are my kids?"

The Private, probably no older than Zack judging by the eager alertness in his eyes and the sharp tautness of his jaw, pointed his gun to the floor. He raised a pacifying hand up to Peter.

"Your kids are safe," he said. "We stitched your daughter's lip and put ice on her bruises. Your son is with Major-General Lapierre. It seems he has a plan?" He said it as though questioning the idea.

"Your daughter went with them, but she's been checking on you from time to time." Private Brewer's brown eyes were compassionate. "She's been pretty worried about you."

It figured that Kayla would think about him instead of herself. In the thick of battle he hadn't realized how badly that thing had hurt her. She'd been so brave and it had all happened so fast.

Peter realized this soldier had been studying Peter's brow for a long time.

What was he staring at?

The young man made eye contact with Peter, blushed a light shade of pink.

He nudged his left sleeve up to check his watch. "You've been out about three hours." That answered one question for

Peter. "You had a head injury, but we weren't able to give you much medical attention."

He studied the ground, giving Peter the impression he shouldered the embarrassment for that.

"We're a little short staffed right now. The infirmary is full, and all medical personnel have been working non-stop."

Peter had already picked up the screams coming from another room. Several voices rang out in agony. He could imagine what kind of injuries they suffered from.

"Yeah," Peter nodded, remembering the violence he'd witnessed on the pier. "These bastards live to eat. I understand completely."

Shouting voices burst into the room, distracting him.

"Medic! We need a doctor ASAP." Two soldiers carried another on a stretcher. The man lying on it between them shrieked with raw vocal cords. His arm had been patched haphazardly with squares of gauze and a tight tourniquet prevented him from bleeding out.

Peter saw teeth marks scratched on the bone. Poor guy. Hope he wasn't right-handed.

The combined odors of blood and antiseptic brought bile to Peter's mouth. The man's hoarse screams haunted Peter all the way down the hall until the poor man was finally sedated.

Peter was pretty damn lucky all things considered. He explored the skin above his left eyebrow, marveling at what he touched-Or rather, what he *couldn't* feel.

Smooth skin greeted his fingertips, no swelling, no scarring; as if the wound never happened.

That explains why the boy couldn't take his eyes off his face.

"We had a doctor look you over, and he couldn't find any serious trauma." His eyes had a disbelieving narrowness. "Maybe that wasn't your blood we saw."

"Oh, it was my blood alright."

So why wasn't he scarred up like Frankenstein's monster?

"Those ugly fuckers out there don't bleed" Peter said. "They turn to dust. Trust me, I did the bleeding here."

Yet there were no injuries, only a sense of well-being, and the warm axe in his hand.

He lifted it to inspect the dangling pendant. "That was your doing again, wasn't it?" he asked the stone. "You healed me while I dreamed."

Not that he expected the jewelry to answer him. He glanced at Private Brewer, who all of a sudden found the tile much more interesting to gawk at.

Just wait for it kid, he thought. You're gonna see stranger shit than that before it's all over.

A thought occurred to him. He wondered why he had his weapon.

"How come you didn't disarm me?" he asked. "You let me keep my axe. Why?"

The young private's expression shifted to chagrin. He peered around to see if anyone could overhear the conversation.

"I, uh, couldn't take it from you." The kid mumbled, staring at the ceramic some more, immune to the demons pounding on the windows.

"What?" Peter wasn't sure what he said. "You couldn't take it from me?"

Private Brewer winced. "You wouldn't let go." Then he told Peter something strange. "It was like your fingers were welded to it. I couldn't pry them off."

His eyes beseeched Peter. "Your fingers were stiff and cold, but I swear I could feel something pulsing through them."

Peter shifted his view to the holy weapon. "Like an energy force?"

Private Brewer nodded, "Almost like electricity running under your skin." The kid couldn't suppress a shudder. "It creeped me out."

Peter stood dumbfounded. His hand rubbed the wound that wasn't there once again. A grin crept up on his face.

"I'll be damned." He could really learn to like having the little rock around.

"Daddy." Peter saw a streak of blonde before the wind got knocked out of him.

"Oof!" The smile he wore widened, and he threw his arms around Kayla. He inhaled the sweaty sweet smell of her hair while she tried to squeeze his oxygen away.

"I was so scared," she said, her speech slurred by swollen lips. "You're injured. You shouldn't be up." As an afterthought, "Sorry I tackled you, I just missed you, and I was worried-"

"It's okay, princess," he said, but he heard the hiccup in

her breathing. "I'm just fine. How are you doing? Where is your brother? That's a nasty-"

"He's making plans with-" She scrutinized his forehead even as he inspected the injuries on her face with a delicate touch. "I don't get it."

"Yeah, I don't either." Private Brewer said.

"What happened to that huge gash in your head, Dad?"

Peter's hand shot up, but he reminded himself to quit touching it, the lack of scabbing could be temporary. The pendant might have only been able to partially heal him, but he doubted it. It seemed pretty good to him.

"Did God do it?" she asked, tiny fingers reaching out to fondle the shining crystal. The minute she did, the bruises on her jaw faded, and the subtle lines of pain at the corner of her eyes disappeared.

Peter stiffened. It was a strange thing to watch, even the stitches fell out. But he decided to shut up and be grateful. "We'd better go find your brother."

Kayla took the hint and pressed her lips closed, not even aware that she did so without pain. He didn't know this soldier, and the less said in front of him, the better.

Not that he didn't trust his own military, but they weren't given to otherworldy ideas. They might lock him up after all if he told them he'd been sleeping with an angel and God was his co-pilot.

Kayla led him through a maze of desks, cubicles and hallways. The walls were all the same shade of ivory, egg shell-whatever. Beige.

The tile under his feet had the same sleep-inducing

charm. But he wasn't lost. He spent enough time here to be familiar with the surroundings.

"Zack's been talking to this guy," Kayla said. "General Laplander or something like that?"

"Major-General Lapierre,' Peter corrected.

"Yeah, they said he was pretty major," she said.

She kept babbling. Peter barely listened.

His children appeared to be safe, that had been the most important thing on his mind.

Now his lover, a woman who hadn't been that important last night, consumed his thoughts.

"Have you heard from Thoeba?"

"What?" Kayla's wide azure eyes met his for a blink. "No. Nobody knows where she is."

Peter dug in his heels, and used the arm Kayla gripped to pull her to him, "Did you look for her?"

She took a defensive stance, not meeting his stare. Kayla bit her lip, callousing it with her front teeth.

"We were too scared," she said. "I thought you were dying and, and there were demons coming out of the sky. I just ran-" her words choked off.

Peter folded her into his arms, stroking her hair with one hand while clenching the axe with the other. "Shhhh. It's fine, princess." He shouldn't have asked. "You did good. We're okay now."

She sniffled into his chest. "For how long?"

“God only knows.” He kissed the top of Kayla’s head. He’d never let her, Zack, or the deity out of his sight ever again.

“Too bad He can’t tell us,” she said. They embraced in silence while Kayla sighed.

Then she brightened, her somber mood evaporated as quickly as it appeared. “Anyway, I think Zack has some ideas that can help. You know how he’s so smart? He says there’s a place with all these high-tech gadgets-”

Kayla continued her side of the dialog unabated, dragging Peter to the back of the building where Lapierre’s office sat tucked in an inconspicuous corner. He’d heard the man valued his privacy.

Two voices argued on the other side of a thick metal door. One Peter recognized as Zack’s, the other with the slight French-Canadian accent Peter guessed belonged to Lapierre.

Kayla barged in without knocking, bringing Peter into the sudden and uncomfortable end of conversation.

Zack hunched over a map on a desk.

A tall thin man wearing a dark green uniform with a solid gold stripe on his sleeve flanked him on the opposite side. The double gold leaf designs on his shoulder left no doubt to his office of power.

Both glared at Kayla, who seemed oblivious to her intrusion.

“Zack, Dad’s fine you can’t even see where he got hurt. There’s not even a scar and the crystal healed-“

“I see that, Kayla.” Zack favored her with an indulgent smile before addressing the general once again. “Major-

General Lapierre, this is my father, Lt. Colonel Peter Mason."

Peter extended a hand. Although he'd had never met the major-general before, he'd heard good things. Like his fearlessness and his fairness. Unfortunately, open-minded didn't make the list.

Lapierre accepted Peter's handshake with a firm grip, and appeared to be considering Peter as well. He established and kept eye contact, his sliver of a mouth a grim and tight line.

"A pleasure to meet you Lt. Mason," he said. "I wish it had been under better circumstances."

"Yeah. Me too." He wondered how either he or Zack could think straight with demons beating on all the windows.

Then he noticed there were no windows in the office.

But the noise came from everywhere. Lapierre and Zack resumed their conversation to include Peter. They'd obviously become accustomed to it.

"Okay. I've been telling General Lapierre where we need to go." He pointed to southern Alberta on the map in front of him. "Yeah, this is the place." He tapped a finger on a tiny blue lake icon in the corner, near the Saskatchewan border.

Peter's hearing faded again. Zack's voice got fainter. He could hear the thumping of his heart in time with the demons pounding somewhere behind him.

Thud. Thud. Thud.

"Listen. There are a lot of scams and conspiracy sites out there." The general had his hand up, trying to calm Zack, who wasn't ready to give up.

"It's not a scam, and it's not a conspiracy. I hacked into the site myself." Peter wanted to tell Zack to take it easy, just relax, but he suddenly found he couldn't breathe.

He became less aware of the discussion in front of him, and more aware of the noise coming from what he realized was the back door.

Thud. Thud. Thud.

Kayla hugged his arm. He rubbed her hand. General Lapierre continued to deny Zack's claims of a secret military base.

"It's called Area 88, and it's at Pakowki Lake." Zack's voice had clammered to a shout, but Peter had tuned it out.

He noticed the pounding had taken on an exhausted beat.

Thud. Thud.

Thud.

He glanced to the pendant strapped to the axehead. He'd never seen it sparkle so rapidly. He became conscious of another presence, even as he handed his axe to Kayla.

He disengaged himself from Kayla, crept from the room. He had to find that door.

Voices lost all meaning and importance through the roar in his ears, as he stalked the corridor.

Directly in front of him the Emergency Exit awaited him.

Several men and women in fatigues moved around him, but Peter ignored and avoided them.

Almost there. Please don't let anyone stop me, he prayed.

"Can I help you, Sir?" A young man in military garb holding a semi-automatic blocked his path.

He smiled at the boy when he plucked the gun from his grasp, and flung it out of harm's way.

"I'm coming," Peter said.

He grabbed the soldier, tossed the man aside before barreling into the back door.

The heat of the late day slammed into him causing sweat to drench him instantly. Alarms sounded, people screamed.

Peter opened his arms.

CHAPTER NINETEEN

Thoeba had her ear plastered to the steel when she heard Peter's footfalls and recognized his quick gait. She all but wept with relief.

He must've heard her. She could only hope.

Thoeba took two shaky steps back and waited.

She thought perhaps she'd be left to wither there-huddled in the dirt amongst the dead and the demons, wondering if she would find him before she succumbed to her injuries.

She imagined the beasts picking at her flesh while she lay struggling to breathe, seconds away from salvation.

Then the metal slab burst open, and a wide-eyed Peter braked to a halt. His arms spread, and Thoeba dropped into his embrace. She no longer held sufficient strength to support herself or keep up the invisibility spell.

He dragged her inside, screaming orders. "Someone get that door shut. They're right outside."

A man carrying a long black gun complied before Peter finished yelling, yanking the door handle into the closed position even as frustrated demonic screeching filled her ears. The abrupt banging that followed brought quiet to the room. No one spoke. Seconds ticked into minutes before anyone dared to move.

Thoeba dared a glance to see fist-shaped dents form in the steel portal. She heard more aggravated howling, and then it faded.

More than likely they'd gone after easier targets. Demons did not play waiting games, and they were sore losers.

Their departure brought her no solace, but several people, including Peter let out a breath. The sound whispered like a breeze, and their relief washed over Thoeba.

She shivered in the abruptly cooler air inside. Peter freed a hand to rub her back, bringing welcome warmth. She dropped her head to his shoulder, allowed him to comfort her.

The bustle returned. People went back to work. Two soldiers flanked the emergency exit she had entered, weapons at the ready.

"Whoa." Thoeba registered shock in Zack's voice. "She looks like hell."

"You think so? She's lucky to be alive," Peter said.

Zack loomed into view, his face pale and distressed. Kayla revealed herself next to him, her frightened eyes out of place in a stiff mask of bravery.

Thoeba tried to reassure them with a grin, but she heard the whispering crackle of dried blood, and tasted iron. It didn't put the teens at ease either, judging from the disgusted curl of their lips.

"Are you going to be alright?" Kayla asked.

"I feel better already," Thoeba said, and she meant it. The close proximity to the deity in Peter's grasp eased her pain like a balm. "I just need a minute."

She shut her eyes, enjoyed the serenity of her lover's hold, blissful in the understanding that her god lived.

She heard Peter's heart beat in time with The Energy's loving power. Her humans were alive, and the whole room radiated a willingness to fight together to defeat the common enemy.

Too bad it's not that simple, she thought.

"I kept It safe," Peter said, bringing the axe up for her to see through her swollen left eye.

The crystal looked shinier than she remembered, or perhaps her vision worsened.

No, the Energy gleamed and pulsed stronger than before. She hadn't seen it that bright since their stay at the cabin, and it brought her happiness.

It meant that evil, for the time being, couldn't touch It. The positive outweighed the negative.

She smiled into Peter's collar bone, inhaled his sour adrenaline and sweat. "I knew you would."

"What happened to you?" he asked. "Where have you been?" She barely heard his voice over all the activity going on around them. His love and concern rippled from the depths of his soul.

"Where is your sword?" he asked.

"I lost it when I fell off the back of the vehicle."

"That explains a lot," he said, and hesitated. "That means we only have one holy weapon on the entire planet, right?" He scowled at the space in front of him. His thoughts churned loudly once more.

"You'd better keep this." Peter handed her the axe. "You need it to heal, I know. Besides, I need both arms."

She hugged the weapon to her chest. He placed his other elbow beneath her knees, lifting her from her feet.

Even though he'd been careful not to disturb torn skin, she whimpered at the motion. The pain in her side swelled.

Peter winced. "We have to find you some place to lie down. Zack, tell Lapierre about Thoeba. Kayla find some clean cloths and some water."

Part of her suffered shame at her weakened state. She didn't want Peter and the kids to see her like this.

But it had taken courage and strength to persevere, she had to remember that.

Yes. And you've been in worse shape than this. You've done well, Thoeba.

An ordinary person might have been killed, or at least wouldn't have survived her injuries without immediate treatment, but she'd made it to safety.

The left-hand side of her body had skittered across asphalt, leaving her skin shredded, oozing blood and pebbles. Some ribs might be fractured. Her nose broke on the first impact, but her cheekbone stayed intact.

She had limped for miles, letting the pull of her god drag her to her intended destiny.

It was a terrifying journey. Half blinded, she'd been unable to find her sword, could barely see her path. Only her will and determination allowed her to remain invisible. She hadn't the strength to fight.

"They knew I was there the whole time." She wanted to block out the images, but she couldn't stop talking. "They were everywhere, sniffing the air." A shudder of memory swept through her. "I used the blood of the dead to mask my scent. I'm sorry. I had to."

"Shhh," Peter's kissed her forehead, reassuring her.

"I couldn't run," she said. "I could barely stand, but I could feel you and The Energy, far away."

"Shhh. You'll be okay for now," he said.

"But I made it here." She sighed. Her divine being sent benevolent healing vibes through her aching flesh, knitting marrow and calming flaming nerve endings.

Kayla returned with clean towels. "How did you get here anyway?"

At the sound of the girl's voice, Thoeba experienced gratefulness, hers not Kayla's. The girl's concern surprised her.

"There were men and women dressed in green," she said. "They all possessed weapons." She spoke as much as the pain would allow. "They seemed to be the safest people to be with. They looked like soldiers. I was sure they would eventually take me to you."

Happiness seeped through her soul like rain after a drought. Her lover held her, and her god had begun the healing process. She could sense It washing the bruises from under her skin.

Thank you, she told the Energy. She let love rush through her veins.

Savor it, she thought, absorb the moment.

To Peter she said, "I love you."

She licked her desert lips. Her heart sang, and she didn't care who heard her muttering. She had worked so hard to be here, and it just felt good to be alive.

He kissed her mouth. Gently. Carefully. "I love you too Thoeba."

Her uninjured eye flared open. Peter's gaze wore something new, something she hadn't seen there before.

Did he mean it?

Her joy fought to leap from her chest.

It is true. The Energy's calm consumed her. *Now rest. You've given me a lot of work to do.*

But she had questions. Peter sentiments and emotions had changed toward her, but why? She had to learn how, but sleep tried to claim her.

"Will she be alright?" Zack asked.

Peter's response sounded weary. "She'll be fine. The crystal will fix her right up."

"How soon?"

"She's injured pretty bad." Peter's worry invaded her mind. "It'll be a few hours at least."

Zack exhaled, his anxiety bubbling through his words. "We have a problem."

Problem?

"What problem?" Peter asked. She attempted to wake.

Rest, Thoeba. You need to heal first.

What she needed was to find out what's going on. She struggled to surface.

"I need you to talk to the general," Zack said. "He's going to be trouble."

Then sleep dragged her away.

CHAPTER TWENTY

Thoeba awoke to darkness. She clutched the holy weapon tight in her hands, but felt no fear, for the other presence shuffling in the room was a welcome one.

"Peter." The movement stopped. For a moment she heard only distant gunfire.

Then a deep breath. "Hey, glad to see you're awake." His voice spoke in hushed tones of relief. "Not a minute too soon either."

She sat up, placed the axe next to her cot. Dying sunlight streamed in from a tall window, allowing her to see the shelves and the supplies Peter packed.

Some things she recognized, such as gauze and bandages. Some others she didn't, like the little white cardboard boxes that rattled.

Peter caught her staring. "Tylenol. Just in case."

"Why? What are you doing?"

Peter sealed the bag with a *zip* and knelt in front of her. In the waning light he placed a gentle hand on her cheek and rest his lips on hers.

"Are you well enough to travel?"

"I'm fine." A charge rippled through Thoeba's veins, and it wasn't just a result of Peter's tenderness. "The Energy's power works well."

She hadn't been this healthy since she'd left Eden. "I underestimated It's strength."

Thoeba communicated a quick thought-wave of gratitude to her god for the repairing of her body and mind. She inspected her once again flawless skin and thanked the Energy for perfect healing. Even the blood had been whisked away from her flesh.

"Yeah. It was quick too. But I guess It is God after all. Even in a weakened state It's still The Almighty."

She noticed Peter wore the same uniforms of the soldiers. He scrounged around in the front pockets, withdrew a slender brown package and gave it to her.

"Eat this. You need to be fueled up and ready to go. We're getting out of here."

She hadn't thought about hunger, but the words on the plastic promised satisfaction, and the sweet sugary fragrance made her stomach audible and her mouth wet with anticipation. She tore the packaging with her teeth and bit off a third of the bar. She'd never consumed anything so heavenly. She tasted nuts, just like the peanut butter at the cabin.

It made her giddy, which probably explained why it said 'Snickers' on the wrapper.

She swallowed most of the treat before speaking again.

"Where are we going?" Peter planted a finger on her lips.

"Why are we whispering?" she asked.

"We're getting nowhere here," Peter said. "Lapierre keeps telling Zack there is no Area 88."

"I don't know much about it, but Zack tells me Area 51 is a front for Area 88, and that's where the real action is."

Not that it helped Thoeba much. What was Area 51?

Peter got up and proceeded to a closet tucked into the corner of the unlit room. "And he's not willing to let us go for the help we need on our own." He extracted green camouflage fabric from the closet. "Here try this on."

Thoeba caught the jacket he tossed at her. "Why not?" She removed the torn and bloodied shirt, grateful for a clean garment to cover her sweat-chilled flesh. Kayla would *not* be happy with what Thoeba had done to her top. Good thing Kayla didn't like it much.

She'd have to make it up to her later, but Thoeba had more important things on her mind. "I thought you said they would help us," she said.

Peter gave a disgusted laugh. "Apparently he can't spare the equipment or the personnel. Claims he hasn't got the resources."

He took a deep breath, lowered his voice again. "He thinks we should stay here, wait it out."

"Wait it out?"

Thoeba straightened up so fast she knocked the axe to the floor with a muted clatter. The pendant flickered like a dying flame and Thoeba quickly bent to retrieve it.

"We can't do that. Did you tell him the demons will

simply keep coming? That they will flood this land like locusts? They won't stop until they've devoured everything."

"Yeah I tried, for damned near three hours." Peter said, "Dumbass doesn't have a clue what he's up against."

Thoeba squeezed her eyes shut. Turmoil churned all around her-Peter's anger mixed with her deity's alarm. Anxiety invaded her spirit.

"Your children…" Her eyes wandered to the metal portal separating them from the rest of the humans. Kayla and Zack entered through it as though summoned.

"I got food and juice from the cafeteria." Kayla hefted the strap of her bag over her head to rest on her opposite shoulder. "And some bottled water."

Even in the gathering darkness Thoeba could see the large guns in Zack's arms.

"Weapons room was open," he said. "Got some extra ammo too."

"Good. We're almost ready to go." A dark lump landed at Thoeba's feet. "Put the Energy in this bag. Let's get moving."

She obeyed, opening it and placing her weapon inside.

Then it struck her: The Energy. Peter had given her god It's title. He hadn't called It a pendant, or a deity, or hanging-crystal-thingy.

Yes Thoeba. He believes.

She beamed. What did you tell him?

Get out of this alive, and you'll find out.

"Are you ready?" Peter asked.

She grinned. Her lover now knew her, himself and his destiny. Together, they could face anything.

Bring forth the darkness, she thought. I have no fear.

Peter shouldered his load and eased the door ajar.

Nothing had changed since she came into this building. The humans ignored them for the most part, too busy fighting their fears and strategizing for a battle they couldn't win.

Thoeba blinked in the stabbing glare of the overhead lights, waiting for her eyes to adjust.

All around her signs of fatigue showed on the humans. Damp spots appeared under their arms, several of the women had strands of hair falling out of place.

Some of them worried over the safety of their children at home, their parents, their lovers. Too many of them stressed over their own welfare while others dreamed how the crisis would further their careers.

Thoeba experienced all this chaos in her aching head, resentful of their intrusion into her brain and their self-absorption.

Worst of all, the uncomfortable warmth of sweat in the air wafted like a sickly wave.

How long had they all been here, trapped in this small shelter from the horror beyond their windows?

How many humans were left fighting beyond these walls? She couldn't tell. She picked up on the rush of adrenaline mingling with the body odor that saturated the room, but not much else. They all had the same ideas on their minds, like a hive mentality. They just wanted to get through this.

Peter approached. “Thoeba has the only effective weapon against these monsters.”

She had a fairly good idea of what he wanted from her. “That means I lead the way.”

Peter rewarded her with a grin that widened until it seemed to take up half his face. “I was hoping you’d say that.”

Thoeba cherished the love radiating from both Peter and the Energy, but the circle of trust she had formed with the humans, along with her deity, made it that much sweeter.

“Now, the exit we need is over there, down that hall.” He jerked his chin to the left, indicating the other side of a large desk. Three women sat behind it, talking into headsets and multitasking. They took and transferred phone calls, pulled files, and entered data without complaint.

To the casual bystander they were calm, but by the resonance they sent to Thoeba’s mind; they didn’t believe things were under control, no matter what lies they told to a terrified public.

“How do we get past the reception desk?” Kayla asked.

“Good question.” Peter rubbed at the stubble on his face. “We need a distraction.”

“Yeah.” Thoeba’s heart stuttered. Thani used to wear that expression on his face when he had an idea.

That mischievous gleam in the eyes. She found it odd to see it on Peter’s rugged face, but he wore it well.

"Okay, everybody get ready to move." Peter dropped his voice until Zack and Kayla had to lean in to hear him. "On my mark, Thoeba you pull that axe out of the duffel bag, flash it towards the windows over there."

Zack grimaced. "Then what?"

"Then, while everyone's gawking and freaking out, we calmly walk along the wall, behind everybody to the emergency exit, and out the door." His sharp blue eyes locked onto Thoeba. "I need you to go invisible, and cover us while we find a lift to the hangers. Can you do that?"

Now that she'd been restored to health, she couldn't wait. She itched to use her warrior strength again. "I can."

"Good, but don't do it until we get out there." He surveyed the mass of cubicles and desks. "Right now I need to know exactly where you are."

Thoeba glanced at the windows, blackening with the night. She saw precious little, but she had no doubts as to what ugliness lurked on the other side of the panes.

Thoeba slipped her hand inside the bag she carried, ran her thumb across the crystal, concentrated on the love and power tingling up her hand.

"Ready?" She awaited the signal. Kayla and Zack froze beside their smirking father.

His finger went up; slashed down.

"Now."

She yanked the weapon from its hiding place in her duffel, making sure the reflection shone in the glass.

Say cheese.

A subtle flash from the Energy.

Thoeba had no idea what that meant, but the result was profound.

Various screeching noises sent the entire place into chaos.

It began with the talons and teeth scraping glass, followed by a demonic chorus, culminating in human screams. Not a single person remained seated or silent. Chairs toppled and paper flew.

It shocked Thoeba to her core. Not a common experience for her.

"Good to go." Peter grabbed Kayla's arm, and ushered them in the direction of the chosen exit.

Even with her superior senses Thoeba only caught glimpses of the hordes trying to make its way inside. Oversized claws drove grooves into the glass. Several pairs of red coals smoldered just beyond the reach of the soldiers lined up with weapons ready in case they broke through.

Thoeba could barely think. The terror in the atmosphere tasted like old dust.

"Keep going." She did. She had no choice.

Peter's breathing labored in her ear. His fingers curled around hers, squeezing tight.

She could almost touch the door. Soon she would take in fresh air and be free to do something, to fight.

"Lt. Colonel Mason, Sir?" They braked in unison without another spoken word, but several angry, surprised thoughts ran through the minds of Thoeba's entourage. Hope evaporated.

Peter released her hand, put his own in the air. He turned around, they all did.

The soldier addressing them had a very large gun.

"Where are you going, Sir?"

CHAPTER TWENTY-ONE

Peter let out an explosive sigh. He recognized that voice.

So much for getting out undetected.

"Private Brewer."

The young soldier had come up behind Zack, blocking any escape from that end of the hall.

"We were just, uh…" Just what? *Think*. His kids were staring at him. "We were…."

"It looks like you were trying to sneak out," Brewer said.

Well yes. That's exactly what they'd been trying to do, but he couldn't say that. Could he? "Do you have a problem with that? *Private*?"

"No sir," Brewer said. He glanced behind him and his voice leveled to a conspiring whisper. "But I think you should take me with you."

Peter hadn't expected that. "Did you say you wanted to come with us?"

Private Brewer's lips firmed to a grim line.

Thoeba stepped out from behind Peter. "We should bring him." She peered up into the kid's face. Judging by the serene expression on Thoeba's own, she was warming to him.

Peter wasn't sure how she made those decisions, probably that ESP thing she did. But she'd judged Brewer as a worthy ally. Who was he to argue? Still…

"You'll be listed as AWOL," Peter said. "They'll court-marshal you."

"Maybe," Brewer shrugged his Colt C7 into the crook of his arm and checked his ammunition. "But if it's going like I think it is I doubt anyone will be left alive to arrest me."

The kid had a good point.

"But why?" Peter asked, "You're relatively safe here. Out there you can get yourself killed."

"I've seen what that crystal can do." Brewer checked various pockets on the front of his flak jacket. "I heard what you said to General Lapierre. Even if he doesn't believe you, I do."

Peter saw grenades and spare cartridges in Brewer's pockets. Those would come in handy.

"Besides, if what you've been saying is true, no one's really safe," Brewer said.

"And we could use another guard," Thoeba said.

Peter glanced to her hopeful face. He'd been thinking the same thing.

"Okay," Peter shifted the weight of his duffel bag and put his hand on the door jam. "But we better get our asses in gear. Demons are impatient and easily distracted, they won't be at the windows for much longer."

Murmurs of agreement rumbled behind him, and Brewer cocked his weapon. Although loud, it blended in with the clacking of all the other guns in the office building.

"Thoeba, put the Energy back in the duffel until you can do your little disappearing trick," Peter said.

"Will my gun work on those things?" Brewer asked.

Peter winced. "Not very well," but the semi-automatic worked better than nothing. "It'll help if you concentrate all your firepower in one spot. Otherwise I don't think bullets have much effect on them."

Thoeba placed her hand between Peter's shoulder blades and he turned to memorize her determined look with the scant seconds they had.

"We grab the first vehicle we find," Peter said. "I'm driving."

Before anyone could argue he added, "I'm the only one who knows exactly where we're going."

"Thoeba, you take the lead. Private, you take the rear. Zack and Kayla stay low." Peter braced himself. "Are we all ready?"

Affirmatives greeted his ears. He gave a grunt before yelling, "Go!" He threw his weight on the door handle and Thoeba sprang in front of him, taking her position.

Then she along with her axe and even her clothing vanished. The duffel floated to the grass to be forgotten.

"Okay. I'm right in front of you," she said.

He heard the click of the door closing behind him. "All clear," Brewer said.

Peter set the pace at a jog, resisting the urge to run full tilt. His kids might not be able to keep up. Not to mention it might draw attention to them.

It wasn't as dark as it had seemed from inside the building, but the sun sat low on the horizon. True darkness wasn't far behind.

Peter congratulated himself on his timing. If he'd waited even an hour longer, they wouldn't be able to see where they were going. At least not here, not with all the trees and the moon shining at a quarter.

Demons littered the skies like flak. Their eyes made them appear as though they barely escaped fire with a few embers clinging.

He guessed Thoeba's location remained consistent. Her breathing came to his ears steadily.

A hot wind in his face brought the smell of old blood and rancid sun-baked meat.

The odor of fresh vomit twitched his nostrils. Zack tried to muffle his heaving without success. He heard Kayla weeping.

Peter groped for her hand until her delicate fingers curled over his. "Be strong, princess."

A sniffle. "I'm trying, Dad."

Not as many monsters as he feared. Thank the Energy for their short attention spans. Most of them seemed to have either been killed off or else they....

His heart dropped to his bowels.

Or else they flew away and spread out. Everywhere.

The gravity of the situation hit him. He didn't believe for a minute the military had destroyed that many of the things. No, it sure as hell seemed likely they'd gone to tastier pastures.

How far? How fast could they fly? As far as Bonnyville? Edmonton? Farther than Calgary? For all he knew they'd flown west and were ransacking Vancouver right now.

"There!"

Thoeba's shout jerked Peter from despair, if only for a second. Something grasped his chin- her hand he hoped-and directed it toward the dim outline of a jeep.

"Good eye," he said. He would have missed it in the twilight. Good to have a superhero with elevated senses in the mix.

"Almost there," he said. Peter could hear all of them, including himself panting like bloodhounds. They'd only been jogging for a few minutes, but the heat left over from the day made them all start gasping in loud gulps.

Dripping sweat made him feel like he'd been dipped in soup. Great. May as well ring a dinner bell.

Dirt hit his heels.

"Kayla!" At Zack's outburst Peter whirled to see his daughter lying face first on the ground.

When he neared, he saw she hadn't stopped crying, but now she held her knee in both hands. "I tripped."

Just beside her foot a human head came to rest. Zack's

gagging sounds amplified.

Peter swallowed the acrid taste of his rising lunch, and kicked the half-digested skull out of sight.

"Can you stand?" he asked.

Thoeba winked back into visual perception, hand extended, which Kayla took. Zack held Kayla under her other arm, dragging her up.

She took a baby step and cried out, causing Peter lurching grief in his gut.

If she couldn't walk, let alone run-

"I got her." Brewer's hulking body blocked Peter's view of his girl until he bent down. Kayla's head and slim arms appeared over Brewer's left shoulder before he stood again. "I can carry her, sir. She don't weigh much."

Peter gave the young man an affectionate slap on the arm. "Thanks Buddy."

Better to let the young guy do the lifting he decided. The kid probably grew up lifting hay bales from the looks of him.

"Good work," Thoeba said, giving Brewer a charmed smile. "Now let's keep moving."

She'd been right, Peter thought. Brewer had made himself useful already.

The jeep sat only steps away. Thoeba leapt over the spare tire and ducked under the roll bars to deposit herself in the passenger side in front. She perched her feet on the seat, alarm barely visible on her face in the dying daylight. She stared down at something Peter couldn't see.

He joined her at the driver's side, and found the reason

for her distress. The keys were in the ignition, with a human hand clinging to them. Blood stains sprayed the console, splattered the seats and pooled on the vehicle's floor.

Not for the first time that day, Peter's stomach did a slow roll. The victim hadn't even had a chance to start the vehicle before they were taken.

"What is it, Dad?" Zack asked. Clumsy thuds and grunts came from the backseat.

Peter pulled himself together. He checked to see Zack trying to ease Kayla off Brewer's shoulders without hurting her.

"Nothing," he said. He grasped the keys in one hand and the dead flesh in the other, yanking the two apart.

He dropped the stiff appendage somewhere on the floorboards wishing he could take a minute to wash the grit of dried body fluids off his hands. "Everybody hurry up and sit down."

"Peter…"

He glanced askance at Thoeba, but her gaze wasn't on him.

She brought her weapon up in a fighting stance, never taking her attention off the air. Both hands flexed on the axe handle. She resembled a baseball player poised to swing.

Her eyes determined pain for her adversary.

"Here they come."

CHAPTER TWENTY-TWO

The howling began. It made Thoeba's ears ache, and she longed to cover them, but she had work to do. She lifted her axe and waited for the soldiers of evil to draw near enough for her to swing.

The jeep coughed in reluctance. Peter swore. Each curse punctuated an unsuccessful turning of the key. Again. With each failure Thoeba's heart sank further.

"My God." Brewer brought his Colt to bear on the same two demons she anticipated. "They're a lot uglier in person."

Brewer fired, but the shots only winged one of the monsters. The beast surged forward, rage imprinted on its face, flapping its wings harder and picking up speed. Kayla screamed and buried her head in Zack's chest-- but her brother wasn't in any better condition.

Zack's breathing grew ragged. "Hurry up, Dad." Thoeba smelled the tang of his fear over the blood on the seats. It reeked of bile and regurgitation. "Hurry. Start it, *start it*!"

The engine sputtered once more before it growled to life. Another volley erupted from Brewer's C7, sending hot used cartridges bouncing into the back seat. This time he struck the first demon in the head with multiple shots, sending black ash like snow to the wind.

Brewer's toothy grin shone in the moonlight. "That'll work."

Peter shifted into gear. "Everyone hang on." To Thoeba he said, "Stay visible for now. I want you where I can see you."

Behind them Brewer's semi-automatic rattled off more destruction while he taunted his adversary. "Want a piece of me?" A beastly hiss replied. Another sputter from his gun. More demon soot.

Thoeba congratulated herself for bringing the boy. His warrior heart didn't recognize fear, like he'd been born to this purpose. She wondered if she'd ever been acquainted him in Eden.

With the first threats gone, Thoeba tried to secure her position. This time she grabbed the roll bar, and hung on with all her strength. Getting tossed from a moving vehicle wasn't an experience she wanted to repeat.

The jeep lurched like a living beast, gaining momentum by the second. They rolled over pavement and grass, through ditches and over pathways.

"Killing the headlights." Peter said. He flicked a switch, and Thoeba's throat squeezed.

How could Peter see anything? Could he drive in these shadows?

"What are you doing?" she asked.

He leaned forward, face to the windshield. "We'll be

harder to see this way."

"Full military speed, sir," Brewer said and fired a few rounds behind them. "We've got three more on our tail."

Thoeba grimaced. "It doesn't seem to be working, Peter."

He ignored her. Brewer's words spurned him to drive more aggressively--if that were possible--and with nothing to light the way.

The ride became rougher. Thoeba bit her tongue more than once, hard lumps formed on either side of it. Her head thrashed back and forth as Peter pushed the vehicle to its limits through every bump and dip in their path.

Her hand ached from the effort of holding on to the metal frame. Once she finished her mission--if she survived--she vowed never again to use earthly transportation. If the demons didn't kill her boats, trucks and jeeps surely would.

Brewer whooped from his perch in the backseat. "Got another one."

Thoeba couldn't believe her ears. The boy enjoyed this game, despite being the mouse. Was he brave or crazy? Good thing they needed him to be both.

She checked on Zack and Kayla, saw them huddled together, hands over their ears. Guns clattered around on the floor of the jeep.

"Zack," She tapped his arm until he looked at her. "Get a hold of yourself."

For precious seconds he stared wide-eyed at her. "I don't want to do this anymore."

The lost expression written on his face threatened to undo

Thoeba. She placed a soothing hand on his knee.

"You have no choice," she said. He continued to gawk at her. He waged a different war inside his head.

"I know you want to just shut down, to stop fighting," Thoeba said. "It's *not* hopeless. Not if we stay strong."

"Zack, listen," Peter didn't let up on the gas, and much to Thoeba's dismay his eyes darted from his son to the road in rapid succession. "You gotta watch out for Kayla. Your sister needs you to protect her." It seemed to work. His father's voice seemed to bring Zack around. He sat up and peeled himself away from Kayla.

Thoeba relaxed. The maelstrom of emotion churning in Zack's mind dissipated to be replaced by determination.

"Okay," He pulled one of the guns off the floor of the jeep. The other toppled out and disappeared into the night. "I can do this." He glanced above Thoeba's head and fired. A shriek and a shower of dust followed.

Brewer lay back, using his legs to brace himself by wrapping them around anything fastened down, the spare tire and the struts of the roll bar. He fumbled in pockets for his ammunition. "Are we there yet, sir?"

"Should be there soon," Peter said.

Nothing else pursued them for the time being, but Peter didn't slow down.

Thoeba repositioned before standing up. Tears streamed from her eyes from the velocity of their run, but there wasn't much to see anyway.

The sun had abandoned them to the night, its setting one of the few Thoeba had ever experienced. Strange to not see the skies, she thought. All that remained were the red fireflies dancing in pairs. Even the stars disappeared behind a growing blanket of cloud.

Something new lit up the evening.

She bent down to be heard. "There's lights up ahead." She checked again.

What she'd thought to be bright stripes revealed themselves to be small lamps in lines on the ground. "There are two rows of blue."

"Then we're almost there," he said.

She liked the warmth and hope that filled him. She found it did the same for hers in spite of the dark.

Thoeba swiveled to Zack and Brewer.

Kayla sat holding her knee, her face crumpled with creases of pain.

Thoeba risked letting go of her own secure spot and placed her hand on Kayla's arm.

"Hang on," Thoeba said.

Brewer got up to scout ahead of the vehicle. "Airport," he said. "Sweet."

Even Zack and Kayla's mood shifted at the words. It had a somewhat calming effect on them, Thoeba thought. Perhaps 'airport' meant safety to them.

They passed to the left of the azure domes. Minutes stretched, yet Peter continued to speed forward without caution.

Forked tongues of electrical discharge laced the horizon.

Small fires provided very little to see by, but ahead of them lights on stalks blinked to life in the growing darkness to illuminate unusual elongated domes.

Thoeba had never seen such strange structures before, could not imagine what miracle they housed. She guessed from Peter's desperate race toward them that their importance couldn't be underestimated.

Something in Peter's demeanor changed. She searched her surroundings but they were in no danger that she could see.

Nevertheless she sensed his distress like a spider crawling up her spine.

"Oh shit." The tension increased with Peter's words. "That's not good."

CHAPTER TWENTY-THREE

Emotions ran rampant. Fear and anxiety from her allies intertwined together in a symphony of growing despondency. Thoeba didn't understand why.

"What? What's not good?" Brewer scrambled from the back seat, maneuvering around Zack and Kayla until he stared out the front alongside Thoeba. "Aw crap."

"I don't understand. What's wrong?" She saw nothing unusual, no imminent danger. But she seemed to be the only one for when Zack and Kayla leaned forward to join them, their expressions stayed grim.

What were they looking at?

Dread hung in the air. The wind grew colder and lightning flashed. The corresponding thunder rolled in the distance. The scent of ozone strengthened.

"Nothing," Peter said.

Thoeba's frustration rose to a crescendo. "It's not nothing. I can tell something's wrong and I-"

"No, I mean there's nothing," Peter said. "All the aircraft

are gone or destroyed."

He decelerated.

As they neared the odd buildings Thoeba got a better view of the disorder.

Bodies littered the ground, various bits and pieces half chewed, femurs with teeth marks. She'd long ago been desensitized to that. Death had become a casual acquaintance.

Fires burned sporadically around structures she noticed appeared empty.

"What do we seek?" she asked.

"We *were* looking for a plane to take us out of here." Peter drove down a stretch of pavement eyeing every building. "If we can't get off the ground, we're sitting ducks just like everybody else." For a tense moment no one spoke except for the gathering storm.

"So what now?" Kayla asked.

Peter sighed. "We need to regroup."

He took a glance at the dark clouds forming over their heads. Stray drops of rain kissed the furrows in his forehead. The jeep slowed to a crawl.

"Dad..."

Zack's discomfort and fear began to chafe at Thoeba's nerves.

"What are you doing?" she asked.

"Hang on." Peter stopped the vehicle, put it into park. He cocked his head, listening. He jumped on his seat, scanning his surroundings. "Where did all the demons go?"

Thoeba and the others checked the skies with him. The storm journeyed at a quick pace. Strong winds slapped Thoeba's hair around her face, the rains raced to touch them. Lightning charged the breeze and brightened the evening like day.

None of the monsters graced their presence.

Thoeba couldn't help it. The urge to laugh overwhelmed her, and she let it.

She raised her hands to the rolling clouds and drops of water streamed off her face like grateful tears. She smelled pine needles, honey suckle and wet earth.

The timing couldn't be better.

She had to pull herself together. Waves of distress and irritation beamed from the humans around her, and all four of them gawked at her.

"Demons hate water," she said, and watched with pleasure and no small amount of joy while her statement sank in.

As if the Energy Itself had planned it, a crack of thunder broke the clouds and the downpour proceeded to drench them.

The entire vehicle shook with their merriment, whooping in happiness, hooting and chuckling in amazement at their luck.

Kayla reached all the way over to squeeze Thoeba in a quick hug.

Zack raised his hand to Brewer, who slapped it then

shook it in a gesture Thoeba had seen humans do in times of camaraderie.

Peter sat down and took Thoeba in his arms. His strong aggressive kiss demonstrated his exuberance as though he would burst from it. He jumped to his knees, and bear-hugged Kayla, then Zack. He extended a hand for Brewer, which the young man slapped with cheer.

Thoeba opened her mouth to taste the welcome wine from the heavens and thought of her home with a pang of loss that quivered in her soul.

She caressed her axe, kissed the crystal holding her god. The Energy radiated Its love to her, to all of them.

You still need shelter. This is Alberta. The weather could change in five minutes.

Did you design it that way on purpose? she asked.

I thought it would be interesting. Do think I overdid it?

Thoeba had to admit it came in handy, and her happiness swelled before she collected herself. She placed a hand on Peter's shoulder.

"Is there somewhere we can go?" she asked. "We need to make a new plan."

Her reminder sobered him into the driver's seat. Zack, Kayla, and Brewer subdued themselves, sat back in their respective places. Peter's noisy thoughts began to grind in competition with the heavens.

"Can't your god keep the rains coming?" he asked. "Can't It just hold these things at bay with the storm?"

Thoeba let her shoulders sag. "No. The Energy has no

power beyond the crystal of Its prison. Our safety is temporary."

Already the rainfall let up to a small torrent, the titanic rumbling diminished to a dull roar.

The buildings waited with their open and empty mouths, some of them damaged with charred remnants cast everywhere. Nothing that could provide them with any protection.

Peter massaged the bridge of his nose.

Did his thinking hurt him as much as it did her? Thoeba wondered.

Of course it did. He had loved ones to lose and now they waited without a plan for the squall to end. When it did, the monsters would return and the nightmare would begin again.

"We should keep driving," Thoeba said. "Maybe we'll find something along the way."

Peter peeked at her sideways.

"No matter what, we need to keep moving," she said.

"I think she's right, Sir."

"I think so too, Private." Peter reached down, took the jeep out of park with a squawk. "We'll follow this road until we find something."

"Like what?" Thoeba asked.

Peter shrugged, his eyes surveying. "Like solid shelter, or a decent way out of here."

Only the purr of the engine and the gentle pattering of the rain broke the unexpected quiet. They rumbled along in an uncomfortable hush.

Thoeba searched the night for answers but found nothing useful. Only more of the odd-shaped buildings.

There were more rows of sky blue lamps as well as red ones placed on poles.

The air was so still, it seemed as though they were the only beings alive.

Thoeba. Do you see it?

She found her attention drawn beyond their vehicle and to her right.

That one. We have to go there.

Thoeba would have missed it had the Energy not pointed it out. The building had no distinguishing features, every bit as ordinary as the rest of the elongated half circles.

She placed a hand on Peter's shoulder. "The Energy says we should try there." She pointed through the drizzle to the shadowed construction. "What is it?"

"That?" Peter steered where Thoeba indicated. "That hanger is used for repairs." His optimism had a nice vibration. "With any luck there's something we can use in there."

"What is that? A half a kilometer?" Zack asked, "We'd better get going. The rain might let up."

They looked up as one. The dance of water drops slowed to pattering. The resounding thunder echoed from a great distance, more of a murmur now.

Peter cursed under his breath and the jeep accelerated with a jerk.

Thoeba found their wariness to be infectious. Red lights held position like ominous satanic guards making Thoeba question her vision.

They could be right on the edge of trees, lying in wait for their turn to strike. For she knew these minions of darkness had no patience, but they had no love of water either.

She remembered the first time she'd seen steam fizzling from a wet demon.

It had been in Eden, next to her favorite waterfall. The beast had caught them napping in the sun, unarmed. Only evasive flight into a cloud of mist had saved them. Its unholy screams of torment had almost deafened her.

No, they would not brave the downpour. She and her human entourage would remain untouched only while precipitation fell from the sky.

The hanger loomed into view, but no cheering erupted. The moment Peter stopped the vehicle, Thoeba and Brewer sprang to the ground.

Brewer's discreet tone set the mood. "How's your knee?" he asked Kayla. "Can you walk on it?"

Kayla tested it, straightening and bending the sore leg before pulling a face. "I can probably walk a bit, but I won't be able to run."

"Let me know if you need me to carry you."

Kayla allowed a shy smile. "Thanks Brewer."

Zack slipped out of his seat, trotting around the front of the vehicle to hold his hand out to brace her as she eased out. "Let's hope like hell you don't have to," he said.

No doubt he'd meant his eye contact with Brewer to be meaningful but a smirk teased the corners of his mouth.

Peter shut off the ignition and joined them. "Just keep moving." A quick glimpse at the trees on the edge of the airport. "And keep an eye on your whereabouts."

Brewer approached the door, gave the handle a jiggle. "Locked." He took two steps back and punished the door with a deliberate kick.

The resulting boom resembled thunder, but did nothing else.

Frustration curled his lip when he addressed Thoeba. "Hey, you with the axe." With his arms occupied by his gun, he motioned her over with a jerk of his head. "Could you give it a try?"

She came forward and studied the doorknob, with its traditional keyhole. The blinking red light next to it didn't look familiar, but nothing in this era did anymore.

Let me try. Let me touch the metal.

Thoeba obeyed, bringing the side of the axe up until the Energy's stone made contact with the lock. Thoeba heard a fizzling crackle before the red light died.

A burnt metal odor tickled her nose as the portal surrendered entrance.

"Huh," Peter said. "It can override security alarms and unlock doors, but It won't make it rain."

'The Energy cannot touch the clouds," she said. "Otherwise It would."

Peter arched his eyebrows at her before pushing open the

door. He ran his hand along the side of the wall. "Must be a switch somewhere..."

Brewer moved in. Thoeba motioned for them to continue while she helped Kayla and Zack along. Kayla's knee had swelled twice its normal size.

Once inside, Zack locked the door and she eased Kayla further into the warmth and dryness of their new shelter.

When the three of them caught up, Peter and Brewer had discovered something occupying most of the space.

Thoeba had never seen anything like it, was at a loss to describe it. It might be the ugliest or the most beautiful thing she'd ever seen.

"*Yes*." Peter looked so happy his eyes and teeth gleamed. "Yes!"

Beside him, Brewer glowered without mirth. "I dunno, Sir."

"Oh no. No,no,no,no,no." Zack backed away from the monstrosity, regarding his father with astonishment. "You can't be serious?"

CHAPTER TWENTY-FOUR

Thoeba didn't understand. Was this a human's idea of a joke? If so, it wasn't funny. Peter's laughter hurt her ears and confused her.

He swiveled his head to stare at Zack. "What? It's perfect."

"It's a death trap," Zack said. "It's an ancient bucket of rusting rivets and warped metal."

"Nonsense." Peter strolled over to the silver behemoth, running his fingers over it while the group huddled next to the door. "The C119 Fairchild was the workhorse of its time." His gaze lingered like a lover's. "They don't make them like this anymore."

Zack chortled. "Yeah, there's a reason for that."

"That thing's older than *you,*" Kayla said.

"Let me put it this way…" Peter pushed a stepladder to the pilot's side to a hatch, climbed the steps and popped it open. "Has anyone got a better idea?"

No one said anything. Even Brewer seemed uncomfortable.

Zack broke the silence. "But if they parked it here, that means it's under repairs or a restoration process, right?"

Peter appeared to consider Zack's words for a minute before he leapt off the ladder.

"True." He made his way to a countertop nestled in the corner behind the Fairchild. "They'll have an invoice for it."

He thumbed through folders and various loose papers. "I'd say whatever it was, they're done." He gestured to the aircraft with his chin. "She looks good for an old bird."

A sound of rustling pages and buzzing overhead lights occupied the room. The pattering of rain created a false sense of peace.

"It would help a lot if you guys started the 'walk-around'," Peter said.

Thoeba had no clue what 'walk-around' meant, but Zack and Kayla must have heard these words before. Zack handed Brewer his gun and made for the front of the Fairchild.

Kayla groped for Thoeba. "Help me to the plane?"

Thoeba put the axe in her left hand, supported Kayla with her right.

"I'll guard the door," Brewer said. "Make sure we're alone out here."

"Good idea," Peter said.

While he made a mess of the paperwork, Zack rotated the massive blades on the front of the craft. Kayla pulled herself, one-footed, up the ladder until she disappeared into the front.

Thoeba couldn't see what the girl was doing up there, but it caused metal slats to move up and down on the plane.

Fascinating.

She'd caught a glimpse of other airborne craft before in this world, but she hadn't had any opportunity to see one up close until now. If they were in her airspace before, she'd avoided them.

Twin red stripes ran along the flanks of the silver machine. Two tailpieces were joined together by a narrow slice of metal. A couple of massive engines perched on the... wings?

Such ingenuity. And this aircraft was less than sixty years old.

I told you humans were resourceful.

She had to agree. They would do anything to touch the skies they'd once known in another life.

Which apparently included risking their necks to launch heaps of steel through the air at high velocities.

"Got it." Peter held a pink piece of paper to the lights. "Fairchild C119. Foxtrot Lima Uniform Kilo." His voice carried optimism. "Turns out they tuned her up for the air show in August. She got a bunch of new rivets and a u-joint."

Whatever that means, Thoeba thought. At least it sounded good.

A sad pause seemed to fill the air. "That's Jim's signature," Peter said. "He mentioned he'd been working on an old bird."

Thoeba stared at him, waiting for soothing words to somehow pour from her mouth. But her mind remained blank. Zack appeared to have the same issue. His mouth remained taut.

"At least I know she'll fly right," Peter said. "No one knew aircraft mechanics like Jim."

"That's not going to help us much," Zack said. He held up a tube.

"Why is that?" Peter squinted across the room at him, unable to see the problem. "You got bubbles in the fuel tank?"

"No," Zack waggled the empty vessel. "We got *zilch* in the fuel tank."

Peter dug his fingertips into the bridge of his nose and swore through his teeth. "Fucking great."

He discarded the invoice in a crumpled ball and sent it across the room. He shuffled along the corners of the hanger and searched drawers until he found the correct keys.

"Pump one," he said, reading the tag attached. "They're on the tarmac. Start poking around for jerry cans or something."

Kayla eased back out onto the ladder still favoring her knee as she planted both feet on a step. "Does that mean we'll have to go back out there?"

"*I* will, yes." Peter eyed her bloated appendage. "*You*'re going to stay here where it's dry. You'd better put that leg up."

The crystal sitting on her axe twinkled at Thoeba. She understood at once.

"I'll stay with you," she said. "The Energy wants to help your knee."

Zack approached. "I can't find anything to put the fuel in."

"Even if we could find some we'd need to make a lot of trips to fill 'er up," Brewer said. "I think I've got a better idea."

Thoeba's warrior instinct surfaced and she gripped the axe with both hands. She readied herself for battle, whatever the plan.

Everyone else had different ideas in mind. Kayla whimpered in pain causing the Energy to remind Thoeba of the urgent need to heal her.

Zack retrieved the gun he'd given Brewer, just as Peter held out a restraining hand.

"No, Thoeba," he said. "Not this time. I need you to heal my daughter." He made eye contact with Brewer then back to her. "Don't worry. I'll keep you in the loop."

We will be with Kayla. Your time to fight will be soon enough. It is important that she have the ability to run should it be necessary.

Of course. She needed to be at full strength. They all did.

She couldn't help feeling odd though, letting them do the fighting. It went against her nature, and nibbled her lip until she tasted blood.

They aren't doing the fighting. They are doing the hard work. Save your strength for battle, and let them be men.

She would relent. For the Energy.

"Alright. Kayla, back in the Fairchild -" The name of the metal bird warbled strange on her tongue. "-and we'll mend you."

Kayla complied, boosting herself back into the aircraft, pulling in until she could support her hands on the backs of passenger chairs.

Thoeba climbed into the dark silence to settle in with her.

It smelled like old leather and human, not entirely unpleasant.

Kayla had dragged her leg to the nearest seat and flopped down on it. She'd put her leg across, leaving Thoeba no choice but to take the first available position by the hatch.

The girl's knee swelled red. The gentlest touch made Kayla hiss.

Thoeba smiled. "It's not that serious."

"Maybe not," Kayla said. "But it sure hurts like heck."

"I'm sure it does." Thoeba lined the axe over Kayla's sore leg. "Let's see what we can do about that."

The light of the crystal brightened while Thoeba brought it ever so slowly down to make contact with Kayla's skin.

Warmth suffused over the axe head and Thoeba's hand.

The sigh that escaped Kayla's mouth came from the relief experienced at the god's touch, no doubt. The color began to fade as did the swelling.

Thoeba half-listened, half mind-read the plans being made by the human males.

She once thought their kind enjoyed discord between

themselves, but they demonstrated none of what she expected.

The Energy was correct. They were a resourceful species, capable of cooperation and bravery in times of need. Much better than the warmongering she'd become accustomed to seeing from their kind. Maybe their brains evolved over the past few decades.

She hoped it would be enough that they came together like this.

The storm had withdrawn leaving them with a persistent reminder of time waning. Thoeba became all too aware of the drizzle tapping overhead.

How long would it last?

~~~

Peter, Zack and Private Brewer made the short jog to the jeep.

The rain drummed on Peter's skin, but he wondered if hunger would force the demons out of hiding. It might be his imagination, but he could swear he was being watched.

The sooner they got this done the better.

"Here it is." Brewer's voice brought him back to the task at hand. "I knew I'd seen a winch back here." It sat tucked beneath the back bumper.

Peter hadn't noticed it. "Good eye, Private."

He slapped the spare tire, rooting around in his pockets for jeep keys. "I'll get into position. You guys get the hanger doors open."

Zack and Brewer rushed to follow orders. Peter once
~~~

again braved the blood-soaked seats of the jeep, breathing through his mouth to avoid the stench of death, and started the ignition. He put the vehicle in gear, aware in his peripheral of Zack and the soldier fighting with the lock before Brewer shot it off.

He kept one eye on his position and one on the horizon. That racket would give them away.

If anyone remained to find them.

Bright light poured over his back as Zack and Brewer tugged the massive bay doors open. He threw it in reverse and backed toward the nose of the twin-engine airplane.

For the thrown-together unlikely team they were, they moved like a well-oiled machine. Brewer grabbed the winch and fastened it to the front landing gear of the plane before jumping into the backseat behind Peter. Zack disappeared into the C119 as planned. Peter concentrated on the cockpit until he got the thumbs up from Zack in its windshield.

Peter pointed down. He needed to see if the rudders worked before they made the trip to the pumps, otherwise there would be no steering the several tons of metal down the taxi way.

Zack nodded. He understood. Peter leaned out of the driver's side to watch the landing gear.

Peter let out the breath he didn't realize he held when the wheel of the nose gear turned first right then left.

"The rudders work just fine," he said.

Time to get moving. The pumps were a long way away, and the hungry wailing had begun again.

CHAPTER TWENTY-FIVE

Peter's hackles spiked. The monsters maintained silence throughout the rain, but not anymore.

Not a good sign.

He drove at a crawl, itching to hit the gas and get the plane fueled up--and get the hell out of Cold Lake.

His patience strained. Behind him he heard Brewer cock his C-7 Colt.

"C'mon, c'mon." Peter had no idea whether Brewer was muttering to, him or the demons but the kid's tension didn't help.

"I can't go any faster," he said. He had no choice but to creep at a walking pace. If he sped up he might snap the line.

Worse yet, the Fairchild might gain too much momentum and get away from them. He pictured his new prize ditched in the grass at a kilter, one silver wing aimed uselessly in the air. Then where would they be?

"I know sir," Brewer said. "It's that sound they're making. Gets me antsy." Peter kept his eyes on the pavement but Brewer's nervous twitch rattling through the whole jeep. "They didn't sound like that before."

Peter had to agree. "Now they're getting *really* hungry."

"That's all we need".

Peter pointed to the last hanger. "Check that out."

The others were empty. This one housed four sets of blood red eyes that bobbed and weaved in the darkness. Peter resisted the urge to bury the pedal into the floorboards. It felt like they were passing at the speed of racing earthworms.

The keening they'd heard earlier increased and took on a disturbing mewling tone. They drove near enough that Peter could see the beasts clawing the air only to snatch their talons back from the shower of moisture.

The hunger vibe wafted from them along with the sulphuric smell of used matches. Peter actually *experienced* their desire, it was so powerful. It burned like a hollow starving rage.

"How desperate do they have to be before they'll brave the rain?" Brewer asked.

"I don't know," Peter said. But he didn't want to find out.

"Got a grenade handy?" he asked.

"Good idea."

Peter never took his eyes from the monsters as Brewer placed one in his hand. He lobbed it toward the shelter and it gave him great satisfaction to watch them grab for the bomb before it blew them to bits.

Black dust crackled and spit as it touched the water drops,

reminding Peter of Pop Rocks. He'd never think of that particular candy the same way again.

Brewer whooped. "That worked well didn't it?"

"Yeah it did," Peter said. He couldn't share Brewer's glee. "Too bad we won't be able to use them once we get to the fuel pumps."

Silence followed. It seemed Peter's statement had sobered the youth and crushed his enthusiasm.

He wasn't doing so great himself. He felt cold, drenched and exposed. With his teeth chattering, he wiped the dry-mouth gumminess from the corners of his lips.

He drove so slow his speed didn't even register on the speedometer. Peter strained his eyes, searching for pumps that had to be out there-he'd fueled up there countless times with his Hornet.

He recognized the shape and size of the asphalt. They were on the tarmac now. The silhouette of the call tower loomed to his right. A few red lights flickered, but even from this distance he could see it sat empty. There wasn't anybody left to challenge them.

Or help them.

High-octane gasoline waited for them only a few meters away. Peter could just make out the rectangles like tombstones in his windshield.

He let out a breath. He'd remained calm for the most part, but this familiar sight made him realize how much tension he'd trapped in his aching muscles.

Despite the irritations of the rains, Peter hoped it kept coming. Their lives depended on it.

~~~

Thoeba lifted the axe from Kayla's knee. "How does that feel?"

Kayla tested her knee, bending until she gathered enough confidence to stand and put weight on it.

"Wow," she said. "That feels great." She tried a few steps down the corridor of the plane. "It's like it never happened."

Thoeba watched the young girl tread between the twin rows of seats, pleased at both the Energy's strength and Kayla's obvious delight.

"Even in this state, the Energy is still powerful," Thoeba said.

Kayla lowered her gaze to the crystal. "I could sense it. Like It spoke to me. Tell God I'm grateful."

The pendant blinked three times, causing Kayla to giggle. "Did It just say 'You're welcome?'"

"That's exactly what the Energy said." Thoeba laughed too. It was good to relax and let her guard down, even if only for a few minutes.

The beasts outside were restless-their presence pulsing like an old ache- but the rain would keep them away. Give her and her friends time to rest and regroup.

Kayla seemed to find the same comfort. She seated herself across the aisle next to Thoeba, a pleased smile playing across her lips.

They rolled to a stop. A subtle change from slow motion to stillness, but Thoeba recognized the shift.

Thoeba focused her attention to the front of the aircraft.
~~~

"Are we at the fuel pumps now, Zack?"

"Affirmative," he said. "Dad and Brewer are getting out." He paused. "Dad's going to the pumps, and Brewer's getting back in the jeep." Zack shoved his nose to the glass. "Oh, I see."

Thoeba joined Zack to get a better view. Darkness and droplets made it difficult to see and decades of old dust tickled her nose, but she could make out Brewer taking the wheel of the vehicle.

He steered beneath the wings of the aircraft while Peter disengaged a hose from what she assumed were fuel tanks.

Zack moved to the pilot's window, and Thoeba squeezed in beside him.

"They're going to use that as a means to get back in the aircraft," Thoeba said.

"Yep. Ladder's back at the hanger. Otherwise they wouldn't be able to get in."

Thoeba shrugged. It made sense. After all, they were mere humans. They needed these large metal birds to fly. They couldn't even jump that high.

Brewer waved up to them before taking the keys back over to the pumps. He passed Peter, who carried the nozzle toward the back of the plane and out of their sights.

The previous quiet had been replaced by clunking metallic sounds she could only assume were associated with Peter's activities. A steady drone filled her ears.

"It's okay. That sound means they're fueling up," Zack said.

His unease lifted by degrees, and Thoeba had to admit she relaxed a little more knowing they would be away from this place that much sooner. She had faith this machine could fly higher and faster than their enemies.

While Zack wrestled his worry away with reassurances, Kayla's thoughts were a balm to Thoeba's nerves.

She crept to the back of the plane where Kayla had moved, choosing to sit with the dreaming Kayla rather than the tense Zack.

Besides, Kayla wanted to ask her something. As if the wild waving gestures for her to come over weren't enough to grab Thoeba's attention. Apparently Kayla, like her father, conveniently forgot Thoeba could tune in to her thoughts.

"Do you think Brewer is cute?"

Thoeba suppressed her amusement and kept her expression neutral. "You're only fifteen," she said. "He's too old for you."

Kayla sat up straight. "Yeah?" Her voice developed a squeak. "How old are you?"

The question caught Thoeba off-guard, an unusual occurrence. "I am one of the Energy's first creations," she said. "What does that have to do with anything?"

"Doesn't that make you way, way, *way* older than my Dad?"

For extended seconds Thoeba sat slack-jawed at a loss for words, her mouth gaping like an abyss.

Were all human offspring this precocious? Or just this one?

"Well for one thing"-How should she explain this? She closed her mouth and her eyes, thinking.

She suddenly became aware, and listened.

Something was wrong.

She could no longer hear the rain. In its place demonic roars became louder as they closed in.

She got up so fast she bumped her head on the low ceiling. Biting fireworks made her gasp. "The men are in danger."

"What? How do you know?" Kayla stiffened, her face paled and her eyes widened in horror.

"I can hear them."

"Shit!" Zack's voice carried a shared fear. Thoeba rushed to his seat where he pointed with a shaking finger to red spots appearing on the horizon. "They're coming for us."

CHAPTER TWENTY-SIX

Peter's first mistake? Forgetting the rain. His second - looking back.

Velocity turned hateful eyes to crimson blurs in the darkness. So many of them streaking fast from the east.

They must be ravenous, he thought. Even from this distance he could hear the urgent flutter of leathery wings pounding the air currents. They were getting closer.

The nozzle shook in his hand. He sucked in air to scream but he produced nothing but a faint keening.

Brewer leapt to his right. "*I got 'em, Sir.*" Shots rang out. Hot casings jingled and hissed as the steaming tubes bounced off the wet ground.

Terror strangled Peter. "Get away from the plane," he said. He struggled with the hose, remembered to loosen his grip so the high-octane gasoline wouldn't spray them and the Fairchild. The pungent eye-watering vapors were bad enough without literally adding fuel to an already dangerous situation.

Brewer continued shooting through the dark night while Peter wrestled the contraption out of the hole, let it fall and screwed the cap back on the fuel tank in spite of his violent hand tremors.

He had to get it together. Now would not be a good time to lose it.

"Get in the plane." Thoeba seemed to appear from nowhere. "Brewer and I will cover you."

A metal crunching thump made Peter spin on his heels. A demon drooled at them from atop the aircraft. It launched itself with a recklessness borne out of constant starvation.

Thoeba cleaved its skull in two. Peter tasted the charcoal remains as they pelted him in the face. His body lurched with gag reflexes.

What he wouldn't give for a gallon of water to wash his face and mouth.

"Hurry," Thoeba said. "What are you waiting for?"

"I'm going, I'm going." One extra tight turn of the tank's fuel cap, then he made for the jeep. Another glance back and he knew Thoeba had vanished to fight. Brewer's Colt belched bullets a few meters away but Peter wasted no more time.

He needed to get this machine fired up.

He sprang over the backseats of the jeep, boosted himself over the rollbars, and clawed at the floor of the Fairchild.

Four hands snatched Peter up, and dragged him the rest of the way in where he collected himself.

"What's going on, Dad?" Zack asked. "What was that noise?"

Kayla wouldn't let go of him. "Are the demons back?"

Her grip was clammy and cold.

He ignored their questions, his thoughts centered on flying them out of here. "Get ready to leave."

Zack peered out the hatch. "What about Thoeba and Brewer?"

Peter paused. He couldn't, *wouldn't* leave without them. "Stay by the door. They're going to need your help getting in."

He eased into the cockpit and strapped into the pilot's seat.

Now to find the battery switch.

Peter scanned the control panel until he found a row of twelve levers. The letters were well worn but he knew by instinct which one he needed. It had been awhile since he'd flown anything this primitive but this was a twin engine, and they hadn't changed that much over aviation history. He flipped the second switch on the row of four.

The two on the right of the second cluster were for the engines, and he flicked the left one first, praying as he did.

Peter sighed when the first engine whined to life on the pilot side. Slight stuttering, but otherwise Jim had done some nice work.

He let it gather power and momentum, listening with pleasure to the steady purr.

"How's it going back there?" he asked.

"I think Thoeba's invisible," Kayla said. "I can't see her, but demons are exploding and I don't think Brewer's getting them all by himself." She let out a shriek. "Gross!"

"What happened?"

"We got hit with demon dust." Zack said. "Must've been close, but I didn't even see it."

Peter muttered a thank you to Thoeba and the Energy for protecting his kids before he hit the switch. Engine two gave a grinding moan, making Peter clench his teeth over bitter nausea.

Let's go, baby. Rev up.

With a determined roar the right-hand engine started up. Peter gave himself permission to relax. Both engines sounded healthy enough to conquer the air.

"Zack, Kayla..." He had to bellow to be heard. "Get Thoeba and Brewer on board."

~~~

He needn't have worried. Thoeba heard the command before he issued it. She'd tuned into his fear and worry and when it gave way to triumph she understood that they needed to leave.

Kayla and Zack were shouting from their place by the hatch, but Brewer, battling meters away, wouldn't hear them.

Thoeba took a risk, leaving the children vulnerable and sprinted for Brewer.

"Time to run."

He continued to blast at the shadows with their hateful red glare.

"Brewer," she said. "We have to leave." He stepped back, letting his gun drop from limp fingers but didn't acknowledge her voice.
~~~

She searched his thoughts, experiencing the growing dread and confusion. As brave as this young man had been thus far, fighting these monstrosities now overwhelmed him.

Thoeba willed herself visible. "*Timothy.*"

Brewer whipped his head around to stare at her. His brown eyes were wide with terror and shock.

She placed a hand on his shoulder. "Get back to the aircraft," she said. When he didn't stir she added, "I'll cover you."

That moved him. He picked his C7 up and jogged for the plane. She stayed visible and followed behind pivoting often. The monsters would never slow down.

Brewer for his part shot his semi-automatic as he charged for safety, the *rat-a-tat* volley following him as he went.

The strange craft's engines became a growl, obscuring gunfire and demon screams. Thoeba prayed to the Energy that all the pandemonium would discourage the monsters from coming closer.

The left engine, the one she could see, choked for a heart-pounding moment. She couldn't be sure if she'd seen smoke or demon dust floating from the spinning blades. She convinced herself it had been the latter when the engine resumed its full power and the scent of sulfur tickled her nose.

It allowed her a measure of satisfaction knowing they might have an additional defense while they strived to reach the plane.

In front of her, Brewer strapped his gun over his back and launched himself at the jeep. Thoeba slipped in behind him. He extended a hand to her.

Did chivalrous foolishness prompt him to help her on first?

"Save your manners for the dinner table," she said. Above Brewer, Zack and Kayla barked encouragement while the Fairchild snarled all the louder. "For I am a warrior." Thoeba grabbed Brewer under his arm and by the back of his pants and heaved.

Zack and Kayla latched onto his jacket and dragged the surprised Private into the back of the plane, and extended arms to receive her.

She didn't have to read the terror in their minds. Demons were coming up behind her. She could tell by the wide-eyed horror on their faces that shouted like silent screams.

She needed to buy more time.

The disembodied hand Peter had thrown away waved to her from the floor of the jeep. On impulse she retrieved it.

She tossed her axe into the space between Peter's kids. Then with as much power as she could muster she threw the body part. Like hellhounds, the demons played fetch.

Thoeba turned back, braced both knees and sprang with all the strength in her legs. Her well-aimed and well-timed course of action brought her into the aircraft to taste the rubber flooring as her jaw banged down hard.

Through the haze of pain in her mouth she couldn't help but be pleased with the quick actions of Zack and Kayla when she heard the hatch slam shut and lock with a clang.

"Got it?" Kayla asked.

Zack confirmed. "Got it."

Scratching and squealing from outside filled her ears. A frustrated and angry demon had been deprived of her flesh.

Not this time, she thought. A kernel of triumph snuck into her throat and she gulped down the victory shout.

"Have we got everybody?" Peter asked from the cockpit.

"Yeah Dad," Zack said. "Thoeba and Brewer are safe."

"Good. Everybody strap in."

Thoeba followed the humans' example and made her way with them to the back. She placed herself and the axe into passenger seats.

She copied Kayla and buckled the seat belt across her lap. The same didn't work for her axe so she had to content herself with bracing it against the window.

Thoeba didn't think it possible, but the engine's bellowing became so obnoxious she placed both hands on the sides of her head as the craft began to move.

Humans and their noisy contraptions. Did they need to make all their machines so ear-piercing?

The lurch of the Fairchild steering toward the runway made her long to hold the Energy, but she didn't dare expose her ears.

But covering them didn't prevent her from noticing the thuds of the beasts pounding steel, trying to get in.

She guessed only the water clinging on the metal stopped them from latching on and attempting to bite through. It seemed unlikely they would eat the metal anyway, but she couldn't be sure.

The craft gained speed, the motion manifested in her

stomach as a rattle that threatened to disgorge her meager snacks.

Be at peace Thoeba, the Energy said. *Humans have been doing this for over one hundred years now.*

Only one hundred years? Bile flooded her teeth.

The C119 Fairchild seemed to leap to the air without a goodbye to the ground below.

Too late to bail out now.

~~~

"Sir?" General Lapierre heard the soldier. The man had addressed him more than once, but he didn't want more bad news. He'd been trying to plot his next attack ever since the storm offered a reprieve. Now the enemy had come out of hiding and had resumed the assault tenfold.

The voices and body odor and the constant beeping gave him a headache that persisted for hours. He tried to smooth the throbbing in his temples. Nothing worked. He'd lost too many good men and women today in ways he could never have imagined.

What the hell next?

"What is it, Private?" he asked with a snap that crept into his voice.

"I thought you might like to know…" The young man wet his lips, and Lapierre tried not to bite the kid's head off. He couldn't help that he intimidated people.

Perhaps it had something to do with his six-foot four height. Or his habit of scowling until his face felt pinched. He rubbed the tightness between his eyebrows, and tried to
~~~

smile reassuringly.

The young soldier took a breath, and let it all out in a jumble. "Someone's taking off from runway six."

Lapierre felt his jaw slack. "What?" He hadn't expected that. "Who? We haven't got anything left."

"We can't see it very well yet, sir." The soldier said, "But someone on the flank identified it as a C119."

A Fairchild. The puzzle pieces started to fit together. That pilot and his boy seemed pretty determined to head south.

He raised his voice to address the room. "Has anyone seen Lt. Colonel Mason lately?" Unexpected quiet greeted him. "Came here with his kids? No one's seen him?"

That son of a bitch took the restoration project.

He pointed a finger at the Private who'd brought him the news. "Have you made radio contact?"

He shrank back. "No, Sir."

"Then I suggest you do so." Lapierre rifled through the papers on his desk. He needed a pen.

"Shall we prepare to fire, sir?"

"No. Hold your fire. Save it for the monsters." Lapierre found a pencil and a blank post-it, and jotted a few numbers on it. "When you establish radio contact make sure they have these coordinates."

He handed the yellow paper to the young private. "Tell them to contact Dr. Thompson. Go!"

When the young man rushed to carry out orders, Lapierre excused himself to make a phone call. He hadn't taken many breaks today, only to get a bite to eat and the rare bathroom trip.

For this, he would need the seclusion of his office. He shut the heavy door behind him, careful not to draw attention to it by slamming.

He sat down in his supple leather chair inhaling the comforting scent of it while he dialed a number he'd memorized, but had never found reason to use. Until now.

The line connected and rang. General Lapierre picked up the family photo on his desk, caressed the images of his wife and daughter while he waited for someone to answer on the other end.

He feared for them, for everyone.

Mason's son had discovered the facility's existence. He had no idea what the kid had in mind, but if he was aware of Area 88, then he might have a way out of this mess.

God knew *he* didn't. He found himself at a loss, unprepared, and it scared him.

Mason had found the last functioning military aircraft left in all of Cold Lake. The rest had been lost to the enemy. If he could fly her through, never mind find a way to defeat these hellspawn at the secret base, more power to him.

Someone answered on the eighth ring. "Yeah, give me Dr. Thompson," he said.

Lapierre didn't know what else to do.

But he prayed to God that he'd just done the right thing.

CHAPTER TWENTY-SEVEN

Once in the air, the cacophony around them abated somewhat, but Thoeba knew it wasn't over yet.

The aircraft yawed left and right at unpredictable intervals while gaining altitude. Thoeba heard the axe clatter to the floor, but she couldn't reach for it. She needed her arms to stop herself from slamming back and forth in her seat.

When the occasional violent thud shook the entire plane she could tell Peter had failed to navigate around another monster and hoped it wouldn't be enough to knock them out of the sky.

Peter's adrenaline affected her, along with the terror misting off the passengers. Pain and nausea once again tried to claim her stomach contents- a half digested snack bar stung the back of her throat.

She worried the change in air pressure would break her skull, and all the human emotions she endured would spill out with the gore. The visual didn't help her swallow the taste of vomit.

A new voice caught her attention. It took a minute before she could make out the words.

"Lt. Colonel Mason, please respond."

So, someone had figured out who they were. Peter ignored them, much to her relief. Considering how they bounced through the sky in this queasy manner she hoped he'd keep his attention on getting clear of this mess.

The thrashing of the old aircraft ceased and Thoeba noticed they'd stopped climbing. The drone of the unknown voice continued.

"Do you intend to answer them?" She wasn't sure if he heard her.

"Do you really think I have the time right now?" he asked. "This isn't as easy as it looks."

She let her ears pop, working her jaw to hasten the process. She risked a peek through the round glass window, relieved to see the tops of rainclouds.

Moonlight shone through wisps of twinkling silver, making her think of the misting waterfalls of her home in Eden. She could see nothing for miles but the velvet sky and diamond stars laced with the storm.

She wasn't aware she wept until moisture spilled to her chest like twin heartbreaks.

She bent down and searched with a pawing hand to find the Energy. It's warmth found her, and she brought it to her damp face to embrace the smooth surface.

So this was homesickness.

It no longer represented a human emotion for her. She sat choking on a sob and her mouth tasted the brine of regret.

Thoeba placed the holy weapon on the seat beside her and

unbuckled her seatbelt.

"Kayla." She stood to make her way to the young girl across the aisle from her. "Where did you put the water?"

Kayla groped beneath her and pulled out a duffel bag. "Right here," she said. "Are you hungry?"

The thought of food caused Thoeba's stomach to clench.

"Not right now," she said.

Kayla smiled in understanding and handed Thoeba a bottle. "Don't drink too much," she warned. "This crate doesn't have a bathroom."

In the cockpit Thoeba heard the voice repeat its demands over the radio. This time Peter replied.

"This is C119 Lima-Uniform-Kilo. What do you want?" A pause followed. Thoeba opened the bottle and listened while she shuffled toward Peter.

"Lima-Uniform-Kilo what is your heading?" The storm scratched the transmission with unseen lightning.

"Who wants to know?"

The answer came immediately "General Lapierre. He told us where you're going."

When she got to the cockpit Peter gave Thoeba an incredulous frown before sending his next message.

"Is that so?"

"Affirmative." The crackling voice continued. "I've been instructed to make sure you've got the correct coordinates."

Judging from the surprise reverberating from Peter, that

reply wasn't what he expected. He stared at her as she placed a hand on his shoulder.

"You don't believe him," she said. It wasn't a question. "Do you think it's a trap?"

"No." He rubbed a hand down his jaw. Thoeba handed him her water and he gulped a mouthful. "That wouldn't make any sense. But it also doesn't make sense for them to give us the right location to a secret military base they've claimed for two or three hours didn't exist."

He pressed the button to relay his message to the ground. "Why should I believe you?"

Thoeba heard desperation in the other man's voice. "He's hoping you know something we don't. He thinks you might have the solution."

A wry grin crept over Peter's features. "Can't argue with that," he said. "Go grab Zack. I'll take note of these ones and see how they stack up to his." To the radio he said, "Fire away."

Thoeba made her way back to the passenger section while Peter adjusted the radio. The plane flew parallel to the ground but it would take time before her inner organs caught up. The occasional pocket of turbulence didn't help.

Her steps were careful and her hands sought stability on the curves of cracked vinyl and tweed seats.

Her ears had adjusted to the new air pressure, and she drank in stale oxygen despite the smell of dusty fabric.

She found her other comrades at the very back of the fuselage. Kayla tended to a frightened Brewer offering sweet words and food. Zack crouched next to her searching for snacks until she caught his attention.

“Your father needs your opinion,” she said. “They are sending coordinates. He wants to see if they’re the same as yours.”

She understood what the raised eyebrows and twisted smirk meant. “They want to help *now?*”

“That’s why he wants to talk to you,” she said.

Zack pocketed a granola bar. “This should be interesting.” He nudged past Thoeba and marched to the front with the practiced ease of a man that spent a lot of time in an aircraft.

The succulent scent of peanut butter drifted from the duffel and tickled Thoeba’s nose. Her insides relaxed long enough for her appetite to return, and she kneeled to find the source of the welcoming fragrance.

She glanced up to Kayla, who poured bottled water on a cloth and touched it to Brewer’s forehead and lips.

“How’s he doing?” Thoeba asked.

“It looks like battle fatigue,” Kayla said, “I don’t know how bad.” She poured more soothing liquid on the gauze. “I don’t really know what I’m doing either.”

Thoeba rubbed the girl’s arm, trying to ease her worried thoughts.

“You’re doing fine,” she said.

She found an orange package that reeked of peanuts and possibly chocolate. She tore it apart to find two delicious brown disks which she devoured while Kayla spoke.

“He just stood there frozen,” she said. “All those red eyes coming straight for him, and he didn’t move.” She sat back on her heels and stared at Thoeba.

"How did you do it?" Kayla asked. "How did you bring him back?"

"I called him by the name his mother gave him," Thoeba said. "His name is Timothy."

"He told you his first name?" Kayla's envy oozed through her voice.

"No, he didn't," Thoeba said. "The Energy told me."

This seemed to mollify Kayla, who went back to Brewer's aid, a small reassured smile playing on her mouth.

She appeared to consider something. Her lips parted and her eyebrows climbed higher on her forehead.

"Do you think maybe-"She looked at Brewer's face then to Thoeba's. "Do you suppose maybe your axe could help Brewer? Maybe if he held It?"

Thoeba wiped her hands on the wet remains of her clothing as she got to her feet. "It's worth trying," she said.

The meager light of the aircraft's cabin led her back to her original seat where the Energy waited.

She hoped her god had the strength to help Timothy Brewer, but a lot had been asked of It today.

She should have expected the healthy shine she saw.

Bring me to him.

She wrapped her hand around the wooden handle and held her god aloft.

So strong came the light it bathed the seats and windows and dazzled the steel walls.

The inside of the Fairchild wasn't pretty. The glow did nothing to flatter the rickety metal or the faded plaid on the cushions, but Thoeba paid little attention. Just the pure beauty of her god lifted Thoeba's spirits. Like having her wings back.

As she brought the axe to Brewer and Kayla she wondered at the Energy's present radiance. She felt a deeper sense of calm as well.

A quick glance out an oval of glass offered only the night. She saw no demons above the clouds where the air thinned and its flow could not be controlled by leather wings.

They were safe. Nothing could touch them this close to heaven.

Thoeba. Her attention focused on her god. *Timothy needs me*.

"Of course." She hastened to bring the weapon to the downed soldier.

She handed it to Kayla, noting as she did how the Energy sparked joyously in Kayla's hands.

It seemed to have a special fondness for her, or maybe Brewer?

Jealousy does not suit you, Thoeba.

The words jolted her. She most certainly was *not* jealous. That would be a human feeling.

But the Energy did not concern Itself with anything else but Brewer now. Her god had ended the conversation.

The young man sighed when Kayla placed the weapon in his arms. His expression brightened for Kayla, and Brewer dropped away into a deep sleep.

Kayla rose from the floor to seat herself across the aisle where she could monitor Brewer. The shiny circles under her eyes concerned Thoeba.

“You should get some rest too,” she told Kayla. The girl grinned her agreement and settled in. Even as she watched, Kayla’s eyes fluttered shut and her breathing slowed.

Thoeba let peace float through her as they relaxed in sleep. She wanted it to continue.

But she had responsibilities. She left the slumbering pair to go see Peter and Zack.

She decided while navigating her way along the narrow corridor of the Fairchild that this wasn’t as bad a mode of transportation as she first feared. Now that they glided on stable currents, only the occasional hiccup of air interrupted an otherwise smooth journey.

She arrived at the cockpit without incident.

Zack had pulled out a flashlight and an enormous sheet of paper. He’d unfolded it and spread it over his lap. Red, yellow and blue spread like capillaries over every surface. He tapped a spot near the bottom.

“Yeah, they’re the same ones,” he said. “What did I tell you? It’s for real.”

“Don’t get cocky,” Peter said.

“I’m just saying,” Zack said. “You should trust me a little more often.”

“If I didn’t trust you, we wouldn’t be up here in the first place.”

Thoeba's superior eyesight searched around Zack's finger. She saw a black dot labeled 'Medicine Hat' above it, the words 'Cypress Hills Provincial Parks.' Zack indicated a blue dot that seemed to stretch out for them with pale arms.

"Whatever," he said. "This right here is the place we need to go."

"It appears to be welcoming us," Thoeba said.

Peter peered over to where Zack described. "Yeah, that's weird. Like a stick man holding out his arms." He sat up and checked various equipment. "That's straight south from here, isn't it?"

"It is," Zack agreed. "Pakowki Lake. Home of Area 88."

CHAPTER TWENTY-EIGHT

With flight plan decided, Zack retired to the passenger cabin, leaving Thoeba alone with Peter.

For long moments she enjoyed the silence between them that should have been awkward, but felt as familiar as love.

The Fairchild hummed to herself in contentment. A single red light bathed the cockpit in an eerie volcanic glow while they sailed through an ocean of misty clouds.

Peter held her hand and she let her fingers slide over calluses he'd earned in his brief human existence. Her kind didn't have skin like this, not even the men. She caressed the scratchy texture, so much like stone.

She remembered those rough hands sliding over her sweat-slicked body, and a quick delicious shiver raced through her pulse.

"Now you know," she said. "You understand your true nature." Euphoria bathed her senses.

"The Energy told me," Peter said. "It gave me a dream while It healed me." He hesitated, seemingly unable to describe the experience. “It was like being there.” The grin he offered melted any misgivings she harbored.

“I accepted it as truth,” he said.

Thoeba saw it in his eyes, let it rush through her veins like a burst of opium.

If only she could freeze the moment in time; just live forever in this perfect peace.

“When did you recognize me?” he asked.

“Not long after I met you,” she said.

“I thought you seduced me as a way to bring me to your cause,” he said, and she sensed his guilt in the admission.

Rather than be insulted, Thoeba found his sheepish smirk amused her.

”But that’s not how it feels.” The heat from him brought a flush of desire to Thoeba’s face.

“I can’t explain it,” he said. The overhead lamp caught his faraway gaze. “I didn’t want to admit it to myself, but it was like…” His nose crinkled, as though an unfamiliar taste touched his tongue. “Destiny.”

Peter chuckled. “I hate that word.”

Thoeba smiled, waited for him to continue.

“You knew when you made love to me,” he said. “What was it about me that gave it away?”

“After the demon attack.” Thoeba kissed the weather-beaten knuckles of Peter’s hand. “You called me by my name when I had never given it to you.” Peter’s mind twisted like a tornado, pitching and rolling as he tried to remember, but his thoughts hurt Thoeba less than usual, a dull tapping rather than a throbbing ache.

"Yes you did." But his tone suggested he couldn't be sure. "You must have."

"No. I wasn't ready to trust you, even if you did smell of clover just like Thani," she said. "It's been decades since I've been to this realm of existence. All of my experiences with humans involved wars among yourselves, killing your own species."

Peter sighed. "Can't argue with you there."

"So you can understand why I wasn't assured of your honor."

He winced and let go of her hand. "But it was perfectly okay to jump into my bed," he said. "Can't trust my intentions, but you can fuck me anyway."

Humans, she thought, so easy to offend.

She didn't point out how he didn't love her when they'd had sex. She didn't have to. His statement destroyed the comfort she'd enjoyed with him.

"You angels have a skewered idea of morals."

Her response, immediate and terse blurted carelessly from her lips. "And you humans have a bad habit of putting us on pedestals."

Peter didn't say the words, but she heard him as though he had.

"Well, we're not. We have the same needs and desires as your species."

"So what sets us apart?" he asked. At least he didn't

sound as angry. More like bemused.

Thoeba's heart sank. Too bad the Energy hadn't explained this to Peter in the dream.

"It's a long story," she said.

"It's a longer flight."

True enough. Though she didn't understand Zack's map, the distance on paper looked vast.

"Where do I start?"

How much could his mind comprehend? Should she tell him angels die? Or the vastness of Eden and how it differed from Earth with its mere three dimensions? Would he care?

"How about, why are we here?" he suggested. "Everyone always wants to know that one." He made eye contact with her, his features curious, no longer infuriated. "You said so yourself. We have it all wrong, we've got it backwards."

Yes, she'd said that at the cabin.

Where to begin?

"You are here because you died in Eden," she began, and took a sip of tepid water when her throat squeezed shut.

"This realm and others like yours are a means to come home, to rehabilitate."

"When our kind dies, it could be for many reasons. Some die fighting off demons from the void, some die by their own hand in a misguided desire to become human, to be free to experience a different world. Some come in through the portals in their original forms to become gods-"

"Whoa, wait," Peter placed a hand up. "Angels

committing suicide?"

"Yes." A ripple of disturbance gave Thoeba pause. "That shocks you." She wasn't the least bit perturbed.

"Well, yeah." Peter scratched his face. He stared out at the night, lost in thought, but his genuine fright wasn't dismissed by Thoeba. "I thought that was the ultimate sin."

"It is," Thoeba said. "And they get their wish. They come to realms like yours."

Thoeba sipped at her water and let Peter absorb the information he'd been foolish enough to ask for. When he rubbed at the white film at the corners of his mouth she handed the bottle over.

He took a long guzzle before saying, "I grew up believing angels were perfect."

"Nothing is."

"God isn't perfect?" Peter asked.

"The Energy is flawless. Not perfect. There is a difference." She placed fingers to the bridge of her nose. She'd made it worse. The mayhem in Peter's brain came at her in sporadic, painful flares.

"The elements, chemicals, dark matter and other components that give the Energy life are without fault. They are a precise balance in which if one were out of sync, the Energy could not exist." She sensed she'd made headway into Peter's ideas. Her headache abated.

"But It is *not* perfect. The darkness and the void is a by-product of the Energy's creativity. If the Energy were, the darkness would not exist. If the hellspawn had not come to the heavens you and hundreds of thousands like you would never have died. You would be home in Eden with me."

Peter put the cap back on the water, and tossed it aside to squeeze her fingers. Tears cascaded to her lap like falling stars.

"My world is lost forever and I accept that," she said. "But I thought I would never see you again, and it nearly destroyed me."

He kissed her palm. "Wouldn't I have joined you back in heaven eventually?" he asked, "When I died?"

Thoeba's grief continued to roll down her cheeks. "That's the problem," she said. "So few learn enough compassion and love to come back. Humanity's contempt has spread. Not only does it prevent your kind from coming home, but it makes the darkness stronger."

"Wow," Peter said. "I wondered why you didn't seem to like human beings much. We really screwed things up, huh?"

"It's not that I don't like your kind..." That wasn't true. She had to admit to it.

"I've lost my compassion too. I deserve to be here."

Peter leaned in to kiss the saline tracks on her face, then her mouth. "I'm glad you are," he said, and the reassuring quiet they'd lost earlier returned.

Thoeba enjoyed the rest of the trip. While flying in this manner lacked the tactile sensations of clean air and turbulent winds rustling her feathers, she liked it a lot better than any other mode of travel on this planet. Better than boats or jeeps certainly. She savored the relative smoothness.

She checked on Brewer and the kids often. All were asleep, even the Energy sat docile and silent. It had worked hard since they'd arrived here and should recharge as well.

She and Peter talked long into the night until morning brought peach-colored skies. She told him tales of their lives together in Eden, how they'd gravitated to each other at the beginning of their existences, aware they were created for each other.

In the explosion that announced their birth they'd been magnetically drawn like moths to flame. She remembered all those centuries ago how she'd peered into his soul and found her place there. Just as surely as an empty chamber of her heart belonged only to him.

He told her about his failed marriage, his children, his grief of losing Jim and his love of flying. She realized more and more how much he had in common with the being she'd left lifeless in her world. He hadn't changed much.

When the clouds cleared they stared at the wreckage of small towns and cities. It resembled a burning green and yellow tapestry, the most disturbing sight below them being the dense clouds of demons swarming like flies. Thoeba lacked words to describe the devastation, so she sat hushed, consoling Peter by touch.

Peter's suffering outweighed hers. He checked the radio, tweaking it to seek another voice.

"Lima-Uniform-Kilo…." He called over and over into the handheld device. "Anyone out there?"

They heard nothing back. The dead air extended from Cold Lake past Calgary.

Peter twisted knobs to read new numbers and communication codes. They kept trying, but it wasn't until they passed a place Peter pointed out as Medicine Hat that they made contact.

"Lima-Uniform-Kilo this is Pakowki Tower. What is your position?" Peter's surprise at hearing those words alerted a dozing Thoeba.

She hadn't realized she'd slept. "What was that?" she asked. "How does the tower talk?"

Peter held a restraining hand to her. "Pilot-speak," he said. "This guy represents the place we're landing at."

Then he put the mouthpiece to his lips. "Pakowki Tower this is Lima-Uniform-Kilo we are fifty miles out of Medicine Hat. Closing in on your coordinates."

Thoeba sat poised at attention, trying impatiently to follow the verbal dance Peter engaged in with the other.

"We've been expecting you," the voice said, "We'll keep runway twenty-two clear for you, but as you can see, we're swamped. You'll have company."

Peter peered through his window to the black masses undulating below. "I noticed." To the disembodied voice he sent, "Roger that." Then he tempered the air speed.

The Fairchild's growling engines lowered in pitch, and Peter pushed the steering column in to start their descent. Thoeba's stomach lurched with the abrupt change in altitude.

He leaned over and kissed her mouth as though he did so for the last time. He let his tongue slide along her bottom lip.

"Go back there and make sure everyone is buckled in," he said. She didn't like the hard edge in his demeanor. He clicked his seatbelt across his lap, and Thoeba understood his need to focus everything on the task at hand.

"You too," he said. "This is going to be a hard landing."

CHAPTER TWENTY-NINE

Thoeba wasted no time. She'd waited too long for action and it would all be over soon. She moved so quick she received another crack on the head from the ceiling.

Growling in pain and rubbing the swelling lump on her scalp, she wobbled to the back of the plane, both hands propelling her forward as she gripped the rickety seats.

Kayla snacked on a granola bar and washed it down with juice. The smell of citrus and wheat wafted through the compressed air. Zack snored into the fogging window while Brewer scratched and stretched from the set of seats he'd slept in.

"Everybody get ready to go." Thoeba bent down to give Zack a gentle shake. His muscles went taut under her hands and he tried to roll from her touch, moaning and grumbling.

He took a feeble swipe at her with limp fingers. "Five more minutes, Mom."

"Zack, we're landing," Thoeba said.

Both his eyes flashed open. "Area 88?" He bolted straight up, adjusting his clothes and tugging his hands through his hair. "We're here?"

"Getting ready to land," she repeated.

She wandered further back, hands pressed to the cold metal ceiling as she went.

Once there, she held her hand out to Brewer. "If you are finished, my friend?"

Thoeba noted with relief that a glow had returned to his skin. He resembled himself again.

With a wordless smile of gratitude Brewer handed her the axe.

The youth around her had become a flurry of activity. Kayla capped her juice and crammed the rest of her breakfast into bulging cheeks.

Zack rifled through the duffel bag Kayla had tossed his way for something to eat and drink before buckling his seat belt. He opened the bottle and a brief fizz announced the scent of oranges as it mingled with the odor of greasy human.

Brewer, his malady cured and forgotten, checked the pockets all over his body, jacket and pants, then his Colt. Kayla tossed him something fruity smelling, and he followed her example by stuffing most of it into his face and chewing while making grotesque smacking sounds.

Thoeba watched this burst of action while holding her mirth in check. They reminded her of a small family of rodents preparing for hibernation. She doubted the comparison would be as amusing to them.

She came back to reality. What to do with the Energy? Should she take it with her where she sat, or strap it down?

The Energy had no such dilemma. *Strapped down, please.*

The request came with a visual of the aircraft yawing back and forth with an axe flying around bouncing off seats, ceilings and people.

Good idea. She hurried to the row of seats behind the cockpit on the co-pilot side.

Her stomach dropped and the pressure in her ears changed. Peter had decreased their altitude. She worked hard using the belts to pin the Energy down, and dared a quick peak out the window.

The sparse cloud cover parted and she could see the land rising to greet them. Buildings once the size of her pinky nail graduated to thumbnail size. She saw the landscape peppered with several hundred of their enemies.

Sickness squeezed her innards. But it had nothing to do with travel this time. How on Earth would they get down from here in one piece?

Have faith in Peter. The Energy pulsed a steady calming stream of light from It's crystal. *Have faith in me.*

Thoeba swallowed the burning sensation in her throat as her ears popped. She would believe. She had to. They needed to land somehow.

Her stomach sank with the aircraft as it descended. She stroked the Energy wishing she could absorb more of It's warmth.

Then she returned to the cockpit.

"What are you doing here?" Peter asked. His eyes never left the control panel. "Go back and snap in with the kids."

Thoeba shook her head. "I want to be here," she said. "With you." She buckled and tightened her lapbelt. "Besides I can help, be another set of eyes."

Peter didn't respond. Surely he had more important things on his mind than where she sat? His thoughts were devoted to landing procedures. But she also understood that her presence bothered and distracted him.

"Peter, I am a warrior," she said. Why couldn't the men on this planet grasp that concept? "I'm not afraid." She watched his face until his features squirmed in the way she expected. His eyebrows lifted while his mouth shifted to one side. She recognized it as the resigned bearing of a man who has lost the argument. His sigh clinched it.

The radio crackled. "Lima-Uniform-Kilo we have you in sights."

Peter craned his neck for a glimpse at the ground. "Copy that, Tower."

The voice said, "We're doing our best to get you clear, but there's a lot of those bastards up there."

"Do you have water cannons?" Peter asked.

The radio squelched again. "Affirmative."

"Bring 'em out and use 'em. We have enough fuel to circle until you get set up along the runway." Peter exhaled, but the tension didn't leave his body as he guided the Fairchild into a left turn so steep Thoeba saw greenery in Peter's side window.

"You lied," Thoeba said.

"Maybe." Peter shrugged, tapped a gauge. "We're getting down to fumes. Tanks weren't quite full enough when we made our getaway."

For once Thoeba experienced more panic than Peter. "Fumes? What does that mean? That doesn't sound very good."

"It means..." He appeared to choose his words with a great deal of care. "It means we're going to be flying a really big glider."

Thoeba bit down her frustration and managed to avoid shrieking. "*What* is a glider?"

Just then an ugly sensation crept up her back. She was acquainted with gliding. She rather liked it as a matter of fact...but she refused to believe that this dense metal bird could soar through the breeze like her feathered brethren.

She peered through her window to the ground below as Peter returned the plane to level flight. Suddenly they were too high for her preference, she saw endless squares of farmland and the demons were thick in numbers like a flock of undead birds blotting out the day.

Strange that she'd be afraid of heights, but being struck wingless then being propelled through the air in a tin tube running out of fuel did terrible things to her nerve.

"It's a skinny plane designed to fly without an engine," Peter answered. It took her a moment to remember the question.

She decided this particular aircraft in no way resembled the 'glider' he described.

"This is *not* a skinny plane," she said.

And to think- she had *insisted* on sitting here.

"It'll work to our benefit," Peter said. "The less fuel we have going in, the better off we are in case something goes wrong." He banked the plane into another left turn. "With that, and the water cannons I actually think our chances are a lot better. If we crash, we won't burn."

Thoeba glared at Peter, but he ignored her murderous sights. "Is that supposed to make me feel better?"

He shrugged. "Works for me."

At least he seemed to be convinced. In fact, when she reached her senses out to the rest of the aircraft's occupants, she discovered no one shared her alarm.

She craned her torso to check on Brewer and the kids.

Zack had his nose pressed to his window. He gave her a brief glance and a thumbs-up before returning his attention to the sights on the ground.

Kayla and Brewer were oblivious to all but each other, chatting like old friends.

Have faith, the Energy said. Did she have to?

"Lima-Uniform-Kilo, this is Pakowki Tower," came the now familiar voice. "We are in position."

Peter pushed the turn to near vertical. "Copy that, Tower. Coming down final."

From her position Thoeba had to look upward to see the long stripe of land flanked by machines spraying massive tubes of water through the air. As hoped, the liquid kept the demons from the runway. Almost as though a halo of purity barred them entrance. The demons shunned that airspace, even fled from it.

But they would be on their own when once they got down to the correct elevation. She didn't like the idea.

Peter knew it too. The musky tang of his fear reached Thoeba's nostrils, and she could see shiny beads of sweat dotting his skin.

The left engine coughed as they lined the Fairchild up to the length of pavement.

Peter slapped the panel a few times with the palm of his hand. "C'mon baby, c'mon."

Thoeba tried to wipe the sticky dryness from her mouth with a shaking hand. The dread began to circulate. Thoeba perceived the others behind them had heard the mechanical twitch and were aware their situation had arrived at a critical point.

Brewer's voice wafted to Thoeba's ears. "Is everything alright up there?"

Peter throttled the engine lower to a restless hum. "Flaps down," he said, his voice barely audible over the snarling motors.

He flipped switches and the plane lurched downward, until Thoeba's organs lodged in her throat.

"Shit!"

Thoeba glimpsed a black streak to the left before Peter sent them into a quick right to avoid it. Startled screams echoed from the cabin.

Too close.

They rolled back to position to the tune of screeching and protesting metal. A snapping twang followed.

"What was that?" Thoeba asked. Somewhere behind her Kayla whimpered.

Peter struggled with the steering mechanism vibrating in his clenched hands. "We lost a flap," he said through gritted teeth.

Thoeba shut her mind to hysteria. She couldn't lose it now. Ahead of the craft's nose she saw everything loom larger. Soon the trees could brush against their belly if they missed the runway. She never thought she'd long to plant her feet on solid ground.

Movement caught her eye. "To your right!" Peter jerked the steering column in time to pull up.

The Fairchild bellowed in protest but managed to find enough power to dodge another predator. The pavement waited with the salvation of the water cannons, and Peter cranked the throttle down until the engines whispered. Thoeba caught sight of individual propeller blades as they slowed.

A solid thud hit them from behind, causing the entire plane to point to the clouds and spin. Thoeba's head slammed into Peter's shoulder from the force of the impact. Both motors bleated before dying, fuel starved and stalling before Peter could resurrect it.

Peter's confusion flooded Thoeba's mind. Shrieks of terror echoed throughout the fuselage as they whirled out of the sky.

"What the hell?"

They were the last words Thoeba heard from Peter before

her spine pounded into her tailbone and the craft slammed flat on the ground.

CHAPTER THIRTY

Consciousness arrived accompanied by the taste of blood and bile. Thoeba's vertebra throbbed as though thrust into the seat. She lay limp and sore and it took tremendous effort to raise her hand to her temple. Slick coppery blood drenched her fingers.

She heard hoarse groaning to her left.

"Peter?" The pathetic whimper coming from her own mouth was frightening, but the sound of his agony weakened her further.

She opened her eyes and grimaced as daylight burned through her brain. The pain in her head rippled. Shying her face from the sun, she searched for her seatbelt with unsteady hands.

Voices she didn't recognize echoed from beyond the twisted metal carnage.

Rescuers? Hopefully. She wasn't in any shape to defend.

Even as she unbuckled, the sudden release caused her body to lurch out of position. This triggered a shot of searing torment to ricochet from her spine through her limbs.

She arched her back in defiance, clenching her teeth against the clicking pops of her bones realigning.

Sweat dripped from her brow. Panting from the queasiness and exertion, she resisted surrendering to oblivion. Her mission wouldn't wait, and she had to check on her humans.

Thoeba slipped to the floor like a falling leaf, causing her vision to dance and double. Not much could be seen through the murky darkness of the fuselage, but she could make out three distinct body shapes shifting with the creakiness of cautious movement.

Zack, Kayla, and Brewer appeared to be all right, for the time being. Peter needed her now.

She crawled through pockets of glass to get to his side, spurred through her torture by the sound of his. Hot pinpricks of pain blossomed from slivers puncturing her hands and knees. She could ignore that. But she couldn't bear the shallow gurgling sigh coming from Peter.

Please be okay. Don't leave me again.

The distant voices grew louder.

She worried about the kids and the Energy, but…

One at a time. She would check Peter first, gather enough strength to return to the cabin-or whatever remained of it.

She lay a compassionate hand on his shoulder, the one she'd hit with her head, and he moaned.

"Peter?" Her throat closed. She swallowed hard and licked blood from her lips. "How bad is it?"

No response.

Ribbons of red stained his face. Although not an expert on human anatomy, certainly his left arm shouldn't bend at that angle?

Her touch made contact with his skull, stroked his hairline. That didn't feel right either. Tears threatened to choke Thoeba.

"Hello?" An unfamiliar masculine voice echoed through the torn wreckage. "Have we got any survivors?"

Zack responded. "We're here." He sounded shaky. Could they hear him?

"There are five of us," Thoeba said. "Zack, are you hurt? How are Kayla and Brewer?"

"Who's up there? Are you injured?"

"Yes, Peter is badly injured," Thoeba said getting to her feet. "How are the others?"

She had to be sure Zack, Kayla, and Brewer were well enough, their thoughts were too hard to read when they themselves didn't know what they were thinking. She separated them with her mind and detected Kayla's intense worry for Zack and Brewer in spite of her minor hurts. A quick prodding into Zack's mind reported mild shock, but Brewer's radiated bad news.

Footsteps lumbered their way toward the cockpit.

Did the Energy remain buckled in? Thoeba had to claim It before someone else did.

Her pain, and everyone else's forgotten, she burst through the back of the cockpit in time to see a soldier bending over the seats touching her secured weapon.

"What have we here?"

"That's mine," Thoeba said. He released the belts and picked her axe, *her* god, off the cushions and inspected its glow in the shadows.

"I'd like it back," she said, demanding with her open palm.

The man regarded her hand straight-faced, jerked his head at another person behind him.

A woman wearing a band on her arm with a red cross on it appeared. "You're hurt," she said.

She reached out but Thoeba wanted to recoil from her. The woman's coffee breath made her gag.

As if she hadn't done enough of that this trip.

"Let me help you," the woman said.

"I'm fine." Thoeba tried to grab for her axe, but the woman restrained her with ease.

"The others need you more," she added. "Private Brewer has cracked ribs and a concussion-"

"They're being taken care of." The lady's voice oozed kindness, and no doubt she meant it, but Thoeba found it difficult to trust the new humans. She had to admit her new attitude of goodwill toward mankind needed more time.

You have no choice.

Thoeba switched her thoughts to the axe with its

twinkling stone.

You must rest and save what little strength you have for the battle to come.

Anger surfaced in Thoeba but she would obey. She had confidence in the Energy's judgment. And she was too sore to rely on others-for now.

Thoeba sighed. "Peter is in the pilot's seat," she said. "His arm is broken and he has head injuries."

She let the female push past her and followed the male out of the crumpled carcass of floor, metal and scattered cushions and into the sunlight.

The water cannons gave the air a bright and shiny misted look, and Thoeba had to squint. The breeze had a strange odor of what Thoeba now recognized as wet pavement combined with hot rubber.

Kayla and Zack stood just ahead of her, holding each other. Brewer lay unconscious as they wheeled him away on a stretcher. They'd wiped his injuries clean and bandaged them, but the pastiness of his moist skin didn't look promising.

She joined Zack and Kayla in their embrace and surveyed the damage to their transportation. They'd landed listing to the left side, hitting the ground hard enough to decimate the landing gear along with the bottom of the plane.

"What happened?" Thoeba asked.

One minute they'd been approaching the runway, the next they'd been yanked down and pummeled into the ground.

"Never seen anything like it," said the soldier who held her axe, stopping to gawk with them.

He tipped his cap back to regard the wreckage. "Two of them monsters tackled you by the tail. Dragged you right outta the sky." He shook his head, disbelief evident in his face. "You people are lucky to be alive. Come to think of it, if you'd had any fuel left on board, you'd be burnt bits of skin and bone and we wouldn't be having this conversation."

Medical personnel lifted Peter from the broken body of the Fairchild. Kayla wailed in anguish and squirmed from Zack and Thoeba's arms.

"Daddy? Daddy?"

Zack and Thoeba came forth as Peter raised his good arm, and managed to give her a weak upturning of his lips.

"Hey princess." It came out a raspy croak, and Thoeba placed a hand on his torso while Kayla's sobs continued.

"You're gonna be okay, right?" Kayla asked. "Promise?"

She took her father's blood-crusted fingers in her hand, and Peter gave it a squeeze. Bits of crimson flaked off and blew into Kayla's chest.

"I'll do my best, sweetheart," he said.

"Enough," said the nameless soldier, peeling Kayla from Peter as they marched him away. "We're taking you all to the infirmary."

Thoeba had to agree-it sounded like a good idea. Time to recuperate. She gathered hope as water from the massive machines streamed over her like rain.

She wasn't the only one. Zack's optimism shone from his bruised face like a torch in the night.

Kayla surprised her by taking hold of her hand. She

leaned close, her voice a stage whisper.

"Tell God that if he makes Dad better, I promise I'll never steal again."

~~~

Dr. Thompson used the touch screen to zoom in on camera three. Pixels winked as they adjusted the view.

About damned time. He'd endured several hours of anticipation for these people to show up, wasted precious research time.

General Lapierre had alerted him to their arrival, saying they might have the solution to their monster problems.

He'd be the judge of that. He sat on the largest technology and weapons base in North America. What could they have that he didn't?

He didn't perceive them to be anything special. Two of the men resembled horror movie props. Whatever. He'd seen worse this week.

He took note of the others clinging together like toadstools in the rain. Two women and one man. Nothing remarkable.

But they knew of the Area 88's existence, and that bothered him. Both the Canadian and the United States government spent astronomical amounts of time and money keeping the location secret. Too much sensitive data and advanced weaponry were kept here to risk exposure.

No matter. He would fix that later. In the meantime, he'd like to share their secrets.

And they *would* relinquish them.
~~~

Camera three projected his new guests, but not the rumored treasure. He noticed one of his men clenching something to his chest.

What did they bring him?

He rotated his headset lenses for a better vantage point, and the images on the screen swelled before him.

What interesting little toy did the Sergeant carry? It could be an ordinary camping tool, but the gleaming jewel on it—-was that significant for some reason?

He tapped a button on a silver and black panel in the upper right-hand corner of his gargantuan desk. "Sergeant?"

The immediate response squawked in his ear. "Yes, Dr. Thompson."

"After you've taken care of our friends, I'd like to see that fascinating piece of equipment you're holding," he said.

"Right away, Doctor."

Dr. Thompson leaned back and steepled his spotless hands. He monitored their body language as they progressed to camera four's range located inside the base proper. He surmised they were on their way to the infirmary.

He took off his headgear and let it dangle from his fingers while he rocked in his padded ergonomic chair. He took a sip of bottled water, letting it slosh around his woolly-tasting teeth.

He should have cleaned up for company. He tugged on the rumpled lab coat, inspecting it for stains. He'd have to change it one of these days, but he had more important things to do right now.

Excitement he hadn't enjoyed in a long time squirmed in his loins. His cupped palm strayed to the front of his corduroys as he pondered the possibility of that kind of power.

Only to retreat when his gaze strayed to the satellite feed.

He opened the door to his lab meandered to the sink in the corner, grasping the well-worn nailbrush to scrub his cuticles, reluctantly losing sight of the monitors.

It was getting worse out there. Human bodies decorated world-reknowned landmarks as the Earth's population dwindled at an alarming rate. Even Christ the Redeemer wore red.

But if Lapierre could be counted on, the solution would be in his hands within minutes.

CHAPTER THIRTY-ONE

The walls were closing in on Thoeba. She hated this place. Though free of monsters, the infirmary's glaring fluorescent lights hummed continuously. The brightness of the white walls could not erase the knowledge they were miles underground. Gravity weighed on her shoulders, and she could smell the brittle scent of absolute sterilization in the air.

She waited along with Zack and Kayla in a tiny bland space, languishing on tan sofas that smelled like feet. The naked boredom might lull her to sleep, if she were not suffering over loved ones.

If the room had a depressing effect on Thoeba, she imagined Zack and Kayla's emotions were downright morbid.

She tried to keep the thoughts of her humans from

invading her psyche. Her pangs of anxiety were plenty without loading theirs along with it. She got up and marched away from the sofa.

The smell of bleach tickled Thoeba's nose. She needed to sneeze. She needed to scream. No, she needed to be with Peter, but they spirited him away along with Brewer to knit bones and stitch flesh.

She had little faith in battlefield medics, having seen several wars and the injuries that manifested as a result. Of course, that had been decades ago. Perhaps they'd improved since then. At least they'd done a half decent job of tending to the injuries she, Kayla and Zack had sustained.

Her legs shook with suppressed dread, her hands rubbing and twisting over each other in a futile gesture of longing.

She had no idea where they'd taken the Energy either, and part of her wanted to bolt from the room and destroy everything, shredding the place apart with her bare hands until she found it.

Breathe in through the nose. Out from the mouth. Control.

They had nowhere to go. She'd already tried to fool the locked doors open by becoming invisible. It didn't work. Nor could she peel them away no matter how hard she struggled.

They were prisoners. For now.

She needed to have faith and trust in the modern day witch doctors. After all, she had their word they would heal her friends. They assured her of the Energy's safety as well.

But that seemed like hours ago, and her optimism now soured in her mouth.

“What time is it?” Zack asked. It startled her. She’d tuned out his brooding. His pacing had become a mind-numbing metronome.

“I was just wondering the same thing,” Thoeba said. “How long does human medicine take to work these days?”

“You’d think with all the fancy technology around here they’d be a little faster,” said Kayla, her tone bitter.

As if summoned by sarcasm a man appeared through the door on her right. His garments were papery and blue. He smelled like blood and chemicals. Thoeba assumed him to be a doctor.

“Both your colleagues will be fine,” he said. “Their injuries were not as severe as we originally thought.”

Kayla couldn’t help her tongue. “Sure took you long enough.”

“Ah, but you’ll be very impressed with our work,” the doctor said, unconcerned by her surliness. “Our technology is a little better than your average Medicenter.” He chortled at his own joke. No one else did. “They’re almost as good as new. See for yourself.” The blue doctor removed himself from the door, welcoming them through with a wave of his hand.

Kayla ran in first, trailed by Zack. Thoeba hurried to keep up.

The next room housed nothing more than the two beds holding Peter and Brewer, but it exploded with joy.

Kayla planted a wet kiss first on her father’s face, and followed it up with one for Brewer.

Zack dropped any pretense of manly nonchalance and

bear-hugged Peter until he puffed out a painful grunt.

"Easy, kid. I was worried about you too." He ruffled Zack's hair with his left hand. Thoeba checked again. His left hand.

"Your arm," she said. "It isn't broken."

Peter let Zack go, and extended the healed appendage to fold her in. She let him, and kissed the salt from his collarbone.

"Not anymore," he said. "It's still sore, but they set the bone and fused it back together. The surgeon's not exaggerating. The care here is *way* better than what you'd get at an ordinary hospital." He turned to Brewer.

"How's the ribs?" he asked.

Brewer's voice sounded shallow. "They've been better," he said. "But not as bad as they were after the crash that's for sure."

Thoeba's lay her head on Peter's chest. His rumbling chuckle made her giddy.

His gentle hand tugged her off to look at him. "What about you guys?" he asked. "How are you all doing?"

"Don't worry, they checked us out pretty thoroughly," Zack said, pulling his sister in a quick hug. "Cuts and bruises. That kind of thing."

Peter grimaced at his kids. "You both look like you've been through a meat grinder."

"It's not that bad," Kayla said. She rolled her eyes and smiled for Brewer's benefit. He repeated the gesture.

Peter brought his attention back to Thoeba. "You look

great," he said. "Like you barely got a dent."

She shrugged. "My kind doesn't 'dent' easily," she said. "And we heal quickly if the damage isn't severe."

"Of course," Peter shook his head. "What with being a supernatural creature and all."

Thoeba smirked. "Trust me, this crash was easier than falling out of a moving truck."

"We got a good view of the plane's wreckage," Zack said, steering the conversation back to the present. "Left hand side took most of the impact."

"Otherwise we might have been in the same shape as you and Brewer," Thoeba added.

"Glad you're not." Peter said.

Two soldiers Thoeba couldn't identify marched through the door.

"Can you walk?" one of them asked. He stared at both Peter and Brewer.

Peter eased his legs to the side of the mattress. "I'm good. Brewer?"

"Good to go." With a wince and a heave Brewer also swung himself off his bed.

"Excellent. Dr Thompson would like to see you now."

Thoeba's heart jumped. Dr. Thompson? The doctor she heard on the radio? The one who requested the Energy?

"We're ready," she said. She couldn't contain her impatience and raced for the exit. She'd brave the claustrophobic tunnels to reunite with the Energy once more…but she'd wait for her friends.

Peter and Brewer took careful footfalls at first, with Kayla nestled for moral support between them. Hope grew evident as both staggered forward. Zack took a spot next to Thoeba and remained there until the rest caught up.

"Either of you need a hand?" he asked.

"Nah, we're military men," said Peter.

Brewer nodded. "We're tough."

"Don't worry," one of the other soldiers said. "It's a short trip."

Gratefulness washed over Thoeba as they departed the germless rooms with its ugly furniture and entered the earthy-smelling tunnels.

However much she hated the low dark walls surrounding her, she knew it to be demon-free and dry. Her newfound family stayed intact and her mission would, be it a success or a failure, end here.

But the tension was killing her. She bit the skin off her chapped lips until she tasted coppery flakes beneath her teeth. The droning echo of their footsteps tortured her ears, but the worst had be the creeping feeling something wasn't right.

She just couldn't place it.

She sensed the thoughts of her humans. In fact, they seemed much more settled than usual, peaceful even. Relieved.

The soldiers flanking them, however, gave her pause.

She found their outward calm eerie. Not that their

thoughts were boisterous or violent. Maybe that's what made it so strange.

So maybe all humans weren't crazy like the ones she loved. Perhaps she wasn't used to normal people after meeting Peter and his kids.

But underneath the skin Thoeba could sense a tension and alertness that didn't quite seem normal. Too quiet.

They came to a door on the right, and their escorts stopped. One of them slapped his right hand on a green panel. He then placed his eye right to the wall, where Thoeba noticed a hole directly in line with it.

A stripe of radiant swamp gas green flared forth into the soldier's skull, but he made no sound, nor did he drop dead.

"Identity confirmed." The voice jangled Thoeba's nerves. She'd never heard anyone speak like that.

Peter must have seen her trepidation. "It's just a computer," he said, rubbing her arm. "Perfectly normal."

"And not exactly new," Zack said. The door hushed open and let them pass. "Thought this place was supposed to be high-tech." But he kept his mutterings at low volume.

When they strolled through, Thoeba's eyes were assaulted with wall-to-wall images of destruction. Dozens of visual boxes flashed shots of demons killing and eating humans. Flesh flew in meaty chunks while dribbles of blood decorated the world like finger paint.

Most were aerial views from high places. She recognized little of the architecture, but enough to understand that they came from other places on this planet.

Some landmarks were too distinctive for Thoeba to

mistake them. The Eiffel Tower wore bodies like grotesque Christmas ornaments. The Leaning Tower of Pisa lay in ruins. The beasts hadn't been content with causing death. They had to destroy anything of beauty as well.

Kayla began to cry. Peter's arms swallowed her in a hug, sheltering her from the horrendous sights. Zack and Brewer made sounds of disbelief, gasps of anguish.

Peter slid a shaking hand down the side of his face. "I can't believe this." His voice held tears. Thoeba became aware of a wetness trailing down her cheek.

Zack shook his head in dismay. "They're everywhere, all over the world."

"They found the other portals," Thoeba said, her voice hardly more than a whisper.

"It seems our common enemy has gone global." Thoeba hadn't noticed the bald man at first. He sat hunched behind black machinery, but he rose to greet them. "I've been expecting you."

He extended his hand first to Peter. "Lt. Colonel Mason is it?" Peter gave him a hesitant glance, but took it all the same.

Thoeba couldn't blame Peter for his uncertainty. The man's hygiene suffered from neglect. His hands appeared clean but he smelled like the couches in the infirmary, and his breath had the rotted enamel odor of tooth decay.

"And you are?" he asked.

"Dr. Thompson," he said, after a firm shake. He continued to the rest of them, including Thoeba, grasping them in the common Earthling greeting. "General Lapierre told me you were coming here with a possible solution to this..." he waved his fingers to indicate the scenes of chaos behind him.

"Difficult situation."

Thoeba tread forward. "Yes, the Energy," she said. "It's the key to everything." She perceived her god to be near. She couldn't stop her hopes from rising.

"When we crashed the plane, one of the soldiers took it with him to bring to you. Do you have it here?" She reached out with her heart until her deity answered her...

From right in front of her. With the man they'd just met.

And something was wrong.

Get out. Run.

"Why, yes. I have it right here." He dipped into his lab coat pocket and extracted the pendant, leather strap and all.

Run!

Thoeba shook her head. Not without the Energy.

She lunged for It, but the doctor snatched it back with a mean-spirited giggle as their escorts yanked her away, aiming their rifles at her temple.

All pretenses of friendliness disappeared from Dr. Thompson's face, replaced by a sneer of contempt. "Arrest them," he said.

CHAPTER THIRTY-TWO

"*What?*" Thoeba understood exactly how Brewer felt. The incredulous expression on his face might be considered comical if their predicament not so dire.

"Are you out of your mind?" he asked.

Four more troops appeared like ghosts from side panels in the walls. Multiple pairs of boots tapped a disjointed rhythm on the floor and echoed through the bleak space.

Peter's worry for Kayla masked his confusion and anger, and he clutched her tighter. "What's going on?"

Zack threw both hands up, shaking them in front of Dr. Thompson as tension between them escalated. "You don't understand," he said. "We're here to help you. Don't you get it?"

Thoeba heard the confused ache in his heart. He jabbed a finger toward her. "This woman came from a different dimension with the life force of the universe to save our world from the same fate as hers."

He's wasting his time, Thoeba thought.

This human wore the stench of arrogance along with other cloying odors he'd collected from days without bathing.

But Zack's passion forced him to plead his case. He dared a lunge forward.

"We can do this," he said. "Let us work with you. I'm really good with computers-that's how I found out about this place. I uh, hacked in." He studied his toes, and Thoeba could almost see the chagrin on his face. "I can help if you'll let me."

"I don't need your help, boy." Thompson put an aloe-vera scented hand in his rumpled pocket, and withdrew a small pistol. "Save me your *tortiliquies*."

Tortilliquies? Thoeba hadn't heard that word for decades, not since medieval times. It meant 'false speech.'

Perhaps the way the doctor used it caused Zack's reaction. Could it be the obscure word itself? She didn't know, but its effect on Zack staggered her.

The color disappeared from his eyes, his pupils and irises spun back in his head as his thoughts emptied, draining away like water through sand.

Peter tossed Kayla to Thoeba and rattled Zack by the arms. No reaction. "What the hell is wrong with him?" Zack's head bobbled with the motion, but gave no sign of life.

Peter whirled on Thompson, braving the smaller man's stench and his weapon to grasp a handful of his jacket. Thoeba experienced the burn of Peter's rage like a molten volcano, but his speech was low and lethal. "What did you do to my son?"

Thoeba concentrated on Zack's mental faculties. Never before had she experienced a mind hushed so profoundly by a single word, but the young man's thoughts were gone, leeched away to nothing.

Silent.

Thompson seemed to fear nothing. He favored Peter with a sleazy smile. "Get your father away from me, Zack."

Zack advanced, slammed both hands on Peter's shoulders, and slid him across the floor.

"Now take the pistol," Thompson said, and Zack obeyed. "Put it to your sister's head."

Zack positioned the muzzle of the gun against Kayla's temple, dismissing Thoeba with a bruising shove. She landed in Brewer's embrace as his colorful swearing scorched her ears. The air thickened on her skin with the tension.

The unpleasant tang of urine tainted the air. A warm river flowed from Kayla's shorts and created a puddle on the tile, spotting her legs and feet.

Peter wore the physical and emotional trauma stretched across his lips. They crinkled, wiggling downward and threatened to scream while his eyes watered.

"Zack, what are you doing?" Peter's tremulous voice and the wild fear in his thoughts pierced thorns through Thoeba's heart as he regained his footing. "Get that gun away from your sister."

"He can't hear you," Thompson said. "He responds only to me."

Peter glared poison at him, fingers curling into talons as he raged toward the snide little man. "What did you do to my son *you bastard*?"

Thompson raised one finger toward Kayla. "Don't make us kill your daughter."

Peter's shoes squeaked to a halt.

Thoeba bore witness to Peter's intense fury-he vibrated with it. "What did you do to him?" Spittle flew from his lips.

Soldiers wrestled him away from the doctor, clenching his arms behind his back, but not before Peter rewarded two of them with fists to their midsections and jaws.

For the first time Thoeba could recall, her emotions were torn.

Did she jump in and defend him? Or would that force the doctor's hand? She froze, frustrated with her inability to make a decision.

Brewer ventured forward, no doubt with heroic intentions, and stiffened beside Thoeba when the cold metal of a rifle muzzle dug between her shoulder blades. Brewer appeared to take stock of his chances for triumph, then a begrudging step back when he realized he couldn't win. Not without a price.

Thoeba admired his restraint. It clearly galled him to stand down.

Thompson gifted them the only genuine smile he'd offered since their introduction.

"It's highly experimental," he said. "A little something I wrote up for security measures."

He sauntered back and forth in front of his massive black desk. His nonchalance infuriated Thoeba.

Judging by the violent thoughts streaming from Peter's and Brewer's head like hurricane winds, she wasn't the only one.

"You see he's not the only second rate computer geek to discover Area 88," Thompson said. "It isn't easy, but it can be done." He ceased pacing to make eye contact with Thoeba, Peter and Brewer in succession. "I had to include some additional programming."

"Is that what you did?" Peter asked. "You *programmed* him?" Peter's fists clenched, his skin mottling an unpleasant crimson.

Thompson sneered at Peter. "You should thank me," he said. "The others were not so fortunate. They all died by their own hands." He shook his head. "Wasteful. What was I thinking?" He resumed a patient gait.

Thoeba's loathing heightened. No remorse ate at his conscience for the suicides he'd inflicted, no second thoughts. Only regret for lost resources.

"Your son, however," he said, "He got additional sub-routines when he tapped in."

Thoeba hated this human, strutting in front of them, flaunting his power and control. She'd never seen such conceit, such self-absorption. It made him dangerous.

She would have to destroy him.

But how? Zack had Kayla at gunpoint, his mind like that

of a golem, and this megalomaniac held her god in his pocket. She'd been foolish to trust.

Have faith. I am not helpless, and neither are you.

I wish I could share your confidence and optimism, she thought, but right now I'm not sure it's appropriate.

The Energy didn't waver.

Thompson marched up to Zack and waved a hand across Zack's glassy gaze. "I would say the experiment was a complete success," he said, and Thoeba longed to stretch Thompson's lips from his ugly teeth. "Wouldn't you?"

She wanted to squeeze his throat until his veins bulged. Her urge to strike this demented excuse for life frightened and appalled her.

"I lost a lot of soldiers in those early attempts. It was a lot of work." Thompson continued preening. "I don't usually get the opportunity to gloat."

Calm down, she told herself. If not for the Energy, then for the innocent mortals in the room.

She couldn't let this creep, this *slimy rodent* cloud her judgment.

Breathe in. Breathe out. Think.

Thompson waved dismissively. "Take them to the brig," he said. "I have work to do."

Thoeba received a sharp poke in the spine. "Move along," someone said.

Outnumbered and outflanked, Thoeba sacrificed her will and allowed the military men to lead her back toward the tunnels.

She shuffled ahead. Peter and Brewer eyeballed Zack as he manhandled Kayla, drool seeping from his mouth like a dying man's last curse.

Patience and faith.

Yes. She would have to exercise both. They'd come this far, why should they give up now? She caught Brewer's eye, and tried to project encouragement with a raised eyebrow. His expression changed to hopeful. She attempted to do the same with Peter, to send him a vibe of assurance. Maybe between them they could create an escape plan and get the Energy back.

"One more thing…" Thoeba glanced back at Thompson who made a show of pondering something, posing with one finger on his chin and staring into space. "I think I'd feel a little better with the young lady here to keep me company." He gestured to Kayla. "Zack bring her to me."

Zack did so without reluctance, never taking the gun from her temple.

Thompson spread his hands in false supplication. "Just a little insurance you see," he said. "I wouldn't dream of you trying to escape."

Thoeba wilted, her heart slowing in defeat. Their ambitions left the room, a guest that couldn't stay. The doctor took pleasure from it, and Thoeba desired nothing more than to shrink the grin growing on his face.

But she had no power here.

Dr. Thompson's henchmen prodded the three of them through the dark chilled tunnels. Kayla would stay a hostage while Zack remained mindless.

She stared straight ahead as they were forced back into

the corridors and away from the Zack and Kayla. She realized, without reading their thoughts, that Peter and Brewer shared her despair. Both hung their shoulders in defeat.

How would she fix this now?

CHAPTER THIRTY-THREE

Dr. Thompson despised kids, hated those foul-mouthed, loud, obnoxious parasites. These two were no exception.

The boy would no longer be a problem. His days of pissing around in other people's affairs and properties were over.

As for the girl...

He glimpsed her snarling face from his peripheral while he made his way to the door of his lab behind the office. He'd probably just get rid of her after he had what he needed. Programming such a scrawny child wouldn't be worth the effort. What would he use her for? Right now her reason for living was leverage, nothing more. He might need her in order to keep the others in line.

They passed the pitch-colored desk, with its bells, whistles and paperwork crammed to fit on the same surface, then to the portal beside the wall of video screens.

Demons continued to rip and shred through human flesh in disturbing video silence.

He listened to Kayla's repeated swallowing sounds. Little bitch already pissed herself. She'd better not puke in his lab.

After placing his palm on the scanning screen, he positioned his eye in front of the laser scan. He ignored the painful urge to blink as the computer confirmed his identity in a monotonous drone and welcomed him in.

"Bring her," he said to Zack. He heard the shuffling of Kayla's protesting feet, her grunt of pain as her brother dragged her into the cluttered and busy room.

Thompson surveyed his domain. Spending endless hours and days here never failed to comfort, and he preferred it to the spartan living quarters he'd been issued on the other side of base. He considered the lab his true home.

Few unoccupied spots peeked from the clutter of machinery and unfinished projects.

One corner housed microscopes of various magnifications, right next to the hand-washing sink and a couple of refrigerators.

One of the appliances contained food and water, while the other housed organic specimens for experimentation.

It got harder each day to tell the difference between the two.

But a titanium machine dominated the room. It took up an entire wall, and it would play a large part of Thompson's work with his new toy.

"Put her there," he said, pointing to a worn yellow chair placed next to a work island in the middle of the cramped space.

Without a word, Zack pushed Kayla down until the sound of her ass hitting plastic smacked in Thompson's ears.

A vertiginous giggle rose in his throat and he gulped it down, but he couldn't help the way it manifested as a stretched grin on his face.

His first true brainwashing had been a complete success.

Subliminal messages and well-timed flashpoints combined with hypnotic programming were inserted into everything from access codes to latent files. Finding obscure trigger words had been a lovely stroke of brilliance. He'd covered all bases, and won.

The potential for this application could be astronomical, and Zack marked only the beginning. Why program intruders to shoot themselves when you could program them to serve? With this application he could amplify his control of the military as well.

He took a left to step up to his most powerful microscope, chuckling at how his perspicacious nature served him so well.

"Laugh it up while you still can," Kayla said. "We're gonna kick your ass."

Thompson regarded the disheveled teenager slouching in the seat to his right. "You're pretty brave for someone sitting in her own piss." To his intense irritation, she shrugged.

"It was a long trip without a bathroom," she said.

One way or another, he would wipe the smug from her face.

He extracted a pair of latex gloves from a convenient drawer. The acidic scent along with the powdered residue tickled his nose as he pushed one hand then the other into the fingers.

Thompson slipped into his pocket searching for the warm smooth pendant. Once he located it, it seemed cooler to the touch than it had before.

He brought it out, gazed at the dimming light.

The waning glow disturbed Thompson. The last thing he needed would be for the power to drain out of the thing before he had a chance to harness it for his own.

If this truly was the solution to the demon problem enveloping Earth, then it would mean a tremendous windfall for him and his government. He'd be a hero.

A very *wealthy* hero.

He checked on Kayla and Zack. Kayla sat with legs akimbo and arms folded, glaring at him with daggers in her eyes.

Zack hadn't moved. Thompson became aware of the urge to giggle creep up again. The boy held the muzzle of the pistol against his sister's temple as instructed. His face stayed blank. If the young man blinked, he did so rarely.

Thompson brought his attention back to his new experiment. He adjusted the height of the lenses on the microscope. He'd start on the weakest magnification.

He carefully snipped the leather strap from around the crystal, noting as he did the distinct drop in the pendant's temperature. Thompson didn't truly believe the creator of the universe lay in his hands, but he couldn't shake the impression that the rock didn't *like* him.

He gave his head an absent shake. Absurd.

"I'm not scared you know." Kayla's grating voice interrupted his parade of ideas. "This isn't the first time I've been a hostage."

"Really." Interesting if true, he thought. He dropped the glowing stone on the microscope and adjusted his sights. He had to squint. Even though its shine had waned he found the light stung his eyes.

"I killed my last kidnapper," Kayla continued. She leaned toward him as far as she dared. "With a *sword*."

"Wow," Thompson said. Not impressed. "Do you get kidnapped often?"

"Second time this week," she said.

Thompson breathed a heavy sigh. "I can't imagine why. Are you sure your last kidnapper didn't deliberately impale himself?"

Between her babbling and the luminescence shining through the microscope a sharp throb took root behind his eyes.

No matter how powerful the lens, his search proved fruitless. The radiance inside the crystal had no beginning or end. He stared into a shimmering golden void. It set his teeth on edge and made his innards twist.

He snatched the rock from the slide plate and inspected it between thumb and forefinger in the fluorescent light.

He stalked over to stand in front of Kayla. "How does this thing work?" he asked, turning the crystal in front of her nose.

"How should I know?" She had that irreverent expression all over her face again. "You're the science guy. You figure it out."

Thompson straightened, fixed her with what he hoped resembled an intimidating glare. "I can make your stay here very unpleasant."

Kayla's half-lidded eyes suggested she wasn't convinced. "What are you going to do?" she asked. "Make me watch you play 'Revenge of the Sith' with your action figures?"

It took a heartbeat for Thompson to backhand Kayla from her chair. He couldn't be sure what pissed him off more, her insolence, or the fact that he didn't get the joke straight off.

"Pick her up, Zack." His knuckles hurt from the impact, but it had been worth it when he saw the blood streaming from the little slut's nose. "Keep the gun on her head."

He rifled through various cupboards and drawers until he found duct tape and spare electrical wire. Zack waited with the pistol pointed at Kayla's cranium. "Tie her hands behind her back with this." He tossed the red and black strands in the general direction of Zack's feet.

It made him nervous when Zack released the gun to the floor with a thoughtless clatter to obey his orders, but the blow to her face had stunned the wretched teenager into submission and she didn't have much fight left.

Zack hauled Kayla back to the chair like a sack of potatoes and wrenched both arms behind her until she barked in pain.

Kayla didn't take her eyes from Thompson's as she licked the blood from her lips. "My dad is *so* gonna kick your head in."

The air resounded with the rip of tape rolling away in a generous strip. Thompson tasted the chemical gooeyness of the adhesive as he cut the tape with his teeth.

"I don't think so, sweetheart," he said and slapped the silver rectangle across her mouth. "After I get what I need here," he gestured to the dark chrome machinery with its coiled cables and flickering lights. "I'm going to give him and your friends back to the medical team for dissection."

He relished the torment and futile seething flashing in her bulging blue eyes for a moment before rushing to the sink to scour her blood from his skin. Much better.

"Come along Zack," He swiveled back to his computers and lab equipment. "It seems I'll need your help after all." The excitement returned to his day. "We've got a lot of work to do, and I'll need another set of hands."

CHAPTER THIRTY-FOUR

She had no choice. As several pairs of shoes squeaked and tapped down the tiled floors of the damp corridors Thoeba agonized over her decision. But nothing held more importance than the mission, and she couldn't accomplish it if she let them lock her up. She hoped that Peter and Brewer would understand.

She seized Peter and pressed his lips to hers. She kissed him like she'd kissed Thani for the last time. She let her body melt into his, ran her hands through the silky stubble of his hair, the sharp bristles along his jaw. She tasted the sour dryness of his fear with an eager tongue as though it were sweet wine. She lingered, squeezing her hardened nipples against his chest…

Then wrenched herself from his grasp. "I love you," she said.

She left him holding the memory of her touch while agitated voices filled the air.

"*What the hell?*"

"*Where did she go?*"

The soldiers spun in every direction, pointing their semi-automatics at shadows, stunned expressions stamped into their faces.

Peter took a deep easy breath, licking his lips. "Oh, didn't we tell you?" he said. "Thoeba can disappear at will." She loved the mischievous glint in Peter's eye.

Behind him Brewer let out an appreciative chuckle. "I love it when she does that."

The tension left Thoeba's neck. Peter and Brewer would be okay without her, and that would make this so much easier.

She didn't move. Not yet. She plastered herself against the seeping concrete walls, the damp collecting in her bones. Something cold and wet dripped in her hair. She sucked her stomach in, just out of reach of the muzzles of their weapons. Each time one passed her abdomen she resisted the urge to run.

"Shit," the soldier covering Peter said. He waved his gun under her lover's nose. "Where is she?" Thoeba quivered but held her ground. Everything counted on her remaining motionless and silent.

"How should I know?" Peter sounded nonchalant, but his nervousness rattled her as though it were her own.

"She never tells us the plan," Brewer added. "Not much of a team player, that one."

The first soldier let his arm go slack, his gun now pointing to the floor as he wiped his free hand down his chin. Thoeba would have recognized the human gesture of frustration even if it didn't ripple off him like sound waves.

Thoeba could smell the dusty sweat beading on his skin. "What the hell do we tell the doctor?"

"I don't envy you," Brewer said.

"Shut up, Private," he said. "Save it for your court-martial." He pointed to two of his fellow soldiers. "You and you, take them to the holding cells." Thoeba noted their appearance and their direction, but didn't hold out much hope of remembering such details.

Not that I could find them through this maze, she thought.

Maybe she'd have to borrow a tactic from the doctor, and force one of these people to bring her to them, but right now she needed to concentrate on the leader.

She could sense his hesitation. His mind blared with indecision. Apparently Dr. Thompson's experiments had left scarring that made independent thought difficult.

She waited and studied him while the tall fellow and the moustached one led her friends away.

Thoeba prayed she'd find them again.

Later, she told herself, don't let your emotions get the best of you now.

The lead soldier's nametag labeled him Captain Smith. His brown eyes betrayed his trepidation. She hadn't done anything yet, and he feared her.

Her heart told her this wasn't a bad man. Quite the opposite. Even without Thompson's interference his loyalty and patriotism reminded her of Brewer and Peter. In different circumstances the men might be friends.

But for now, she would stalk him like a wraith. He would

eventually bring her back to Zack and Kayla. Peter and Brewer would have to wait.

"The rest of us have to spread out. Search the grounds," Captain Smith said.

"What are we looking for?" the blonde one asked.

"Damned if I know," the Captain said with a shrug. "Look and listen for footprints." He cocked his gun. "She could be anywhere. For all we know, she's standing right behind us."

Or right in front of you, Thoeba thought.

Two of the men startled, eyes wary.

"Just stay alert. Use all your senses," Smith said.

"Should we report the prisoner's escape to Dr. Thompson?" a carrot-headed soldier asked.

Captain Smith stared the speaker in the freckles. "You volunteering?" Much foot shuffling and quiet muttering ensued. "Didn't think so. Now move along. Failure is not an option."

The other three men branched off in different directions. Captain Smith loitered until his troops left him standing alone.

Thoeba froze. This man listened for her to make a mistake, and give her position away. She didn't stir, didn't take a single step. He scanned the room, checking corners and peeking over his shoulder. The murmur of the lights and the occasional drip were the only sounds partnered with Smith's breathing.

He sniffed the air for her scent, rifle pointed in front of

him. *That* frightened her. How well could humans smell? She didn't expect that kind of tactic from a human, but this one had an unusual imagination.

She would use extra care with this hunter.

Just when she believed she might blow her cover by exhaling too loud, he made his move. He backed away holding his gun out in front of his torso.

Thoeba tasted acidic adrenaline in her mouth but she couldn't lick her drying lips or swallow the flavor of doubt.

In order to shadow him she had to step toward him, mimic him. She measured her tread with each rolling footfall. If she made the slightest sound, he would fire. Thoeba bit down a shiver as a single drop of sweat traced an icy finger down her spine.

She couldn't remember the last time she'd had to use such a strategy in close quarters. Probably never.

But she had no choice. Instincts told her to stay close to him. For the Energy. And for Zack and Kayla.

Because his theory involved her heading for the lab.

How ironic. He didn't realize that without him, she would never find her way back, and being invisible didn't mean she could walk through doors.

He would inadvertently lead her back to her destiny.

CHAPTER THIRTY-FIVE

Alone with the captain, Thoeba coiled in readiness.

He no longer pointed his weapon at her and if memory served her, only one lock separated them from the central office.

She would become his living shadow.

Time slowed as both took careful strategic toeholds on the ground in a mute ballet.

The captain, unaware, inched to the tubular walls, likely attempting to make himself less a target and more a ghost.

Thoeba risked such nearness she could hear the reluctant squeal of his shoes, smell the subtle fragrance of leather and canvas mingling with his masculinity.

When they arrived at the white panel the captain spared a glimpse behind. Thoeba's blood sang in her ears when he seemed to meet her gaze.

With calculated slowness she rocked back on her heel.

Too close.

He scanned the concrete without reaction, and her skin cooled as he began to access the lock. He placed his hand on the panel, and his face up to the laser hole.

He doesn't know I'm here, she thought. He thinks I've long gone, and walked through walls.

Good.

The portal sighed open and the captain advanced. Thoeba mimicked his movements and crossed as quickly as possible, rushing to avoid being caught in the door.

Her impatience stirred the slightest breeze. It graced her skin with a flutter. The captain tensed and she dropped to a crouch.

The soldier reacted, whirling around, the barrel of his weapon creating more motion above Thoeba's head.

"I know you're here, lady."

She waited with her hands splayed on the cold floor. Shallow breathing combined with the uncomfortable position started a cramp in her ribcage.

If he walked away she would be alright. If he made a single stride forward he would trip on her.

So be it.

Thoeba grasped his ankle in midstep and flipped him over the bulk of her body.

He yelped, his gun flying from his grip.

Brapt! It rang out in the vast expanse of the room. It dented the tile when it bounced and an ugly string of holes blackened the ceiling. She straightened her legs and jumped over the flailing human, kicking the Colt out of range.

Thoeba straddled him while he squirmed to his back, but the fight hadn't left him. He bucked between her thighs like a man possessed, and she clenched them to his sides until his hip bones ground into her skin.

He tried to grab her wrists, wrestle her off him while grunting, growling and squirming.

His hands were strong, but she wrenched free. She had to quiet him before he sounded an alarm.

She ground her left hand down on his chest, her right fist connected with his jaw.

The crack from the impact resounded in the quiet space and he went limp beneath her. Only then could she indulge in a huge gulp of precious air.

The divine sensation of oxygen filled her starving lungs and brought a spell of dizziness. She allowed for several more cleansing puffs as she peered down at the captain's unconscious face. A single drop of her sweat landed on the bridge of his nose.

She gave herself permission to reappear. Invisibility required concentration she no longer had and she needed a break.

She listened for reinforcements. None came.

Hadn't anyone heard anything? She paid attention for sounds of running or yelling. Nothing but silence. Perhaps the walls were thicker than she'd thought.

She took stock of her surroundings, noted with satisfaction that he'd brought her back to where she wanted to be-the main office.

Black frames flaunted their awful images, but the rest of the white void remained uneventful and quiet as falling snow.

"Sorry, Captain," she said into his ear. "But I need you to stay out of this."

Thoeba swung her leg off his torso and slipped her arms under him, lifting him as she regained her footing.

She couldn't just leave him vulnerable on the hard ground. She had to find that tacky couch. She turned the open corner to her left and found the waiting area outside the infirmary.

She lay the soldier down on the tan cushions and leaned in to his lips to ensure that his breathing stayed slow and steady.

The gentle snore on her cheek signaled he'd be fine. Probably bruised and humiliated, but otherwise alright.

Thoeba studied the relaxed slopes of his face, the lack of tension around his eyes. They all resembled children regardless of their age when they slept.

Zack and Kayla. Peter's children. She had to find them.

But where? She retraced her steps, but blinding white walls and unremarkable metal doors made up the landscape.

Great, she thought, and I just knocked out the man who most likely could have helped me.

Thoeba rubbed her gritty eyes.

They hurt with the twinge of unshed misgivings.

Don't cry, don't come apart now. Think!

But she faltered. This entire building and its monotone color scheme dulled her brain cells and stifled ideas. Every detail suffered from a painful lack of imagination or originality...

Except for that door in the south corner. It had a window.

Why would that one have a window when the others didn't? Not much to go on, but better than tasting tears.

The doctor didn't strike her as the type of person to need a view. It had to be installed for the benefit of the people working here. If *she* were forced to deal with a man like that, this would be a good way of checking in on the troll without the discomfort of having to engage him.

She tiptoed toward it, mindful of the soft impact of her borrowed sneakers tapping on the tile. She doubted anyone could hear them, but everything rang louder in this enormous and empty stretch. She could hear the captain slumber around the corner behind her like a hurricane wind.

She willed her body to vanish before sneaking a peek through the thick glass on the portal.

Her heart ached. Zack and Kayla were there alright, along with the deranged Dr. Thompson.

She saw the Energy lying on a clear platform between engine parts Thoeba didn't recognize. A clear tube encased It, imprisoning her god's light.

Too dim, she thought, swallowing distress. The Energy's diminished flickering demonstrated Its weakened state.

Kayla's body faced the door in profile, and Thoeba sickened at the chafing rope burns on Kayla's tied wrists as well as the silver tape across her mouth.

Zack had his back to her, his movements slow and methodical as he positioned himself to attach wires to other wires to screws and plugs.

He's still in there.

As the familiar communication made contact with her soul, happiness leapt through Thoeba's bloodstream and energized her.

My Lord, she asked, are you well?

For the time being.

Thoeba took her mind off the Energy to read the minds of Peter's children.

Kayla remained defiant, the flash in her eyes telling the world what her censored lips could not.

Zack performed his tasks without a glimmer of true consciousness. His mind held only Thompson's recent commands and nothing more. His memories, his personality, everything that made Zack unique ceased to exist.

Are you sure he's okay in there?

Yes. He's in the dormant part human's don't use. You will have to break him out of it.

The Energy sent a wave of urgency.

We're running out of time. Millions of demons are swarming this realm, and Dr. Stuart Thompson will blow this part of the universe to cinders because he doesn't understand the true power of what he's dealing with.

Can you stall him?

Surely the Energy could give Thompson a few good shocks when he tried to touch It?

No. The equipment here is too sensitive. An electrical charge in this room could destroy the machines we need.

Thoeba rest her forehead on the window, her hands flattened on the door. She tried to probe a mind every bit as closed to her as the metal slab she leaned on.

How could she mentally communicate with a *human being?* Their brains didn't operate that way.

Not true.

Thoeba peaked at the platform holding her god. She saw signs of life in a subtle blink.

How so, she asked.

Zack's conscience remains in the part humans never use.

Yes, she thought. I understand. Please continue.

That is the part of their minds where they keep their latent telepathic abilities. Very few humans can access this power.

She wanted to hope. Even with a mortal as bright as Zack, could she find him?

Zack's intelligence is locked up with the rest of his psyche. He is merely functioning.

Thoeba watched his liquid movements take lenses and other unknown components and place them in the correct order with a strange thoughtless grace.

After tightening a blue wire to another part of the machinery, Zack stood apart from the contraption. His brainwaves were unnerving, like the dead air she'd heard on the radio.

You have to do this Thoeba.

Desperation burned her cheeks, saliva evaporated from her mouth. Her god needed her to act *now.*

Thompson dabbed his sleeve to his forehead before parking in front of a keyboard. His fingers skittered across its surface. Words and mathematical equations appeared in front of him. More information Thoeba couldn't fathom.

He reached up for a lever with a red plastic handle. He shot Kayla a triumphant stare while Zack gawped.

Thompson flipped the switch.

CHAPTER THIRTY-SIX

All at once Thoeba learned the true horror of Thompson's madness. In split seconds she read the intentions behind his eyes as twin streaks of a demon's glare shot from metal canisters straight to the crystal.

Lasers again? They must be.

The brightness intensified. Thompson donned dark glasses while he shoved Zack out of his path to the control panel.

Zack took two shuffled steps back, his glassy eyes watering from the radiance.

Kayla squirmed, tugged at her restraints. Her face crumpled in an effort to block the intense heat. Her head thrashed back and forth nearly toppling her chair. Sweat spotted the floor, the desk, her clothes.

Thompson's glee seasoned with Kayla's terror erupted around Thoeba like insistent ghosts. She forced them out.

No one could help her now. If she couldn't bring Zack

back to reality, the crystal with all the Energy's otherworldly strength inside of it would explode, wreaking untold havoc on the solar system.

She opened her senses to the black void of Zack's mind. The nothingness she found there oppressed her, the sudden quiet so abrupt she wondered if she'd been struck deaf.

She'd endured the loss of Eden's never-ending meadows and clouds. She'd tolerated the narrow confines of the flying tin can Peter referred to as "air travel", and she'd braved the cold shivering hell of this subterranean nightmare. But locking her own psyche into the corroded narrows of an Earthling brain for the purpose of finding his soul?

I've lost my mind, she thought.

And why not? She'd lost everything else she'd ever known.

No. That wasn't the answer. It would be this or oblivion.

What could she do to bring him back? What could coax a man from catatonia back to reality?

She rationalized that her race valued love above all else, and humans were an earthbound version of her kind. She needed to believe Zack and most of his species prized the same thing.

She couldn't waste another minute. Thoeba allowed for the emotional coziness of her god to wash over her, letting her eyelids droop and her blood to slow. She dipped into Kayla's tumultuous thoughts, gathered them to her like a ribbon of light.

Zack? It's Thoeba. I'm here with Kayla.

She tried pushing through the psychic wall. He didn't

budge. Kayla's distress didn't move him.

Thoeba couldn't believe she'd complained about the loud thoughts of humans. Now she'd give anything to hear Zack's intelligence break through.

It scraped her nerves. She didn't want to traumatize him any more than he had been already, but she dug in further, tried harder.

Her extrasensory perception searched Area 88 through barred portals, through desolate corridors, and into the vague distracted minds of various other men until she found Peter and Brewer.

Which did nothing for her sentimentally. Brewer tried to project a positive attitude he himself had no faith in, while Peter's despair threatened to eat him. She wanted to ease it for him, to tell him she was there. But she didn't have time to try. He probably wouldn't hear her anyway.

She'd never experienced such loneliness. Surrounded by so many minds, but unable to communicate with any of them.

She collected the streams of anguish with her and projected them to Zack along with her own misery.

Zack…

Her heart tightened as she pleaded for his deliverance.

Please, can't you hear me?

The metal beneath her hands warmed, distracting her. She opened her eyes, noting as she did that she could not longer concentrate on being invisible. It didn't matter anymore.

She could see Kayla's sweat drenched hair, how she

struggled for a full breath in the heat. Zack's clothes clung to him as rivers poured unchecked down his face.

Thompson ditched the white jacket and stomped over to sit behind his desk. Damp spots stained his armpits, neck, and back, but his tight confident posture denied worry on his part, his belief stayed unshaken.

I should never have come, Thoeba thought. I'm not good enough or strong enough for this.

Thoeba's hope unraveled. The self-pity she'd been trying to stave off enveloped her.

I should never have involved them.

She covered her sobbing mouth with shaking hands that smelled of a long journey through water, air and earth. And now it would end in fire.

I should have run off into the night and spared them. First I get their dog killed, and then I-

A spark of life in Zack's mental acuity interrupted her rant.

What had she said to make Zack do that?

He hadn't responded to the thoughts and emotions of his loved ones, and he certainly hadn't responded to her despair....

She visualized the limp and twisted body of Crash the dog. Flies dancing over a clouding eye, his furred carcass discarded like tainted meat.

Zack *twitched*.

The muscles in his back convulsed with his forgotten grief. Something awoke inside him.

Interesting.

Love wasn't the only way to a human's heart after all. Sometimes love brought pain and rage. Like the passions racing through Zack's mind right now.

She pursued her line of reason without hesitation, hoping someday Zack would forgive her abuse.

A demon killed Crash, Zack.

He'd heard her. His body quivered with fury as he shifted to….confront her? She hoped so.

And they'll kill everyone and everything you love.

Eye contact.

The hostility warping his smooth young visage made her stomach weak. But she couldn't let up.

We have to stop Dr. Thompson first. Help me defeat him.

Zack shuffled toward her, his arms flaccid at his side like rotting leaves on Deadly Nightshade. Blood escaped from a nostril to pelt the floor. Behind him, scarlet lights blinked unheeded while Zack pondered her through the glass.

Thompson left his seat and approached Zack. "What are you doing?"

Thoeba plastered herself against the wall away from the window, slamming both hands to her ears. She reeled from the abrupt rush of voices, sirens and clattering machinery.

When they didn't abate she realized she could hear through Zack's senses.

He'd returned to the living world.

“I didn’t tell you to move,” said Thompson.

Irritation undulated from the doctor, so she chanced a quick peek through the window.

Thompson opposed Zack with his back to her, waving in Zack’s face. Thoeba could smell his halitosis fanned by the breeze he generated with a swishing hand as though it were on her cheeks, not Zack’s.

But Thompson’s attempts for control came too late. Thoeba almost had him, and Peter’s son locked his attention to her once more.

He is not your master, she said. You are your own master.

“What the hell are you staring at?” Thompson spun around to peer up at the window. “*You.*”

He whirled in the direction of his desk. “Security!”

You have to stop him Zack, she said.

But he seemed in no rush. His face frozen in a caricature of confusion and uncertainty, he processed his thoughts with excruciating detail, as though they were new to him.

Thoeba tried again.

Look what he did to Kayla, she mentally implored him.

Seconds ticked by like days as Zack regarded the teenager tied to the plastic chair. His lip curled as he noticed, for the first time, the tape on her mouth, the raw skin on her wrists. His eyes tinted to darkness as he noted her feverish blush.

Something inside his mind connected in a snap, releasing him at last.

He lashed out with a primitive roar, backhanding Thompson across his shoulder blades. The bald man gasped like a fish before he collapsed, his feet waggling as he tried to gain footing.

But Zack had more revenge in mind. He grappled the doctor in an adrenaline infused headlock and dragged him to his feet.

"Zack, stop," Thoeba pounded on the slab separating her from them. "There's no time for that."

He glared up at her. She couldn't be sure if he was quite himself yet. He resembled a mindless beast more than he did a man.

"Stop the machine," she said. "*Stop the machine or we all die*."

Comprehension dawned on Zack's face. He relinquished the slack Thompson, unconcerned about the little man's painful grunts and pathetic coughing as he banged his knees.

Thoeba ceased to breathe. Zack considered the machine before him, one hand shielding his eyes as the sweat evaporated from his features.

"On your left."

Thoeba sent it to his thoughts as well as shouting it. She couldn't tell if he could hear or sense her or both. Or neither. "It's red. I saw him using it."

Time crawled. Whichever Zack understood, he found the lever and yanked it down.

Thoeba fogged the glass on the window with a previously held exhalation. The crisp light of the room had settled to a more tolerable level and even through the steel door the warmth dissipated. The sirens faded.

Zack came around, grinning, his sweet jovial personality returning.

"You fool," Thompson said. "Get back there."

Thoeba exercised patience and monitored the snarling doctor. With the danger quelled she could wait until Zack released Kayla. She noted with relief how mindful of her raw abrasions he was, the protective brother once more.

Once he freed her, Kayla promptly stomped over and kicked the shrunken and balled-up Thompson in the shins.

"Told you we were gonna kick your ass," she said. "Where do you keep the water?" She perused the room until she spotted the refrigerators. "Anyone else want something to drink? Eww, what is that?"

Thoeba shook her head. She admired Kayla's resilience. And her faith in the ones she loved.

Thoeba.

She brought her attention back to where the Energy lay blinking.

The equipment we need is here. Zack has the knowledge to make this work.

And time wouldn't wait.

"Zack, bring the doctor here," she said. "I need you to let me in so we can get this done."

He stalked to Thompson who cowered under Zack's baleful stare.

"So much for your tortilloquies," he said.

Through the hazy glass Thoeba saw Thompson's composure turn to impotent resentment.

"You are nothing," he said. "You've ruined my plans, and the demons will destroy the whole world."

Zack seized him, dragging him to his feet and grasping his right wrist while placing him in a headlock.

"Actually, from what I can see..."

Although Zack wasn't a muscular man, adrenaline still lent him strength and boldness. He controlled the doctor without effort.

"Your plans would have blown up our hemisphere. Or worse."

Thoeba clamped her lips over her tongue as he forced Thompson into helping them.

Much worse, she thought.

"You couldn't see the possibilities," Thompson said. "Your lack of vision makes you useless."

Zack slammed the doctor's fingers on the glowing security plate. When it chirped an acknowledgment, Zack peeled Thompson's eyelid open.

"Your arrogance makes you stupid," he said.

CHAPTER THIRTY-SEVEN

Thoeba stalked into the lab like a true avenging angel, storming past the cursing Thompson who struggled in Zack's arms, and straight to the platform holding the Energy.

Thoeba jabbed a finger in the doctor's direction. "Tie him up," she said.

If that scrawny meddlesome excuse for a sub-human hurt my god ...

It perched vulnerable on the warm glass. Faint, but she'd seen her deity in worse shape. It glimmered a little brighter in her presence.

All is well Thoeba. Takes more than Earthling technology to hurt me.

Yes, of course. But the consequences to the population of this planet, and the universe in general....she didn't want to think about it what would happen if the Energy were damaged or destroyed.

She stroked the smooth tube surrounding It, jerking her finger away as the hot surface seared her skin. Pain, combined with the foul odor of her burnt flesh, infuriated and sickened her.

She spun around to Thompson. Zack pinned the man's arms behind his back as Kayla looped the same wires that he'd used on her around his lower forearms, wrapping them as tight as her meager strength allowed.

If she wasn't so angry, Thoeba might have enjoyed the girl's enthusiasm.

"What could you possibly accomplish with this?" She swept her arm, encompassing the tangle of cables and machinery behind her. "You thought this would work, didn't you?"

Thompson fixed her with a stony glare. "Can you imagine, with your pathetic lack of insight what kind of power source we have here?"

Thoeba ground her teeth until a sharp pain stabbed her jaw. This narrow-minded human had no concept of the Energy's power.

"You people ruined everything." His bottom lip protruded, reminding Thoeba of a spoiled toddler. "This was to be my ultimate discovery. If I had been successful in siphoning off the juice from that crystal I could have targeted the monsters at will."

"Yes, I heard your thoughts," Thoeba said. "Believe me, you wouldn't have survived long enough to profit from your plans."

Kayla paused while tightening her knots. "You were going to *sell* this technology?" Her voice sounded incredulous. "What about the people who can't afford it?"

Thompson snorted. "What about them?"

He tried to twist to Kayla, but Zack squeezed his arms tighter in warning.

"Let me tell you something kid," Thompson said. "Nothing comes without a cost." He leveled his gaze at Thoeba instead.

"The meek will inherit the Earth, but only if they can afford it. Money and knowledge are power. It's how the strong survive."

Zack sent mental daggers to the back of the doctor's head, but released his arms as Kayla cinched her last loop.

"Nice," Zack said, and strode away to the refrigerator. He spoke to Thoeba when he said, "Please don't hold this jerk against us. Most of our species aren't so dickfacious."

"Other than the occasional Hitler or Osama Bin Laden," Kayla said.

Thoeba imagined the blood draining from her face and pooling in her stomach. She leaned against Thompson's desk and tried to catch her bearings. Her burned finger throbbed, and she put it in her mouth to ease the pain, but removed it quickly when the salty blister created more nausea.

She'd relinquished the life force of the universe to this megalomaniac. The air chilled despite the leftover heat radiating from the equipment behind her.

"Are you alright?" Kayla asked.

Thoeba glanced up to the innocent and concerned expressions of Peter's children as the room pitched and rolled.

She almost got them killed. Again. Her negligence had almost destroyed an entire solar system. She hated this now familiar aura of failure.

Steady.

Thoeba soaked up the love and assurance of her god until her head stopped swimming.

You haven't failed.

No, not yet.

Weariness weighed upon her like wet wings. When this mission finished, she'd sleep for a week. A long, deep sigh leaked from her, one that settled in her aching shoulders.

Yes, a nice long nap would be in order. If she survived.

Thoeba met the hopeful countenances of Peter's kids.

She beamed at Kayla. "I will be fine," she said.

To Zack she asked, "Do you know what this equipment does?" She waved at the jumble of plastic, glass and metal behind her. "Can you get the Energy free?"

The multicolored wires and blinking lights all looked foreign and menacing to her. She didn't dare touch anything else for fear of hurting herself or the Energy.

Zack surveyed the mess. "I understand what he *tried* to do," he said. "But I'm gonna go out on a limb and assume blowing us all to hell isn't what you had in mind?"

Before Thoeba could answer, Thompson flew into a rage.

"I am not some dangerous hack," he said. A ripping sound brought Thoeba's attention to Kayla, who had torn off a long silver strip of tape. "That power was perfectly contained. This is a top of the line facility and I-"

Kayla pressed it firmly onto the man's face, sealing the duct tape across his now muffled words.

"Thanks Kayla." Thoeba grimaced as the girl wiped Thompson's spittle off her nose.

"My pleasure." She wore a stretching grin as she searched for something to clean her hands and face with. Thoeba stared at the doctor's dour demeanor and decided he didn't like being on the receiving side of the rope and gag. Not that he didn't deserve it.

When she brought her attention back to Zack, he had disconnected several wires and his fingers traced the black boards while he whispered instructions to himself.

"What are you doing now?" she asked.

"I've removed the power source to the crystal." He nodded at the Energy. "Now I have to find the button for that containment field." His eyes widened and Thoeba realized she wore doubt on her mouth.

"Don't worry," he said. "We're not going to blow up anymore." And he flashed a reassuring grin she returned.

"There it is." He slapped a large red square, and the cylinder around the platform hummed up and disappeared inside the mechanical mayhem.

Zack interlaced his fingers and stretched them out in front of him. "What's the plan?" His knuckles crackled as his confidence soared.

Thoeba found it infectious. She savored the tingle it gave her. Like nitrogen in the air before a thunderstorm.

This is going to work, she thought, and her hopes rose to new heights.

"The Energy needs to fix this on Its own terms," she said. "It can't be bullied or broken from the crystal. It needs all of us, our love, to free It and make It stronger."

"You said at the cabin you wanted to send a signal." Kayla had listened to the conversation for such a long and surprising silence Thoeba had almost forgotten about her.

"From what I understand, yes," Thoeba said. "The Energy told me you had the technology to send messages across the entire planet."

A slow grin crept over Zack's features. "I know what we need to do," he said. "We need to talk to satellites."

Thank the Energy for Zack. They would succeed, and they would leave here soon. Thoeba thought of her lover languishing in a locked room where he couldn't see, hear or touch her. Did he miss her as much as she missed him?

She couldn't conceal her agitation. "Please hurry."

~~~

Peter's throat burned. His hands ached.

He found himself clenching the bars of his cell, a scream halfway past his tonsils and a pair of Colt C7's leveled at his torso.

"What's your problem, prisoner?" the short guard asked.

Wish I knew, he thought. Another strange dream courtesy of an earthbound deity, no doubt.

Peter released the cold steel and massaged the bridge of his nose with one hand while pacifying with the other.

"Easy, easy," he said. "I just had a nightmare, that's all."
~~~

"Both of you?" The same man gestured with his rifle to his left. "At the same time?"

Peter followed the muzzle to Brewer.

His rigid stance and ragged breathing caused a drop in Peter's gut.

What the hell?

"You too, Brewer?"

"Yeah, I think so," he said. Brewer swallowed and shook off his tension. "But that was nasty." He sat back down on the berth he'd been occupying before.

"What was nasty?" Peter asked, roaming across the cement to address him. "What did you dream about?"

Brewer dug the heels of both hands in his eye sockets. "It felt like more of a def-com situation than a dream, danger and mayhem, that kind of shit."

Peter pondered the idea. "I think that's what I got too." He glanced at their guards before lowering his voice. "No images. Just a kind of destruction-vibe."

"What's going on?" Brewer asked. "Earlier on, I got this headache, like my head suddenly got crowded. Now I get death threats in my sleep?"

"Interesting way of putting it," Peter said. "I wonder if that's what Thoeba meant by humans thinking too loud."

Brewer straightened his spine. "You think it was her?"

"I think those messages were more than just her," he said. He sat on the opposite bed, staring down the soldiers pretending not to eavesdrop. "I think it's bigger than that."

Their captors shuffled further from the bars, but Peter dropped to a whisper.

"We'll rest now," he said. "I have a hunch we'll need to be alert and ready when Thoeba starts making appearances."

CHAPTER THIRTY-EIGHT

Thoeba admired Zack's efficiency. His nimble fingers twisted wires, typed keys and wiggled over panels while he conducted a choreographed dance around the massive machine before him.

"What are you doing?" she asked.

He didn't answer right away. He continued clicking in codes and numbers while muttering under his breath.

"We have everything we need right here to send a signal to anything up there," he said. He motioned for Kayla's water bottle, which she relinquished. "I just have to tweak it."

"You're not going to be the one blowing us to smithereens though, right?" Kayla asked. She guarded Thompson with arms crossed, doubt dulling her eyes as she tapped a toe into the ground.

Zack drained the bottle, tossed the plastic aside. It bounced off a corner, its hollow warbling thrumming through the confined space. "Nope."

He didn't slow as he perused the wall of blinking jewels.

"There's a big difference between sucking power and sending a message."

He returned to the platform with the waiting crystal containing the Energy. "Fortunately the mechanics are close enough I can just switch some stuff up."

Thoeba relaxed, inhaled the smell of recycled oxygen and ammonia. She caught the baleful stare from the doctor.

Another problem solved.

They still faced the issue of escape when the Energy gained strength and power. Being a benevolent god didn't mean It couldn't be destructive. After all, It had the power to create worlds, but was compressed into the size of a pebble.

And they needed to find Peter and Brewer, free them, all while avoiding Thompson's men.

This could get ugly.

Thinking about it gave Thoeba a throbbing, relentless hum in her temples. Her mouth tasted like sand and the hardly palatable tang of dry ozone fear. She became aware of the Energy's presence filling her sore brain with deep affection.

I know, she said to It, have faith.

Now more than ever. Everything will be alright. I promise.

Thoeba calmed. Her god didn't make promises It couldn't keep. The tension uncoiled from her back and shoulders as she tried to understand Zack's methods.

Kayla paced a respectful distance back, giving her brother

clearance to connect wires and attach clips while he grinned his way through procedures only he enjoyed. He didn't notice Kayla huffing her bangs in mock irritation at his odd scuttling.

Thompson observed Zack with blatant interest and jealousy.

Wishing you'd tried that? Thoeba thought. She checked his mind. Yes, he is a lot smarter than you gave him credit for.

Zack proved to be smarter than *she* gave him credit for.

Having faith in Zack didn't mean Thoeba wasn't frightened. She had the skill of invisibility, but she hadn't figured out how she would sneak everyone else out of the building.

What a human thing to think.

She strolled to the door and pressed her pulsing forehead to the cooling window. Farther down and out of Thoeba's line of sight, a tan sofa cradled the captain. She sensed his continued slumber.

No other soldiers patrolled the area that she could see.

Thoeba smirked. Of course not. All the men were busy searching for an invisible fugitive, and none of them were brave enough to tell the doctor they'd lost her.

I should go to him, she thought.

He'd been sleeping for quite some time, and she'd struck him with superhuman strength. She hoped she hadn't broken any bones. Perhaps she should pick up that gun she'd thoughtlessly kicked away so she'd have some kind of defense. She pushed at the door.

Locked.

Thoeba stared at the panel next to the door with its emerald grid smudged with human oils and the portal with the pinhole laser for additional security.

Like every other way in or out of this facility, it required a hand print and an eye scan before it would open.

The thought made Thoeba want to pull out her hair.

She regarded Thompson with new contempt. She couldn't just leave this little monster, with his dog breath and rancid sweat to engineer his own escape.

No, he would have to come with them.

He'd help them out from this maze. Whether he liked it or not.

Judging from the loathing on his face, she guessed she'd have to use force.

A wicked grin slipped over Thoeba's lips. But at least that might be fun.

Zack rubbed his hands together. "Finished." Thoeba heard the pride in his words as he said, "One more command and we'll be world wide."

She joined him at the communication device, amazed at his absolute control of it, his confidence. When she reflected on the marvelous contraption in front of him she didn't see the solution to her mission. She saw a whirring beast whose language she couldn't speak.

Good thing you brought the humans into this after all.

She sighed. Indeed. Serendipitous as well that she'd picked the right ones.

Yes, you're always right, she said. No one likes a show-off.

"Let me show you how this works," Zack said. "See this?" He pointed to a set of blue cords he'd connected to the lasers. "I've tapped it like a power source, but I've hooked it up to send out a program instead. Does that make sense?"

It didn't, but Thoeba let him continue. He droned on, explaining things she had no hope of comprehending. She took a glimpse behind her.

It seemed Kayla didn't either. Her lost expression was a stone tablet on her face.

Thompson, however had shifted in his seat, trying to view Zack's lecture from around Kayla's back.

Thoeba's attention wandered beyond Thompson's lab. Zack's chatter faded to a mosquito's buzz.

Just outside this enclosure on a barrier of screens, scenes of murder and flame played endlessly with relentless clarity.

She didn't need to see it. The lapse in action allowed her to tune back into the vibes of the world around her, and she could almost smell the blood of the dying and brimstone scent of her enemy. She stared at the graying crystal wrapped with swollen manmade threads of scarlet and sapphire.

No wonder the Energy had lost It's sheen. The weight of this planet's loss threatened to bury her and the deity.

She swallowed thick tears. They would end this soon, she reminded herself.

Zack had stopped talking. She peered back at him to see his empathy as he shared the sorrow he no doubt saw on her face. Sadness trembled his chin.

"I hope this works," he said.

"The Energy promised it would," she said. "God never breaks Its word."

Kayla's arms wrapped around Zack's waist and squeezed. "That's reassuring."

Thoeba frowned as her god blinked encouragement. "What does 'thumbs up' mean?"

Zack and Kayla studied her with amusement before both stole a peek at the rock on the platform.

"It means all systems go," Zack said.

Thanks for the clarification, Thoeba thought. Not that I understand any better.

The siblings disengaged from each other, and Zack returned to the black monitor before him.

He placed his right hand on the same crimson lever Thompson would have used to drain the Energy of It's power. "Once I pull this lever the lasers will read the vibrations off the crystal." He placed his left hand over the keyboard. "Then I'll give the command to broadcast. Are we ready?"

Kayla waited at her post behind their bound and gagged hostage. "Ready."

Thoeba lunged forward, placing a gentle grip over Zack's.

"Please understand. When you set this event in motion, we will need to leave here. Quickly."

Her touch found him shaking. "I thought if we did this, we wouldn't blow up," he said.

"No, we won't blow up," she said. "But the Energy will break free."

"What does that mean?" Kayla asked. Thoeba could hear the worry even as it wafted to her like a wave of misery.

"It means the controlled power of many suns will have to leave this room," Thoeba said, "The Energy will not destroy this world, but we should be well away when It escapes." She studied the tension apparent on all three faces in the room. "It's going to get hot in here."

No one spoke. No one moved. She could see Thompson's trepidation behind the tape. Thoeba surmised she wouldn't have to coerce him too much to help them after all.

"Kayla, untie the doctor," she said. "He's going to 'escort' us out of here." Kayla obeyed without question.

Zack hovered over the switch he hadn't engaged yet. "You could have said something," he said.

"Would you really want to know that kind of thing ahead of time?" she asked. "While you're trying to work on a machine to stop millions of demons and from devouring your entire realm? Did you need the additional pressure?"

Zack blinked rapidly. "I guess not."

Thoeba softened her speech. "It will be alright. Trust in me. Trust in the Energy." She stroked the arm holding their destiny in a vibrating hand. "We are wasting time."

She closed her fingers over his.

"Let's do this," she said.

Zack nodded, and together they yanked the lever down. Zack pressed one button on the keyboard, and a note answered in kind.

The screen projected '*Send all*' before a howl of activity clammered from the gears and engines.

Numbers and letters rambled across the monitor too quick to read. The plastic counterpart of the metallic behemoth started grinding a new chant.

"It begins." Thoeba said.

Zack backed away from his bellowing accomplishment. "No turning back."

CHAPTER THIRTY-NINE

Fiat lux.

Thoeba began to vibrate. From anticipation or the motion of the Energy, she couldn't be sure.

The machine purred in the manner of a contented cat. The pressure in the air buzzed through her teeth, like a mouthful of bees. Wonder seeped through her rattling heart as the true voice of her god rang out with the words in the ancient language of her kind.

Fiat lux!

She remembered the first time the Energy had used this phrase. Words of creation spoken to give birth to new realms, planets and solar systems.

Fresh urine assaulted her nostrils this time from the doctor. His fear was justified.

Fiat lux!

"What does that mean?" The question came from Kayla, who froze with hands clamped down on the back of Thompson's chair, her face and knuckles bloodless.

Thoeba opened her mouth to answer, but her throat closed and stifled her words. She didn't realize until now how she'd longed to witness this moment.

"It's Latin," said Zack. "It means 'Let there be light.'"

"You can hear It?" Thoeba asked. "You hear the Energy speak?"

Kayla whimpered behind her. "How can you miss it?"

Thoeba wanted to comfort her, but Kayla's attention focused on the brightness touched by lasers. Her azure eyes twinkled with brilliance and...love?

Thoeba let her gaze wander to Zack. He slouched with his mouth gaping.

"My Lord," he whispered, as both hands drifted upwards.

"The signal," Thoeba said. "It's working. You are one with the Energy!" Joy threatened to consume her, but wait-

She considered the doctor, who hadn't stirred from his seat.

Thompson-potential despot, megalomaniac, hateful self-absorbed pillar of arrogance-had tracks of sorrow etched down his reddened cheeks.

The transformation in the room was all the evidence Thoeba needed. She let herself weep, safe in the knowledge she had fulfilled her destiny.

She bathed in the intimate devotion of her god.

I could die here, she thought.

The lab heated once again. The equipment whooped and thundered as it transferred electricity and heavenly thunder.

Thoeba began sweating. She wasn't the only one judging by the scent of sun-kissed flesh joining the ammonia of human waste.

It didn't have the menace of a potential explosion, more like a warming hearth.

That didn't mean they were safe. On the contrary, they would have to *go*.

Run.

Thoeba crept to Thompson. His tears pulled her forward like a magnetic force. Sweat had loosened the tape from his face. It required no effort to remove it.

He took a deep shuddering breath. "What have I done?" His mouth curled downward in mortification. "*What have I done?*"

Thoeba stroked his wet brow. "Nothing so bad that you can't earn forgiveness," she said.

He ducked his head, away from her and the Energy. "I'm so ashamed." Thoeba reeled from his truth, even though she'd hoped for it.

"You can make it alright," she said. She smoothed her hand over his skull, caressing the tiny bristles of hair poking through his soft skin. "We need to get out of here. Will you help us?"

Thompson gave a sharp snuffle, swallowing before meeting her gaze.

"I will, I need to." Flecks of greasy sweat shook off his brow as he nodded, hitting her like greasy rain. "For the Energy. For all of us."

The promise in his watering eyes were caused by the Energy's signal growing in strength. Thoeba knew it.

"Kayla." She peered up at the transfixed girl, not sure if the girl heard her. "Kayla, help him up."

As if in a dream Kayla drifted toward them, bestowing a serene expression of happiness and affection at both Thoeba and the doctor.

"I understand everything," she said, crossing the distance between to give Thompson her hand. "I know who *I* am, and the Energy has never stopped loving me."

Kayla brought Thompsons palm to her cheek. "Just as It has never ceased to love you. It just doesn't like what you do."

Thoeba watched her use a gentle touch to tug the rest of the ropes away, stopping to soothe Thompson's wrists as she did. He accepted it without complaint, gazing as though hypnotized at his former captor's ministrations.

"Great." While she welcomed their newfound compassion for one another, Thoeba couldn't help wishing they'd discover it a little quicker.

"Thompson? Open the door, please." She turned to Peter's son. "Zack?"

She saw him as a silhouette against the shining sun of the Energy's power. His head swiveled side to side, back and forth from the Energy on the glass platform, and the computer monitors on Thompson's desk.

Thoeba took hesitant strides forward. His thoughts were the same brightness as those of Kayla and Thompson, but he remained rooted to the spot.

"What is it?" she asked.

His deep sigh disappeared in the roar of the machine. Zack's words were a whisper of awe. "The signal's gone global."

She became aware that Kayla and Thompson came up behind them, but the event before her commanded every ounce of her attention.

* * *

The Energy gloried in It's growing strength.

At last.

Finally It would be free of this prison. Free to cleanse this blue-green jewel of the menace that had so wrongfully tipped the balance of good versus evil. It was too late to save Eden, but the darkness would not taint any more of It's creations. There would be no more death and suffering at the talons of these enemies.

Thoeba could not know how her bond with what she called her *humans gave It a storage of power. How her acceptance of their flaws, and their growing affection for her sustained It, or how they banded together to fight for the mission and for one another gave It fortitude.*

These powerful emotions were the true nectar of a god, and it was sweeter than any mortal wine.

As It's song echoed across the ozone via space-age technology, the Energy could sense the impact of It's words, and It's love.

While these mortals before It merely watched It glow, the Energy experienced so much more.

It came to the young mother in Wisconsin who heard the signal from the closet where she had hidden with her children, her fireplace poker in hand, as the television blared unattended from her living room. She heard the Energy's words and emerged to receive a blessing for her weapon before engaging in battle.

The Energy recognized the British anchorman and his camera crew who abandoned their telecast when they heard the music of the creator coming through their headphones. They rallied, racing from the safety of their studio to march against the demons with newly bestowed props and tripods from the set design.

It heard the war cry of the Brazilian carnival dancers when they raced from their shelters, saw their plumage like a dangerous rainbow as they swarmed the dark minions with knives, stones, and anything they could fight with.

In Thailand the Energy's power swelled as Molotov cocktails and instruments of revolution were consecrated and thrust upon the evil that spawned all hatreds.

Even the birds and the beasts, with their direct ability to commune with God fought back.

All this and more occurred as the melodies of God awakened the inhabitants of this shiny little pebble of a planet. They all listened to the Energy now, be it radio, television or internet, they learned the message.

It's children discovered themselves and recognized their god. The Energy received the love of this world, and It fed, absorbed the worship.

Indeed, there would be Hell to pay.

CHAPTER FORTY

Vadere.

The single word broke Thoeba and the others from their trance. "You heard the god," she said. "Go. Get out."

"Wait." Thompson rushed behind his desk and flipped up a chunk of wood. A whirring hum announced a new machine climbing from the depths of the corner. It continued to rise until a triangular slab perched before the doctor.

Zack took the extra time to wander to the back where an assortment of ferocious weaponry graced the walls. Kayla sidled up, her hands gracing a slender black pistol.

"Hey Doc?" Zack asked. "Do these things work?"

Thompson spared him a glance. "Yes. Very user friendly, but be careful, they're experimental," he said, and stabbed a large red button.

An ear-drilling whoop commenced. It seemed to be coming from everywhere.

He pressed a smaller white button and leaned his face into an opening. "This is Dr. Thompson. Evacuate the premises. I repeat, evacuate the premises."

Thoeba squinted at the Energy but couldn't keep watching. The deity became difficult to look upon with It's white-hot brilliance, and the hum in the room changed pitch, roaring louder and higher.

Kayla and Zack made for the exit, new acquisitions hugged to their chests.

The doctor's greasy palm made contact with another radiant lime panel, this one placed on the formerly hidden minicomputer. He struggled to keep his sweat-slicked digits from sliding off while he aligned his face with the coinciding eye scan.

Thoeba thought she understood the importance of the ritual, but Thompson wasted precious seconds typing more keys. He leaned in, voicing a series of numbers in an articulate chant.

"What are you doing?" Thoeba asked. The warmth and brilliance in the room made her uncomfortable, impatient. They had yet to rescue Peter and Brewer, and she'd been away from her lover for far too long.

In answer, the exit across the room sprang open.

Thoeba let her mouth drop. "Oh."

"The thing about getting out of here," Thompson said, "is that you need to override *all* the locks." He grabbed his lab coat, used it to wipe his brow before discarding it. "Lucky for you, I'm one of the few people here with that kind of authorization."

Good thing we kept him, Thoeba thought.

Zack and Kayla glowered at them from the main office,

waiting with tapping feet, prompting Thoeba and Thompson to proceed.

Thoeba gave the area a once over, visually and mentally. It pleased her that Captain Smith no longer occupied the couch.

Had he sensed the signal in these dense walls? Or was he hunting her?

She checked for the captain's gun. Where had she sent it? They could use an extra gun right about now. Especially with the Energy blessing anything remotely resembling a weapon.

No such luck.

"Forget it," Thompson said. Had he heard those thoughts? "We've got a whole room full of toys we can use, but we have to get out in fifteen minutes."

Kayla and Zack ran for the first open door, the one leading to the jails, if Thoeba recalled correctly.

"Why?" Thoeba asked. "What happens then?"

"The whole building will go into lockdown," he said. "It will be impossible to get in or out."

She didn't need further encouragement. Thoeba and the doctor darted from the bright space to their escape in the dank tunnels.

She raced with them in the corridors, trusting her instincts to guide her while her pupils adjusted to the shadows.

The small group had become a pack of wolves on the run.

Thompson kept pace at Thoeba's side, panting to keep up.

Zack sprang like a gazelle, freed from mortal coil by a

new awareness most humans never possessed.

And Kayla, an older spirit than either mortal, sprinted to reunite with a love as ancient as Earth.

Thoeba absorbed it, the unity, the sharing of empathy she hadn't experienced since she fled without her brethren from Eden.

And it was good.

Something sparked in Kayla's being, and Thoeba realized its source, since the sensation rippled through her as well.

In front of her, Kayla plunged forward, gaining momentum until she appeared to fly.

Thoeba's footfalls became quicker, urgent. Fleeting steps brushed cement with whispered slips of movement. Echos faded with her flight, until darkness gave way.

And she plunged into Peter's arms.

~~~

Peter squeezed Thoeba until she struggled for breath. He let her go, and gave Zack the same. He waited to hold Kayla, annoyed that her reunion with Brewer took first place over hugging her father.

It would be hard to think of her as his little girl now, learning the things he had through the Energy's message. He wondered just how many lifetimes she'd spent loving that young man.

Good thing he liked the guy.

But the lovefest would have to wait. The urge to be free of these tunnels wasn't due to claustrophobia.
~~~

The little man… Thompson? Yes. He nodded his understanding to Peter as though his words were spoken aloud.

"This way," he said, and the group began to jog to his direction. "We need to make a stop."

"For weapons," Thoeba said.

"Yes," Thompson replied. "The demons are at the entrance. Can you sense them?"

Peter tuned out the tapping of running shoes and concentrated. The temperature climbed around them.

Not only could Peter feel the weight of evil around them, he heard screams of death and the rattle of weapons fire, the rattling ping of flying cartridges hitting cement.

He searched the faces of his companions.

Old mortal habit, he guessed. He wondered what he hoped to see when he could read their minds so easily.

He'd been certain that the situation would change after the dream, but developing a sixth sense wasn't something he expected for himself, never mind sharing it with everyone in the entire complex.

It made it a lot easier to convince the guards to let him and Brewer out.

Before him Zack and Kayla held strange guns with white knuckled grips.

A low moan escaped Brewer's lips. "I hear them dying."

"We can't help them without more firearms," Kayla said, compassion thick in her voice. "Two high-tech laser blasters won't hold off an army of darkness."

"Getting there," Thompson said.

The voices were louder, and in the flickering luminescence of failing electricity more shadows darted to and from a hole in the wall.

"Doctor," someone called.

Peter recognized that voice. It belonged to the captain... Smith or something.

The man appeared in the waning light. Peter recognized him for more than his human form. Peter realized he remembered many of the men and women working here from life in Eden, just as sure as he knew Thoeba, Brewer and his children. Warriors, all of them.

What a time to get all warm and fuzzy. He nearly laughed.

"There's still a few handguns," Smith said. "We need all the help we can get out there."

They filed into the cramped quarters, which once bristled with weaponry but had now been picked clean of all but the simplest of guns and grenades.

"How are we faring?" Thoeba asked as she fingered the wall, trying to choose something useful.

Smith favored her with a gentle sadness. "We are overwhelmed and our numbers are dwindling," he said. "Even though our semi and fully automatics have been graced, we don't have the strengths we had in Eden."

Thoeba paused to make eye contact, and something passed between them, Peter noticed. She had the human's respect, and she'd wished for forgiveness. Smith rubbed his jaw, and Peter took note of the purpling.

But the bond became instantaneous and their inner circle swelled to include the soldier.

What a weird non-conversation, he thought. If you could call it that.

Smith instructed Thoeba on the use of her chosen pistol while the doctor gave Kayla and Zack pointers on theirs.

"Is it getting warmer in here?" Brewer asked.

"It is," Kayla said.

Peter noticed the waves of heat wafting at them from the halls they'd left behind. Sweat beaded on his upper lip, and he licked the salt away.

He wished they'd come sooner when the selection was a little better. He just hoped these weapons were more effective than the movie props they resembled.

He pocketed several grenades and ripped a new toy from the displays.

He searched the faces of Thompson and Captain Smith. He had to stop reading facial expressions; it wasn't necessary. "How do we get out of here?" he asked. "Which way is out?"

"This way," Thompson said. "We're running out of time."

That spurred everyone into action, like an inner stopwatch had suddenly started ticking. The rumble of feet bounced off the round concrete as the makeshift troop left, and Peter made sure no one was left behind before exiting the weapon's room himself.

He gasped as the rolling hotness turned his forehead buttery and made his limbs melt. It sapped his will to escape, his desire to run.

Ahead of him, through waving lines of heat, he saw the plodding steps of his lover and his children, also struck by lethargy as they pressed their bodies to a slowing trot.

Turn left. He heard the voice inside his mind. *Don't surrender now, you are so close.*

Peter immediately spurred himself onward with confidence. The Energy would never lie to them, and as promised, an opening waited for them on the left hand side like a darkened well.

His children, his woman, and his new friends were swallowed into that black hole as he trudged toward it.

Almost there.

Then Brewer's hand shot from the gloom to take his shirt and suck him in.

What followed could be described as an oasis in the desert, at least it shaded and cool like one at night.

Peter's eyesight couldn't adjust. Not with the flashing between sporadic lighting and complete shadow. But he counted heads.

Tried again by counting presences. All were accounted for.

He sat against the concrete wall, noting its growing warmth, and shuffled to the surface opposite where everyone else recuperated.

"Ohhhh...." Peter thrust his forehead into the welcoming damp of the tunnels underground cooled cement.

"Enjoy it while it lasts," Smith said. "The other side's

already heating up, and we only have seven more minutes."

"Everybody just catch your breath, and get ready to move on," Thoeba said.

"Does anyone have water?" Kayla asked, and a chorus of groans echoed throughout the tunnel. "Sorry. I shouldn't have brought it up."

Peter ran a dry tongue over sticky teeth, tasting his own stale breath. Lack of elbow room forced him to inhale the stench of his and everyone else's body odor.

If he ever got out of this alive, he'd take a three-day shower.

His breath came in gulps, and no one else spoke, each lost in their fears and thoughts, which were inevitably shared.

The halogens above their heads shone two brief flashes before giving out for good.

Thoeba ventured further down the corridor, deeper into the gloom. Peter followed her with his gaze, disturbed by her rigid posture.

"Can you hear it?" she said.

Peter straightened. He made his way to her side, Kayla and Zack falling in position on his right.

He strained his eardrums, but all he heard were the shuddering respirations and shuffling feet of terrified humans.

Smith had edged so close on his right, Peter endured the breeze of the soldier's dry mouth on his neck.

Then came the faint sound of machine gun fire.

More fire. Closer. Now accompanied with shouts and dying screams. They reverberated throughout the enclosure, taunting the ragtag group with their promises of slaughter.

Despite the rising temperature a chill squirmed its way down Peter's spine. This only meant two things.

"They've breached our defenses," Smith said.

Thoeba's swallowed alarm travelled to Peter's ears. "Yes. They are coming."

CHAPTER FORTY-ONE

Thoeba allowed rage to wash over her as a low growl throbbed in her throat.

The demons would soon learn they were too late to stop her god. No matter what happened now, the Energy would swell and break free, and these monsters would be nothing more than a bad memory.

Her life, even the lives of her chosen allies paled in comparison to that triumph.

But I want to live, she thought. I want these humans to survive.

I am sick of running, sick of hiding.

Tepid sweat dripped from her upper lip to her tongue.

And I'm sick of tasting my bodily fluids.

To her left the concrete wall pulsed with growing heat, and an insistent hum flowed through the humid air. Breathing became laborious.

Two pairs of red dots wobbled toward them through the murkiness. They were on foot. No room to fly with these low ceilings. Which meant no added advantage, either.

Thoeba studied the sleek black lines and the aerodynamic shape of her laser pistol. It might have been considered beautiful to some, but not to her.

Such an ugly graceless weapon, she thought. It will have to do.

She switched the safety off as Thompson instructed her, listening with sadistic satisfaction as it whined to life in her grip.

Thoeba thrust the muzzle of the firearm before her like a challenging sword or a *momento mori*.

"*Deo Optimo Maximo*." To God, the best, the greatest.

She squeezed the trigger.

The emerald light show that ensued rocketed the others to action. Thoeba heard the howling of more weapons powering up, while machine guns rattled and chimed a melody of destruction. More stripes of lime-colored death slashed the darkness.

Thoeba advanced when the first sets of demonic rubies vanished only to be replaced by another four pair of guaranteed carnage.

And there were more. She shuffled close enough to see the puffs of dust as she and her friends poked holes in their ranks.

A new pitch added to the growing racket threatening to break Thoeba's eardrums. She was sure it came from the lab. The Energy would break free any second.

They had to get out now.

Yet the demons kept coming.

“There’s too many of them,” she said.

“I got it.” Zack’s presence at her right introduced a welcome blast of cool air that graced her arm as he elbowed her from the front line.

The chrome monstrosity squealed with eager intent as Zack aimed and Thoeba shivered from the icy draft it gave off.

Foom!

Zack stumbled from the recoil and a blue sheet rippled down the tunnel and over the horde of demons.

Ice coated the concrete, ceiling to floor. The instantaneous freezing turned the beasts to black frost, then to a sudden eruption of soot. The beasts disintegrated with such force they coated the walls.

After a blink to absorb the sight, the hall echoed with mirth, human laughter a concussion of victory.

Zack blew a wisp off the barrel of his weapon. “I love this thing.”

“It served its purpose well,” Thompson said. “Revenge is a dish best served cold.”

Peter favored him with a smirk. “Trekkie.”

“Zack?” Thoeba placed a hand on his shoulder. “Could you lead with that?”

“My pleasure,” he said, stomping forward, grinning while he scanned for more enemies to vanquish. The others hurried to follow.

Thoeba took the rear along with Peter.

"Everyone, when we get outside just run, get as far from here as possible." She gave Brewer a gentle push forward, urging him to go faster. "And don't look back."

"Why?" Kayla asked, "Will we turn into a pillar of salt if we do?"

Loose chuckles filled the corridor. Thoeba didn't get it.

Less than two minutes later, they approached the surface.

Bright sunlight seared Thoeba's brain. Her entourage sprinted forward, shielding tearing eyes while trying to escape the overheated facilities of Area 88.

Thoeba spun to watch their backs, firing her blessed laser pistol through the oppressive heat, satisfied that every demon she hit died without much effort.

Perhaps she could like these clunky guns. Judging from the victorious howls of her comrades, they also enjoyed good hunting.

She hadn't paid much attention to the outer appearance of Area 88 upon arrival, but she noticed now.

It warped. What few windows it had popped and shattered from intense structural damage as melted curves made the walls resemble molten lava.

A gaping hole had appeared off-center in the building, right where Thoeba assumed the lab had been. Black bubbles boiled up from what remained of the roof, she could smell the tar.

More importantly, beaming like a torch from the crater, a

white light purer than virgin snow on Mount Everest glittered. It outshone the sun, bathing the landscape with uncontrolled radiance.

She didn't see the runway in front of her, didn't even think about what lay ahead as she ran. Thoeba stumbled over the asphalt and landed with tooth-jarring impact on her rear end.

"Thoeba!" Peter rushed to her side, nearly yanking her arm out of the socket in an effort to get her to her feet, his grip tight enough to bruise.

But she sat transfixed. Time crawled. Thoeba couldn't hear Peter, couldn't feel the insistent rough tugging. All else became unimportant.

With a mighty groan, what remained of Area 88 split in half and peeled away from the holy star. The sacred spirit climbed into the sky like a rising sun.

The Energy was *free*.

CHAPTER FORTY-TWO

Thoeba filled her lungs to scream.

"Everybody down!" She dragged Peter to his knees, heard him swear as the pavement scraped his exposed skin.

Thoeba took her gaze from the raw power of the Energy long enough to see demons taking flight in any direction that would remove them from the glorious glow. She watched the humans obey her command as they flattened their bodies to the ground on the other side of the runway.

She lay drunk on the wet tarmac, swooning from the pulsing love of her deity. It didn't matter if she lived or died. The humans, all of them, had come through.

They had won. Nothing could stop the Energy now.

The god pulled into Itself, and Thoeba braced for what would come next.

The Energy bleached the sky, and Thoeba squinted from the intensity. Emoting heat scorched her skin. Peter leaned over to shield her, but she feared nothing.

And it happened.

The world silenced. Every bird, every breath, every rustling of leaves was stolen from the air as though they'd never existed.

It lasted for a single second before concussive thunder shook the planet. A milky ripple washed through the atmosphere, shredding the demons out of their skins. Thoeba braced as it slammed her and the others against the vibrating earth.

A chorus of agonized hateful screams announced a black snowfall.

But none of it hit the ground.

It waited, suspended in mid-air. Thoeba could see the whorls and shapes of dead monsters as time ceased...

Only to begin again as gravity lied, and the demonic dust flew straight up to disappear past the ozone and into space.

Cheers exploded from everywhere on the base. Sounds of life returned louder than before, as birds sprang into song with men and women throwing weapons to the ground and caterwauling along with them.

The air smelled pure, like the day Earth was born. No sins of man or demon tainted it.

Infectious joy filled her as Peter covered her body with his, not to protect, but to share.

His kiss raised the hair on her arms as he sipped her breath. He took his time, not caring who saw, and she had to push him away before it became a stronger need.

She got to her feet with Peter's help, smiling at all the

military men and women hugging one another in celebration. Brewer and Kayla sneaked a quick kiss before they wrapped Zack in their embrace.

Dr. Thompson stood alone, his mesmerized gaze locked to the skies. Thoeba saw rapture in his whitewashed face.

The sunlight.

No, too bright for sunshine alone....Thoeba followed the doctor's line of sight.

The Energy in all It's strength and glory waited.

But for what?

Choose.

Choose? Choose what? Choose who?

Then she understood.

Should she return to Eden to cleanse and rebuild for the sake of her race and her god?

Or should she stay here among the humans? To become mortal? To grow old and eventually die?

Her place should be with her god, as a true guardian of the Energy, and together they would reclaim Eden.

But her weariness grew. She'd nearly failed this mission, several times. Did she deserve her title?

Peter's presence touched her before he took her hand and squeezed it.

Thoeba sucked in a deep gulp of air, and made her decision.

EPILOGUE

Thoeba let out a profound sigh. Every morning when she gazed at the sight before her she experienced exquisite delight for the coming day and all the possibilities that came with it.

Pink skies mingled with peach mists, and the hush invited quiet contemplation.

A lot had happened since that day two months ago, when she'd fled her home, alone and pursued by demons.

The signal of the Energy found every crevice of Earth. Even the untamed corners without radio, television, or computers. The love that grew from the knowledge of It's existence encompassed the world like a blanket, destroying hatred and creating a cocoon of understanding that affected every man, woman and child.

Celebrations, ceremonies and rituals went on for days all over the world. People celebrated unity, mourned the lost.

Earth became a different place.

Some remembered that day as Armageddon. Scandanavia named it Ragnarok. More likened it to the Quaran's Jihad. But everyone understood it as the final battle, and that they had a greater enemy than each other.

While the telepathy the humans experienced during the fight faded, the sentiment it invoked didn't. Compassion became the key component in peace talks, power and territory became less important than life.

Even now, with her own telepathic abilities waning, Thoeba detected changes. The world just seemed nicer.

"Hey you," Peter said, his voice groggy from sleep. "It's too cold. Come back here."

Indeed, the chill raised gooseflesh on her skin, turning her nipples taut. She savored the sensation.

As she did with all things in her newfound home.

She tread barefooted from the balcony back to the warmth of Peter's...no, *their* bed.

He lifted the heavy comforter and Thoeba dove for the coziness there, moaning in pleasure as Peter's body heat soothed her.

"Brrrrr," he said, jiggling the bedframe with his complaint. "Your feet are freezing."

"And you're so toasty warm," she said, laughing as she squeezed closer and nuzzled his chest hair with her nose.

She inhaled his sleepy sweat scent mixed with hers, rubbed her face against it. Her lover belonged to her once more, for the rest of their lives.

And she had a different existence, with new friends and family. She had a son and daughter in Zack and Kayla, with challenges she'd never faced before.

Like disciplining Kayla for stealing, and setting ground rules for when she and Brewer started dating, but *not* before her sixteenth birthday.

Timothy Brewer would definitely be around for that. He hadn't been court-martialed after all. General Lapierre had given him a dressing-down, reminding him he was nothing but a grunt. The government didn't pay him to think for himself, and that kind of thing was reserved for men of higher rank.

Then he promoted Brewer to the level of his insubordination.

Thoeba's giggles began anew thinking of the stern general. "What *was* that awful song the general and the doctor were singing last night?"

"Eye of the Tiger."

"I thought that vein in Stuart's temple would explode on that high note." A new gale of laughter blew forth from the two of them.

"I thought he'd bust a lung," Peter said before getting serious again. "Did I tell you he recommended Zack as his replacement at the new facility?"

"Really?" Thoeba propped herself on an elbow to meet his eyes. "Is he going to go?"

"Yes. Now that Zack got a taste for all that high-tech, I can't see him going back to mundane things like what they're teaching at the Institute." Peter grinned. "But he's making Thompson add a 'no brain-washing' clause in his contract, and he's not allowed to say the word 'tortilliquies'."

"I don't think he has to worry," Thoeba said. "Stuart is a different man now. Besides, he'll probably go to prison, won't he?"

"I think you're right," Peter said. "Still, he's a smart and powerful man. He's also a remorseful man with a good lawyer, so anything could happen."

Thoeba rolled over in the plush softness, and Peter traced the reminders of her former life down her shoulder blades. The impression of her wings were the only physical reminder of what she'd been. What she'd willingly thrown away to be with him.

The sacrifice had been an easy one.

"Thank you," she said.

"For what?"

"For everything." Her throat tightened and tears threatened to dampen her pillow. "For helping me, for loving me, and for my lovely wedding."

Peter stopped the meanderings of his touch and wrapped his arms around her. He buried his face in her neck, brushing his lips behind her ears. "You're worth it."

You are too, she thought.

"I will love you until time stops," she said.

"Time could stop, and I would still love you."

Thoeba's happiness overwhelmed her. Should she scream or shed tears of happiness? Or both?

But she fast became aware of another sensation. The one expanding in size and swelling against the curve of her buttocks as Peter's coarse hands explored her breasts.

A whimper of pleasure escaped as he cupped one and squeezed.

"Is there something else you want to give me?" she asked.

He punctuated his lusty growl by easing her on her back and settling between her thighs.

"Oh yes," he said, pausing after a kiss that tasted of the things he'd done to her last night. All the playfulness disappeared from his face. "I want to give you a baby."

Her stomach plunged.

Parenthood?

As if Zack and Kayla weren't handful enough, do I dare raise a human from seed? She let the thought sift, weighing the idea.

She'd spent hundreds of years as the guardian of God. Battled demon hordes and lived. How hard could it be to bring up one small child?

"Yes," she said. "I can do that. I'm strong enough. I'm a warrior."

Peter let out a mischievous chuckle. "Famous last words."

ACKNOWLEDGEMENTS

I'd like to thank the following people for their help:

Dave Winter of Cold Lake, Alberta for the information on all things military with the exception of the military base. Thanks to you, I got a lot of nice little snippets I would never have known about otherwise. Details of the base were fictionalized by me in the interest of security and post 9/11 paranoia. Any mistakes in the military details are the fault of myself, and not Dave.

Carly and Ashley McEwan for helping me round out Kayla's personality and providing a few Cold Lake locals.

I'd like to thank my publisher Heather Savage at Staccato for all her hard work and thanks to Nicola Ormerod for introducing us. Also, thank you Terra Koster for the fabulous cover.

Also I'd like to thank all the great writers and friends I've met over the last three years through the RWA, Facebook,

Twitter and various other writer pages. Thanks for your help, commentary, information, contacts and for all your support. There are too many of you to mention personally, but you are all loved and appreciated.

Also I want to thank the people of Cold Lake, Alberta. You people and your beautiful town truly inspired me.

Thanks to every English teacher who told me I should be a writer, and to all the friends and acquaintances who believed along with them.

I would also like to thank my muse, Bruce Dickinson-lead singer of Iron Maiden, who is also a pilot, fencer, tank enthusiast and author. He is a true renaissance man.

CPSIA information can be obtained
at www.ICGtesting.com
Printed in the USA
FFOW03n0744020814
6597FF

9 780983 934127